Praise for

MILLION
DOLLAR
DILEMMA

Books by Judy Baer

Steeple Hill Single Title

The Whitney Chronicles
Million Dollar Dilemma
Norah's Ark
The Baby Chronicles

Love Inspired

Be My Neat-Heart #347
Mirror, Mirror #399
Sleeping Beauty #415

JUDY BAER

MILLION
DOLLAR
DILEMMA

Steeple
Hill
Café

Published by Steeple Hill Books™

STEEPLE HILL BOOKS

ISBN-13: 978-0-373-78618-3
ISBN-10:   0-373-78618-2

MILLION DOLLAR DILEMMA

Printed in U.S.A.

A man who works hard sleeps in peace. It is not important if he has little or much to eat. But a rich person worries about his wealth. He cannot sleep.

—*Ecclesiastes* 5:12

CHAPTER

1

Cassia, I'm collecting again. Want to chip in five bucks? If so, leave it in the envelope in my desk. Hope it's a lucky weekend. See you Monday!
Stella

Who is having a baby *this* time?

Sometimes I wonder why I work for a living. Is it to support myself or the office kitty every time someone in customer service or any other department has a baby…or a wedding…a funeral…a promotion…or a zit?

We are the most fertile, engage-able, promote-able and magnanimous division of Parker Bennett Manufacturing and buy more gifts and flowers than the rest of shipping and receiving, human resources and accounting offices put together.

It doesn't hurt that Stella Olson prefers shopping online as an office-related activity to doing her actual work as receptionist and secretary. Of course, I enjoy being part of a group so generous and thoughtful. I like giving things away. Proverbs 11:24 and all.

Some people give much, but get back even more. But others don't give what they should and they end up poor.

My Sunday-school teacher—who also happened to be my mother—made a big deal out of that. She talked a lot about how giving freely could lead to good things and being stingy and hoarding things wasn't all it was cracked up to be. Maybe she was just trying to get my sister and me to share toys, but the lesson went far deeper in me.

At first I dumped all my pennies into the collection plate as insurance that nothing terrible would happen to me, but as I got older I realized that I hadn't purchased any heavenly health insurance after all.

I'm a P.K., a preacher's kid—or if I want to get fancy, a T.O., a theologian's offspring. Money never meant much to us. We always had good food to eat, a nice parsonage to live in and anything else we seemed to need. Now Dad is happy as a clam serving a three-point parish in Wyoming, sometimes eating three potluck dinners in a single day and turning a deaf ear to my mother's lectures on the dangers of high blood pressure. He's been known to have coffee and homemade cookies as many as seven times in a row when he's visiting his parishioners and, because he looks so cuddly with those extra chins, they keep on feeding him. He's oblivious to all but his flock and his faith and is often difficult to engage in conversations about anything other than baptism, church council, salvation or the Sunday-school board of education. Mom, fortunately, loves being Sunday school superintendent, leading Bible study and directing Christmas pageants. They're a little distant at times, but that's probably natural. They spent a lot of time in the mission field while I was growing up, and when they were gone, my sister and I lived with our grandparents.

I blame my grandfather, Benjamin Carr, for my proclivity to donate money to every good cause. I can still envision him—his perfectly groomed white hair, fastidiously trimmed mustache and penetrating gray eyes that pierced right to my soul. I can also hear his rumbling, sonorous voice quoting Luke 6:38. "Whatever measure you use in giving—large or small—it will be used to measure what is given back to you." He led by example—to my grandmother's dismay when she needed grocery money and found her cookie jar empty. But as she reminded us time and time again, God always provides.

I've missed my grandfather every day since he passed 10 weeks ago. Grandma assures me that with time, the pain will lessen. I'm still waiting.

Gramps was a big fan of the Bible first, and of Winston Churchill second. Spiritual, brilliant and with a keen interest in the history of Great Britain, Gramps spent the last fifty years of his life in Simms, South Dakota, a speck-in-the-road town that hadn't substantially changed since the day he and his nineteen-year-old bride arrived, fresh faced and eager, to build a new church.

Gramps believed that Christians are givers—of time, talents, compassion and money. When anyone remarked on his proclivity for keeping so little for himself that he could barely make ends meet, he responded with a quote from Winston Churchill. "We make a living by what we get, but we make a life by what we give." Even those doubting Thomases who took issue with the Bible were usually willing to respect old Winston.

I sighed and turned to stare at Stella's desk.

I'm new to this office and to Minneapolis, Minnesota. I need all the friends I can get. Besides, I take pleasure in the celebrations as much as anyone. I love a good party.

I dug deep to find five one-dollar bills in the bottom of my worn faux leather purse and opened the desk drawer. I need a new purse, but right now I don't have anything to put into it—or to pay for it with, either. What's more, Grandpa Ben praised frugality so much that I actually get more joy out of *not* spending money. Weird, I know—a twenty-eight-year-old woman who doesn't like to shop.

I peered inside the desk drawer. She's meticulous, that Stella—I have to give her that. Every nail-polish bottle is arranged in order, descending from the dark rum-brown to the pale pink haze. Her pens, one of every color except black, which she says is depressing, are also tidily organized. She has lipstick, breath spray, mascara, blush and foundation stored where everyone else keeps their sticky pads and paper clips.

I suppose that's what happens when you are a beautiful Scandinavian with hair the color of lemon juice, flawless porcelain skin, blue-violet eyes that change from the color of a peaceful sea to the angry violet of a nasty bruise in a nanosecond. Stella wants to be a model or an actress, but until she hits the big time she also wants to make a living—hence her receptionist position at PB Manufacturing. She's nearly six feet tall and has a presence that terrifies most men. She says this is a great filter—only the most fearless dare approach her.

Stella also has a private-investigator friend who is always giving her advice—or making her more mistrustful, depending how one looks at it. A woman like Stella, who can have any man she wants, needs a screening system of some sort, I suppose. She's not paranoid like another of our coworkers, but her philosophy is that all men are guilty until proven innocent.

There, right up front where no one could miss it, was her collection envelope with "Fun Money" printed on the flap. More fun when you're on the receiving end of it, I imagine. I stared into my now-empty purse.

"Sorry, Winslow, you'll have to wait one more week for your pedicure." I glanced at the framed photo on my desk of my enormous, taffy-brown golden retriever/Old English sheepdog as I spent the money I'd been saving for his trip to the grooming parlor. I named him after Winslow Homer, the painter who first used watercolors to paint significant art. Although Homer primarily painted the sea, one canvas, *The Rustics,* always reminds me of Simms, the place I still call home. Despite his pink, lolling tongue and patient, benevolent expression, Winslow won't be happy about waiting. He's almost as vain as Stella, and loves coming home smelling like doggy perfume and having a new kerchief around his massive neck. My ninety-day probation period can't be over soon enough for me. That's when I get a raise that will bring me out of poverty level.

Ever since I moved to the twin cities of Minneapolis-St. Paul, I've been reeling from sticker shock. In Simms I could buy a great little house with a garden and double-car garage for a third of what I'm paying here for a diminutive, overcrowded second-floor apartment in a sixty-year-old building with as many creaks and groans as the retired ranchers who populate Fannie's Coffee Shop on Saturday mornings.

As I slipped my five dollars into the envelope and closed the drawer, the phone rang. For me, terminally curious, ignoring it is never an option.

"Parker Bennett Manufacturing. This is Cassia. May I help you?"

"Can you talk?" The voice on the other end of the line was rich, throaty and full-bodied, like French roasted coffee laced with heavy cream.

"It's five o'clock on Friday afternoon, Jane. You don't have to whisper. The exodus from here started at three."

I imagined my perpetually pleasant, five-foot-one-inch sister leaning conspiratorially into the phone, her bobbed hair swinging over her round cheeks and her brown eyes sparkling. I'm the "redheaded stepchild" of my family—everyone else has plank-straight hair that's a lovely traditional shade of brown, and eyes to match. I, on the other hand, look as if I was sired by Henry VIII of England and birthed by Pippi Long-stocking, with my riot of russet curls and eyes the color of, according to my dad, warm caramel.

Jane is envious of my porcelain skin and oval face. I figure the accursed ginger-colored freckles across the bridge of my nose make us even in the skin department. We both, however, have smiles with teeth straight and even as a mile's worth of fence posts across the South Dakota prairie.

"I didn't want your boss to think you took personal calls during working hours. Proverbs 15:3, you know."

The eyes of the Lord are everywhere, keeping watch on the wicked and the good. Jane and I had listened so often to our grandfather's sermons and pithy homilies that as kids we'd started referring to our own life experiences by book, chapter and verse. Just the mention of Proverbs 12:24 can make me shorten my coffee break and get back to work.

Hard workers will become leaders. But those who are lazy will be slaves.

"Are you taking Grandma home to Simms this weekend, Cassia? I forgot a sweater there on my last trip. I'd like you to pick it up if you go."

No way. I'd just escaped from Simms, and had no immediate desire to go back. "There's nothing to do there except to check the basement for mice and kick the furnace. Grandma Mattie isn't interested in the long trip, and the neighbors are looking after things. I thought we'd wait until Mom and Dad come for a visit."

Their vacation is months from now.

"What about Ken? Don't you want to see *him?*"

Talking to my sister on the phone is very frustrating. I prefer to do it in person so she can see me glaring menacingly at her. Jane's a busybody, pure and simple. "I've said it a dozen times. I'm not seeing Ken anymore."

"Does *he* know that?"

"I've told him often enough. Of course, I've told you a number of times, too, and you keep bringing up the subject."

"Touchy, touchy. Did I hit a nerve?"

"I only have one nerve left and you're on it. You know perfectly well that Ken and I were just…convenient. Two single people in a small town. We were invited to the same parties so often that someone decided we were a couple, that's all." Unfortunately no one in Simms believed that we were only friends, not even Ken.

"Maybe that's true for you, but I think Ken has a slightly different perspective."

"It doesn't matter. Ken and I are done."

"Just checking," Jane said infuriatingly. "I'm glad to hear you're hanging tough with him. He'd have already marched you down the aisle if he had his way."

"I know. The story of my life. I never find my Mr. Right, but I have an entire army of Mr. Slightly Wrongs beating on my door. Ken is waiting for me to get lonely in the big city, realize what a 'good thing' I've got in him and come running back to Simms to marry him."

"And pigs will fly!" Jane knows full well my attitude

about the subject, but feels it's her sisterly duty to check my emotional temperature once in a while. She never realizes how many times she's the one responsible for raising it into the danger zone...

"I suppose it wasn't quite *that* bad…"

"Hah! Don't try to pretend with me, Cassia. You only went to Simms because Gramps needed a temporary church secretary. Three months, tops, he told you. If you'd known you'd have to put your master's degree on hold and quit your job at the preschool to help Grandma care for him for eighteen months, you might not have been quite so willing to help out."

"No one knew how ill he was, Jane, least of all Gramps. None of us had any idea that Grandma Mattie and I would be taking care of him until he died."

"Of course not, but I'll bet if Ken offered you a million dollars, a mansion overlooking the James River and a fleet of servants, you wouldn't go back now."

Actually, he *had* offered me that. I'd just never mentioned it to Jane because I didn't take him up on his proposal.

"Ben and Mattie needed me, that's all that's important. Besides, I'm not much interested in money. You know that. All Winslow and I need is food and shelter." I glanced at Stella's desk. *And enough money to buy gifts for my coworkers.*

"Oh, Cassia. You'd be contented in a tree house if you thought that was what God wanted for you. You're the least materialistic human being on the planet."

I propped the phone beneath my chin and removed the clip from my hair. I felt it cascade down my back in ringlets like cooped-up children let out for recess, and ran my fingers through my curls with relief.

"No one in our grandfather's house dared to be acquisitive. Jane, you and I were the only two children in school who were afraid of our own allowance."

"Speak for yourself. I, at least, could suppress my guilt and spend mine, guilty as it made me feel. You'd put yours in the offering plate on Sunday morning. I thought you were nuts."

"Psalms 37:16."

It is better to be godly and have little than to be evil and possess much.

"Having money doesn't make you evil, silly."

"Gramps did warn us a time or two about the dangers of storing up one's treasures on earth, didn't he?"

"I doubt he was thinking of his two scrawny, scabby-kneed granddaughters."

"All I know is that I don't want too much cash. It's more responsibility than I care to have. Besides, I don't need much."

I glanced at my watch. "Listen, I have to go. Winslow is probably crossing his legs and dancing by the front door by now. Talk later?"

Silly question. Jane is as chatty as I can be reserved. It's a wonder that I still have ears—you'd think she would have talked them off by now.

"Okay. Hug Grandma Mattie for me when you see her. Oh, by the way, have you met your neighbors yet?"

"Slowly. Listen, I have to go. Bye."

Hanging up on Jane made me feel both guilty and relieved. I don't want to admit that I haven't met a single neighbor in the building she'd assured me was probably full of people my age and very friendly. According to Jane, apartment living would be a veritable mine of opportunities to expand my social life. Of course, the last time she lived in an apartment, she was in college.

As far as I've gathered from the landlord, most of the residents are elderly or hold night jobs. The apartment below mine, supposedly occupied by someone under sixty, is closed up tight.

The dull mechanical drone of the dial tone hummed in my ear.

Social life. What a novel concept. I'll have to go right out and get myself one. Of course, at this point, I have to admit, any old life would do—they all have to be more exciting than mine.

CHAPTER

2

Grocery stores are the most amazing things, like Disneyland for the hungry and fresh-food deprived. In Simms an apple, banana or orange is exotic, but here…

I felt my control slipping in the fresh produce section and didn't pull myself together until dairy loomed ahead. Even there I felt a tingle over the choices—milk for the lactose intolerant, for the dairy intolerant…next there'd be milk for the simply intolerant.

"Are you a vegan?" the clerk asked, eyeing my kiwi, Asian pears, jicama, pomelos, tangelos, mangoes, plantains, bread fruit and pomegranates.

"No, I'm Swedish. People get us mixed up with the Norwegians all the time."

Jane says I have a twisted sense of humor. Maybe she's right.

I'm also a flower lover, but when one of the fronds of greenery from the mish mash of flowers I purchased tickled my nose, I realized that a dreaded carnation was stowed away in a perfectly nice bunch of tulips, daisies and one strangely exotic bird-of-paradise I couldn't resist.

I don't like carnations. They remind me of the leftover funeral flowers my frugal grandfather had me rearrange for church on Sunday mornings. No matter how artfully I did it or how many funereal bows I discarded, everyone in the congregation knew exactly where they'd come from.

As I neared my Nicollet Avenue apartment I saw that a crowd had gathered on the sidewalk near the front door of my building to watch a tall, dark-haired man carry suitcases and crates into the vestibule. Several bystanders were gathered around a single case, eyeing it with looks of either trepidation or serious indigestion.

Curious, I picked up my pace, telling myself that I needed to get the flowers into water and walk Winslow before he had an accident on the ugly patch of brown shag rug in the foyer that really should have been destroyed decades ago.

"Excuse me, coming through…excuse me, please, I live here. If you don't mind…" I wormed my way through the crowd of spectators apologizing for batting gawkers with my bouquet and obscenely heavy bag of lumpy fruit. I was almost to the door when a growl made the hair rise on the back of my neck.

The sound smoldered out of the crate and circled the crowd like a ring of smoke. Everyone took a single step backward in unison, as though the fiend inside the cage

were about to escape. Low and guttural, it was an un-
domesticated, dangerously feral sound. And too
untamed to be coming from an enclosure that was
about to be carried into *my* apartment building! I've
always wondered what could make one's blood run
cold. Well, that sound wrapped a definite chill around
my arteries.

Instead of following my impulse to run, I pushed
forward, my maternal instincts pumping. "Please, I
have to get through!" Winslow, my baby, was inside
that building.

Feisty as only a redhead can be, I stepped into the
center of the circle of people and came toe-to-toe with
the dark-haired man, who was wearing a battered
leather jacket, perfectly pressed jeans and chamois
shirt so soft and pale it looked like fresh butter. Like a
pricked balloon, my temper leaked away and jelly
settled in my knees. From Attila the Hun to Gumby,
just like that.

"Oh, hello," I said stupidly, all rational thought
gone. The man was Indiana Jones incarnate. Younger,
of course, and without that charming little cut in his
chin, but a heartthrob-with-a-death-wish-type adven-
turer, nonetheless. And he did have a scar over his left
eyebrow that was mesmerizing in its own way.

He glanced up as if a mosquito had landed on his
cheek, and I was afraid he was going to brush me away.
Instead, his faintly stubbled jaw tightened and his eyes
narrowed appraisingly.

As he looked me over from head to toe I felt a weird
internal meltdown. This had to be the most beauti-

ful—and intimidating—man I'd ever seen. It was the eyes, I thought. Dark and searing, sorrowful and soul-searching all at once, they snagged on mine for the briefest moment as he bent to pick up the large gray travel crate punctured liberally with airholes.

Then, through the fissures came a bloodcurdling, unearthly yowl that had the same effect on me as chewing aluminum foil on metal-filled molars.

"What *is* that?" I started as the crate quivered and shook. It appeared an eruption was imminent.

"'That' is my cat."

Crazed fiend from the bowels of the earth, you mean.

"Now excuse me, but he's anxious to be home. If you'll—" a guttural squall and a brown-and-black paw punching its way through an airhole in the crate punctuated his words "—let me by…" An airborne catnip mouse came shooting out of one of the larger holes in the crate and, without considering what I was doing, I picked it up.

This is his home? That…thing…actually lives here? My shoulders sagged in dismay.

Just then Winslow started woofing happily. I could see the top of his moplike head framed in the window of my apartment. Gentle, mild mannered, loving and easily intimidated, Winslow had never met a cat he didn't like. I had a hunch that was about to change dramatically.

"Oh, rats," I muttered, but quickly changed my mind. There'd be no rats within a ten-block radius once this…thing…was on the prowl.

I've never known what musical charm or spell it was that made both rats and children follow the Pied Piper to their doom in the poem by Robert Browning, but whatever that piper guy had, this man possessed in spades. Before my head switched into thinking gear, my feet followed him into the building and to the doorway of his apartment. And I did have his catnip mouse.

He was oblivious to me. The travel crate tipped, swayed and shuddered as its inhabitant rocketed from one end to the other, howling discontent and elevating his owner's already apparent annoyance.

Mesmerized, I stepped into the apartment, unaware of anything but what was inside that crate. I imagined *cat*astrophe—the smells, the sounds, the claws, the danger, the inevitable showdown and the blood, most of which, I quickly realized, would be Winslow's. He wouldn't last a minute if he came face-to-face with the Tasmanian devil hunkered evilly in the corner of his crate.

I'd meant to ease myself noiselessly out of the room after dropping the mouse on a nearby table, but was captivated by the space around me, which spoke volumes—literally—about its owner. Books enveloped the room floor to ceiling like wallpaper. In the corners piles of hardbacks teetered like architecture in Pisa. The reading material was eclectic—history, auto-biographies, nature and what appeared to be college textbooks.

But the books were a mere background for the rest of the room's decor. Framed photos in color and black and white leaned in stacks against the legs of furniture, and magazines littered the floor like carpet samples. A film of dust coated the armrests of his oxblood leather couch and a petrified burger and fries spread out on the coffee table made it appear he'd fled the apartment as if it were on fire.

It was all very exotic to me, who'd spent the past eighteen months in Simms, where no one can disappear for more than an hour without being missed, no one's business is private and all is fair game for coffeeklatch discussion. Of course, this guy was nothing like the men I'd grown accustomed to in Simms. The most mysterious thing about most of them was when they'd last changed their socks and flossed their teeth.

"You've lived in this building for a while, haven't you?"

He spun around on his heel, scowling. "Wha…" He hadn't even noticed that I'd followed him to the apartment.

"Welcome home," I blurted, trying to recover some sense of propriety, and thrust into his face the bundle of flowers I was carrying. The tulips, daisies, daffodils, roses, the offending carnation and wildly out of place bird-of-paradise erupted out of the green florist paper and into his arms.

"They were so pretty that I bought some of each. You can't buy flowers in the market where I come from. It's only on a rare day that you can buy an eggplant…."

Shut up, Cassia.

"Then you should keep the flowers." He gently

pushed at my outstretched hand as his glower morphed into something softer—a grimace, perhaps. Not much of an improvement, but nothing could dim his good looks.

"I don't own a vase to put them in. They won't look like much in a mayonnaise jar. I don't know what I was thinking." I thrust the bouquet back at him. I'm nothing if not persistent. Once I embarrass myself, I don't stop until I've achieved it fully.

He obviously didn't know what to make of my gesture. Finally he raked his dark hair into spikes with his fingers and stared intently at me, as if seeing me for the very first time.

When he looked straight at me, that jellyfish feeling came back into my legs, and I wondered if I'd fall. Perhaps the fruit was weighing me down. I opened my hand, and the sack dropped to the floor. The cage inhabitant howled loudly, but the gorgeous Mr. Mystery Man didn't even flinch.

His unsettling eyes were the color of espresso, and the look he gave me was as disquieting as if he'd pumped pure caffeine into my nervous system. But if he meant to scare me off, he'd met his match. I'd come too far into my folly to turn back without attempting to save face. Besides, I'd traveled in far more hostile environs than these. Anyone who has spent months calling on parishioners who haven't darkened the door of a church since Nixon was president would understand. If my neighbor meant to intimidate me, he'd have to try harder than this.

"No problem." I looked around, trying to think of

something friendly to say before I made my departure on my own terms. The walls of books and heavy leather furniture were masculine and inviting. Ernest Hemingway would have felt right at home.

"It's very cozy in here. Much more comfy than my place. Lots larger, too. I haven't seen you before. You must travel a lot."

My mouth overfloweth. *James 1:26, Cassia, James 1:26!*

If you claim to be religious but don't control your tongue, you are just fooling yourself, and your religion is worthless.

"Let's just say I have enough frequent flyer miles to take free vacations until I'm a hundred and five." He seemed amused. "Now, if you'll excuse me, it's time to let Pepto out of his cage, and it might be a good idea if he didn't see any strangers until he's reacquainted with the apartment."

"Pepto?"

He actually smiled. "After the Pepto-Bismol case in which I found him hiding. He was the king of unwanted strays, fighting, romancing the ladies and living off food from the garbage can outside my bedroom window. I brought him in and fed him in order to shut him up so I could get a decent night's sleep. Somehow, in the process he adopted me."

I had one of those *Awwww...* moments. "How sweet!"

He eyed me as if I were as loony as Pepto. "Right. Sweet. A regular Lion King. I'm going to let him out now, so you might want to step behind a piece of furniture just in case. Or, safer yet, close the front door behind you."

At first I thought he was kidding—about the danger, at least. I knew he was dead serious about my stepping out the door. But before I could get to the entrance of the apartment, he lifted the pin on the travel crate and Pepto was rereleased onto the world.

A shriek that could have frozen molten lava and a brown-and-black blur of fur, teeth and claws shot out of the carrier and ricocheted off several pieces of furniture and two walls. When a floor lamp landed on its side in a clatter, the cat howled as if he'd been disemboweled and plunged himself deep beneath the couch.

. I instinctively hit the floor like a ton of bricks, covered my head with my arms and curled into a fetal position to avoid the thrashing animal. When I came up for air, Pepto's owner was staring at me with alarm. He was as cool and nonchalant as if he risked having his eyes clawed out on a daily basis.

"Are you all right?"

"I'll let you know for sure when my legs stop shaking." I felt my knee buckle, the one I'd hit on the floor as I dropped. "But I wouldn't mind sitting down for a moment, Mr.…"

"Adam. Adam Cavanaugh. Please, sit." He gestured to an antique chair that looked something like a cat itself with animal-like jaws carved into the wooden armrests and paws with claws for feet. It was upholstered in something that looked disquietingly like fur.

But beggars can't be choosers and I was beginning to feel a little queasy. If that thing even *saw* Winslow…

Eyeing the base of the couch, half expecting to see a claw-studded fur ball soar from beneath, I dropped onto it. Dust flew into my nostrils. How long *had* these two been gone, anyway?

"Sorry, I didn't introduce myself." I pointed my finger to the ceiling over our heads.

Something warm and melty flickered in his eyes. "I suspected as much." The room was quiet except for the juicy licking sounds of Pepto bathing under the couch.

His reticence triggered my inner blabbermouth, and suddenly I wanted nothing more than to fill the silences with which he seemed so comfortable.

"I'm Cassia Carr. Most people haven't heard the name Cassia. My mother told me it was Grandpa's idea."

Well, that was profound.

He, at least, was polite enough to acknowledge my chatter. "An interesting name."

"Cassia means 'spicy cinnamon.' I suppose my red hair inspired him. I should actually consider myself lucky. Apparently I had an amazingly loud cry for a little thing, and my grandfather first suggested naming me Calliope. That means 'beautiful voice.'"

That quirky little smile touched his lips again as I plowed on, making an even bigger fool of myself. "With Grandpa being a country preacher and all, I suppose I'm fortunate I didn't end up as Arabelle."

He looked at me questioningly, as if now that this thing on his couch had started to talk, he had no idea how to turn it off. Neither did I. At last, something we had in common.

"Arabelle?" Nonplussed, he folded into the faded tapestry wing chair across from me, definitely the finest example of the male species I'd ever studied, exuding comfort, rugged elegance and simplicity. A no-frills man who looked like a million bucks.

A million bucks. I've never really liked that term. A million bucks is a pile of ugly, lumpy money. There's nothing ugly about this guy.

His eyes fixed on me and I inexplicably felt as though I were the most important person in the world to him, that he wanted—no, yearned—to hear every single thought in my head.

"Arabelle. 'Calling to prayer,'" I yammered. "My grandfather did that a lot—call people to prayer, that is. My sister and I lived with him and my grandmother while my parents were overseas in the mission field."

"And your sister's name is...?"

"Jane."

Much to my surprise, he burst out laughing. "Grandpa didn't have many ideas the day she was born, I take it."

"Apparently not." I felt a rush of blood explode in my cheeks.

"I don't know what's gotten into me," I apologized. "I normally don't follow people around trying to find out what's in their luggage." I eyed the crate. "When I saw that and heard the sounds coming out of it, the first thing I thought about was Winslow, my dog. He's big but gentle, like a stuffed toy almost. Except, of course, for his appetite. His favorite thing in the world is eating. And me, of course. And—" I couldn't help glancing at the base of the leather couch "—cats."

Adam lifted one eyebrow dubiously.

"Do you think that's going to be a problem?"

"Winslow," he echoed, as if unprepared for this on-slaught of information.

"He's named after Winslow Homer, the painter, but I considered naming him Mozart," I yammered. "As a puppy, he loved Mozart's Piano Concerto no. 20 in D Minor. As long as I played it, he was quiet. In fact—and I really hate admitting this to anyone because my sister already thinks I'm besotted about my dog—I leave classical CDs playing for him while I'm at work. Mostly Mozart…" My voice trailed away. "I don't know much about music, but I do know my dog is crazy about it."

CHAPTER

3

"Or just plain crazy," Adam muttered as his new neighbor babbled her way to his front door.

Turning away from the sight, he opened the cupboard to see what he and Pepto would be having for supper. There were two cans of sardines, a can of tomato soup and some mixed fruit he'd purchased with the delusion that he might actually make something out of it. There was probably some of that frozen fake egg goop and bacon in the freezer if he had the energy to find it. Best of all, in the back of the cupboard, shoved behind a double stack of cheap napkins, was a can of the kitten food he'd fed Pepto when he'd first found him. The robust, barrel-bottomed cat now twining himself around Adam's legs had then looked like a starving rat with bad fur and attitude.

"Well, guy, we're going to eat well tonight. Quit kissing up to me, you mangy fur ball."

Adam grinned slightly as he worked the can opener.

Pepto had really done a number on his new neighbor. Maybe he and Pepto were more alike than he'd realized—both good at intimidating women and scaring them off.

He'd felt her caramel-colored eyes on his back as she'd shadowed him into the building. Her gaze had practically seared holes through the leather jacket that had withstood strafing, blistering heat, frigid snow, pellet shot, short knives with sharp blades and, once, even a branding iron. She was definitely a woman who could make a mark on a guy—if he'd let her. But Adam wasn't in the mood to even think about a woman, let alone get entangled with one.

He was bone tired, gravel eyed, hungry and dirty. He'd missed three planes, four meals and two nights' sleep to get home. He didn't want to deal with either a psychotic cat or the big-eyed woman with a mass of astounding red hair who'd apparently rented the empty apartment upstairs while he was away on assignment. His nerves were open wounds, raw, exposed and agonizingly tender. He was exhausted mentally, physically and emotionally, and right now neither the banshee at his feet nor the dewy-eyed feminine apparition who lived upstairs was much to his liking. All he wanted was a bed to collapse into. But instead of indulging himself, he opened the curtains and unlocked the windows to flood light and air into the dusty gloom.

He rolled his shoulders to release the muscles in his neck, but they were so stiff and tight that he felt the movement halfway to his calves. Being a punching bag for the travel industry was not for wimps. Endless hours on the plane, more on the ground in airports without air-conditioning, dehydration and whatever faux food could be hermetically sealed and sold for exorbitant prices from carts in airports had taken its toll. Then Pepto, who'd taken a liking to his babysitters, Adam's cousin Chase Andrews and his wife, Whitney, had thrown a fit at the idea of going back into his crate and had given Adam a full set of toenail scratches on the back of one hand.

And the new little neighborhood cheerleader had given him flowers. He didn't bother to tell her that if he were to get flowers every time he did a touch-and-go in this apartment, the place would be a dead-bouquet graveyard. He eyed the strange conglomeration of flowers that was mostly daisies with a single carnation and a bird-of-paradise thrown in. It was odd, but he rather liked it.

He turned around and was astounded to see her still standing in his doorway. Adam observed her anxious expression, wringing hands and the way she stood like a penitent child. Not a child, exactly. The aquamarine knit top she wore skated smoothly across her curves and the body beneath the crisp white slacks was long legged and fit. All she wore for jewelry was a gold necklace from which hung a simple cross. Her fingers were bare of rings, but she wore a slender gold toe ring on her second toe that peeked tantalizingly from her sandal.

"Now, if you'll excuse me…"

She would excuse him, wouldn't she? It alarmed Adam a little that she looked as though she'd settle in for the duration. She was eyeing his tattered leather luggage plastered with old decals, port-of-entry and customs stamps and held together with a sturdy leather belt, and comparing it to the pristine cowhide carrying case for his laptop computer.

"I don't know what you do for a living," she murmured, "but it must be very interesting."

"Don't mind the bullet hole. A minor accident. No one was hurt."

"Hmm." She bent to drag a dainty pink-tipped finger over a burn mark on the corner of the suitcase. It was a memento of a spirited argument around a campfire during which one of his companions had tried to throw both Adam and his luggage onto the pyre.

Mentally Adam renewed his vow to find another job. This one was just too hard on him.

Though he was tempted to encourage Cassia to mind her own business and get back to her apartment, it occurred to him that there was no casual inquisitiveness or recreational prying in her expression. She was genuinely interested. He could hardly fault her for asking questions, since he made a living doing the same thing. Her face was completely open and without guile, a quality so scarce he'd barely recognized it. Her loneliness and embarrassment were apparent. Adam prided himself on his ability to read people and their emotions. It was disconcerting to realize that, for this woman at least, he actually cared what she felt.

Touchy-feely he was not. Or hadn't been…until recently. But despite the fleeting compassion he felt for

Cassia, he was relieved when she finally backed through the doorway waving goodbye.

Man, oh, man, did he need a shower and a nap.

The little skeleton twitched as though it were still alive. It couldn't be, of course. There was nothing left of the child but tissue-paper-thin skin stretched across an emaciated body. Its skull was too large for the wasted body and the eyelids, like bits of waxy paper, did not quite close, revealing slits of white fringed by sparse lashes.

Dazed and drunk with misery, Adam picked up the shovel and began to dig another grave. Surely he was hallucinating from heat and exertion. The eroded earth was hard and dry as chalk, over-grazed by cattle on this marginal land, leaving it unprotected and exposed to the elements.

He couldn't go very deep with this one. Taking off his brimmed canvas hat, he wiped the sweat from his eyes with the back of his hand. He tasted the saltiness of his lips and felt the visibly shimmering heat embracing him. His water bottle was back in the tent and his tongue was growing thick and parched. He'd have to get this done soon and go back to rehydrate. There weren't many good-sized rocks in this area either. Not enough to cover a grave. He'd used them all for the others. Perhaps there weren't enough rocks and dirt in Burundi to cover all the dead bodies. Even though there'd been a tenuous peace in Africa's Great Lakes Region since the end of the civil war, famine was just as efficient at eradicating life as war had been. Sadly, it took the infants and children first.

He did the best he could, scratching out a shallow hole in the hard earth before turning to pick up the tiny carcass he'd come to bury. He cradled the frail frame in his arms for just a moment. It was like holding a cluster of pencils—tiny sticks of arms and legs, limp and nearly weightless….

Adam heard himself scream as the fragile form moved in his arms. Eyes, large and dark as black holes in a distant universe, opened to stare at him.

"You're dead! Dead!" Adam shouted. But the baby wasn't dead, not quite. The eyes stared at him accusingly, as if he were the one responsible for its suffering.

At least he could wake himself up from these dreams, Adam thought, taking deep breaths. He was on the verge of hyperventilating, shivering and damp from head to toe with sweat and nerves, a sheen of perspiration glistening across his pectorals and the soft, dark furring of his chest. He worked his jaw and willed himself to relax. His pajama bottoms rode low on his hips, and he felt a rivulet of sweat pouring down his backbone to soak the elastic at his waist. As he stood at the kitchen sink slugging back glasses of ice water, he began to shiver. If he hadn't known better, he'd have sworn he had the shaking, chills, muscle aches and exhaustion of malaria. He would have traded the dreams that haunted him for malaria any day. From this side of sleep, a nap no longer seemed such a good idea.

Groping toward the shower, he stumbled over Pepto,

who had stationed himself in the hall in front of the bedroom door. The cat who, abused as a kitten, could be provoked into a frenzy at the sight of anything closely resembling a human attack, didn't even flinch. Even Pepto, the most self-absorbed creature ever born, sensed that Adam had reached his limit.

As Adam stood in the shower, welcoming the sharp pinpricks of water on his body, he wondered anew when…if…the dreams would ever stop.

CHAPTER

4

Kiwi is God's way of cracking a joke.

I peeled another of the hairy little critters, sliced the bright green flesh dotted with its circle of black seeds and added it into my developing fruit salad, to be tossed in a concoction of cottage cheese, black persimmon pulp and honey. The recipe sounds pretty scary, but sometimes it's good to live on the edge.

Cooking helps me ease the loneliness I've been feeling.

I went to church this morning, and came back reluctantly to my empty apartment. I'm "church shopping," going in ever and ever bigger concentric circles in the area of my apartment. I've been praying that the Holy Spirit will give me a big "thumbs up" sign when I find my church home.

The phone rang. I checked caller ID to make sure it wasn't Ken again. Sometimes I'm just not up to being loved by him.

"Hi, Grandma?" I took the phone into the living room and sprawled across the couch I'd borrowed from Jane. "What's up?"

"That's what I called to ask you, my dear." Grandma Mattie's voice was robust and cheerful. I couldn't help but smile just hearing her.

"I went to the market yesterday."

"My, my, now what?"

I suppose she has a right to be apprehensive. I've been going a little overboard at grocery and specialty stores. For me, unfortunately, everything from canned rattlesnake to sushi tastes like chicken.

"Black persimmons—'chocolate pudding fruit'? How could I resist?"

"It would have taken a saint, I'm sure," Grandma said tranquilly. "I've heard that grocery stores and Laundromats are wonderful places to meet men—so clean and wholesome. And men who shop and do laundry at night obviously aren't frequenting night-clubs...."

Visions of men too ashamed to show their dirty underwear by light of day invaded my thoughts. Ewww. "Grandma, have you been talking to Jane?"

"Your sister thinks you're lonely."

"My sister thinks a lot of things. That doesn't make them all true. She's sticking her nose where it doesn't belong."

"That's where her nose has always been," Grandma Mattie agreed cheerfully. "*Are* you lonely?"

There's no use beating around the bush with Mattie. "A little. The people at work are great, but they live all over the city and none near me. My apartment building is quieter than I'd expected. In fact, I didn't meet any of my neighbors until today…and I managed to make a royal fool of myself, too."

"Oh?" Mattie can pack volumes into a single "Oh?"

"I didn't expect the Cities to be like Simms, where I can dial a wrong number and talk for half an hour to whoever answers, but I also didn't realize how much I've missed my friends until I followed a man into his apartment today."

There was a long, potent pause on the other end of the line. "Do you want to tell me about it?"

"There's nothing much to tell, really, but he has the most awful cat…." I unfurled for her my long, wretched story. To my surprise, instead of asking where I'd gone wrong in the common sense department, she changed the subject.

"Do you like your job?"

"It's fine. I'm still learning."

"You'll find something in your field soon. You didn't get a degree in child development to waste it now."

"I need to finish my master's and maybe even my doctorate in child psychology, Grandma. Right now I'm a well-educated unemployable."

"You left school to help your grandfather and me and didn't complain once about your sacrifice. The Fifth Commandment and all."

Honor your father and your mother.

Grandma, too, was accustomed to talking in biblical shorthand.

I recalled the day my grandfather had had his first heart attack. That moment had changed my life. I had known for certain that I couldn't let Mattie struggle alone, and once I realized Grandpa Ben was disappearing in inches, a little each day, it became crystal clear that my place was with my grandparents. I would only have felt remorse if I had decided my own life was "too important" to spare them the time and had missed the opportunity to share so many powerful weeks with Grandfather before he died.

"You and Ben have been like my own father and mother in so many ways. You were there for us when our parents were away, foot soldiers right there in the trenches with us."

"I never considered raising you two a war, dear. Of course, there were a few skirmishes."

I winced, hoping she wasn't thinking of that time Jane and I were so determined to play with the same doll that we pulled it in half. Or that nasty incident with the scissors while we played beauty shop. Of course, that did work out in the long run. Jane still wears her hair in a bob.

I heard a knock and a voice in the background on Mattie's end of the line. Then she said, "Can I call you back, dear? I've got company."

"Don't worry about it, Gram. Call me when you aren't busy."

Because I certainly won't be.

It should be the other way around. *I* should be telling my grandmother how to adjust, not vice versa. She has taken to city life like a duck to water. Mattie turns down invitations from Jane and me because her social life in the assisted living center is so busy. While Mattie is enjoying her social whirl, I already have all my photos in photo albums and my recipes typed nicely and filed in a box. I'm going to alphabetize the spices and the cleaning products next, then refold the bath towels in a new configuration I saw in *Good House-keeping.* I've even started to iron.

The phone rang again. Twice in a day. A new record. I picked it up without checking the ID, only to hear "Are you ready to come home yet?"

The familiar, proprietary voice set my teeth on edge. "Hello, Ken. How are you?"

"Don't play games with me, Cassia. I miss you and I know you miss me. You can be here in time for the spaghetti feed before the baseball game tomorrow if you pack tonight. What do you say?"

"I'm fine, thank you. How nice of you to call. Now, if you'll just excuse me…"

"Okay, okay. I'm sorry I jumped into it like that, but you are driving me crazy, darlin.' You don't belong in Minneapolis. You belong in Simms with me."

I could just see him, hair the color of ripe wheat buzzed into submission, that intentional three-day stubble of beard that so many men wear these days, pristine white T-shirt with tight sleeves stretching over refined biceps. I could imagine his even white teeth with a wad of gum lodged between the back molars and his practiced sneer, an expression he hoped looked just like Elvis's. A fine specimen of a man he is, even if Ken thinks so himself.

"You don't need me in Simms. The game will go on without me."

"So will the Twin Cities."

"We've discussed this a dozen times…."

"And you never get it quite right. I love you, Cassia. I want you here with me."

"But I don't love you. Not like that…"

"Sooner or later you'll realize that love isn't about hearing bells and being swept off your feet. Love is about the time you've put into the relationship, the history you share."

But I *want* bells. I *want* to be swept off my feet. Besides, this romantic deductive reasoning comes from a man who considers venison, codfish and sauerkraut gourmet foods.

"Then you should love your pickup truck and your dog, Boosters, very much. I know how much time and history you all have together."

"I can see this wasn't the right time to call."

Finally, a glimmer of intuition on his part. I'd practically hit him over the head to make him understand that I wasn't going to fall in love with him, but Ken refused to take no for an answer. His persistence had made him an unlikely success in the construction world, and the business he based in Simms had flourished across the state. Apparently when something worked once, Ken figured it would work again.

"If it ain't broke, don't fix it," he says, not realizing that there'd really never been anything between us to fix. But we had dated—showed up at the same places within twenty minutes of each other, actually. In

Simms that counted for something. "Sooner or later you'll have to realize that I'm not coming back to Simms to be your wife. I can't be much clearer than that."

"Sure, that's what you think now, but you'll come around." Gum snapped loudly in my ear. "Hey! The guys are here. Gotta go. We're going skeet shooting at the gun club tonight. You hang in there, babe. Love ya. Bye." And the phone went dead.

My left temple pulsated and the pounding in my head increased. That conversation had been a total waste of time. Ken hadn't believed—or even heard—a word I'd said. He is so convinced that the city is an immoral and inhospitable place to live—and that Simms is as close to Eden as one can get on earth—that he thinks I'll wake up sooner or later and scuttle my little self back to paradise. And he'll be waiting with a told-you-so grin on his face and his latest big showy house, ready to carry me across the threshold.

"I'll build you anything you want, Cassia," he'd told me. "You name it—ranch, two-story, Colonial, saltbox, even contemporary. As many bedrooms as you want and a bathroom in every one of them. I'll put a fireplace in every one, too. You want a pool? Fine. A bowling alley? I'll see what I can do. I'll even build a place for your grandma so she can be back in Simms and close to you. Won't she love that?"

If money or prestige had mattered even a whit to me, it might have been tempting, but grandiose displays of wealth turned my stomach. If Ken had offered to give away some of that money to help others, then maybe…

But he hadn't. He's a good man, but it probably wouldn't occur to him. He looks at the world in terms of dollars per square foot, concrete blocks per basement and the distance between two rafters. That, more than anything, made me sure I could never fully love him. Now I felt more empty and isolated than ever. Mattie was busy, Ken was being obtuse and Jane was doing who-knows-what. And I was all alone.

I built myself up for a great pity party and was planning the exact moment I'd open the Chunky Monkey ice cream in my freezer—should it be before or after I finish the Oreos and the fruit salad? Then a cold, wet nose nudged itself into my palm. Beady black eyes peered at me through a fringe of taffy-colored bangs and a raspy tongue laved my hand.

I knelt and took my dog's gigantic fluffy head in my hands. "You're my best buddy, aren't you, sweetie? I don't need anybody else when I've got you. How about a brushing?"

Unfortunately facing an evening of dog brushing and eating two quarts of Black Persimmon Surprise fruit salad didn't exactly fill my social calendar.

"The city isn't that much different from Simms, Winslow. I'll do exactly what I always did in Simms when I was in the doldrums. Remember how we'd take a plate of Mattie's cookies to the neighbors and have a visit?" But I didn't have any homemade cookies. I would have to make do with what I had on hand.

I wondered how Adam Cavanaugh felt about tangelos and persimmons.

* * *

I almost lost my nerve when I saw that the door to his apartment was open. I smelled frying bacon and heard the coffeepot gurgling. My cheery idea to be neighborly rapidly withered. After deciding that Cavanaugh was probably the last person who would want to see me, I decided instead to offer my salad to the people who lived on my floor. Unfortunately, no one was home. Adam's was the only apartment in the building with any signs of life.

Pepto lay in the doorway like a palace guard waiting to attack anyone with designs on the king. I studied him from a distance, gauging my safety. One incisor hung over his bottom lip, and his mauled, droopy ear made him look like the feline version of a marauding pirate.

Still, the door was wide open and I could see Adam hovering over the stove in overlarge gray sweatpants and an equally washed-out red sweatshirt. His dark hair was damp, his feet bare, and if I had to judge by the sound of pans and lids clanging harshly as he flung them about, his mood was foul.

When I'd moved in, the landlord had assured me that the occupant of this apartment was "a nice guy who works for a newspaper or something." I probably should have paid more attention. That's hardly a ringing endorsement for a person's sterling character, but the landlord also told me that if I ever got into a jam I could safely knock on this guy's door and ask for help. Since I'd had no intention of doing anything that I couldn't handle on my own, I hadn't asked any more questions. Now I wished I'd given my curiosity full range.

Maybe I'd just take my salad home and eat it all by myself.

Unfortunately, the cat chose that moment to yowl like a banshee. I looked down to see if I'd stepped on his tail, and when I looked up again, Adam was at the door staring at me with those disconcerting eyes of his. On the front of his faded sweatshirt were the words Don't Mess With Me.

Wishing desperately I'd heeded that advice much earlier in the day, I did the only thing I could manage. I thrust the bowl into his hands and blurted, "Salad. I made too much. Since you just came home, I thought you might not have anything in your refrigerator."

"But you brought me flowers already. You're too generous." He was laughing at me, so I laughed, too.

"Sorry I'm being such a hick, but this is how we do it back in Simms. I'll just go back to my place now and spend some time getting sophisticated. I'll be back in twenty years or so."

An odd expression flashed in his attractive eyes. "Don't get sophisticated. I hate it when that happens. It ruins perfectly nice people." He stepped back, and with his hand indicated that I should enter. "Want some eggs and bacon?" he offered. "I don't have any bread, so I made a few pancakes to go with it."

"Oh, I couldn't."

"No bother. Come in. Scram, Pepto." The cat slithered away, looking back at me with a disgruntled expression.

Adam pushed his door wide open and beckoned me in. He made no move to close the door after me. Sometimes I surprise myself, but I'm still an old-fashioned girl at heart and I appreciated his thoughtfulness.

He moved to the cupboard, took out two pottery plates and handed them to me. "You'll have to move the mail to one side while we eat."

The table was piled high with important-looking letters and a gargantuan stack of magazines, most of which were news publications and journals, with the occasional glossy print piece.

He peeled back the foil on my bowl and peered curiously inside.

"Fruit salad," I offered, hoping to clarify.

"Not like any I've ever seen." He stared at the oddly colored stuff for a minute before picking out a piece of star fruit. He bit into it and his eyes narrowed. "It reminds me of a soft-shelled crab."

"I went a little crazy in the produce section and bought one of everything."

"I thought that was how you shopped for flowers." He put down the bowl and went to retrieve the frying pan and a stack of pancakes. He set the hot pan on a pile of magazines, his version of a trivet.

"It's getting out of hand. My new hobby is trying out everything exotic in the grocery store—and compared to Simms, it's all exotic. You can't be picky when shopping at a combination grocery store, post office, feed supply, hardware, beauty parlor, pawn shop, you know."

"No wonder you're having fun." Adam slid scrambled eggs and three slices of bacon onto my plate and some onto his own. He rolled an unbuttered pancake into something that looked like a soft-shelled taco, put it beside his plate and reached for my salad. As he dished it up, I winced. The persimmon dressing was not an appetizing color.

"It's not bad," he said finally. "You want some?"

"Since you haven't grabbed your throat and fallen off the chair, I suppose I'll try it. Frankly, I wasn't quite sure I was brave enough to taste it myself." Actually, the prayer I whispered to myself was more a petition for safety—from my own cooking.

"I've eaten stranger things lately," he said enigmatically. He poked at his chipped plate. "I don't have much in the way of dishes. I usually use paper."

"These are fine. I never ate on a paper plate at home. My grandfather didn't believe in waste."

"No kidding?"

"He also hated throwing anything away if he still considered it 'good.' Once we got something, we used it until it fell apart. Then we repaired it and used it some more."

"Why didn't you just buy new?"

"Psalm 41:1."

He stared at me blankly until I remembered that outside my family, giving only a Bible reference was rarely enough.

"'Happy are those who consider the poor. The Lord delivers them in the day of trouble.' My grandfather wouldn't spend an extra dime on himself if he thought he could give it away. My grandmother still jokes that the widows and the orphans had better things than we did because Grandpa was more generous with them than with us."

"Was that a problem?"

"No. It wasn't as though we were involuntarily poor. Poverty was a choice for us, a challenge. How much could we give up in order that others might have more? Believe it or not, Grandpa managed to make it into a game. I learned early how little we actually need."

"Interesting." He stared at me with those velvety chocolate-colored eyes and once again I felt a little weak in the knees. "Probably considered loony in this day and age, but definitely interesting."

As I pushed my chair back from the table and started to say goodbye, a furred cannonball landed in my lap and began to rumble.

"Pepto?" Adam stared at the cat that had just launched itself into my arms. I was equally startled, but Pepto redoubled his purr, turned around twice on my thighs and sat down. "What are you doing, crazy cat?"

"He's fine. I like animals."

"No, he's not. He's never done that before. Even to me."

"Animals and small children seem to like me," I told him as I stroked Pepto's fur. It felt much softer than it looked. "Grandma says it's a sign of my 'pure nature.' My sister Jane says it's because I wear perfume that's a combination of catnip and cotton candy. Either way, I don't mind."

As Pepto tilted his head upward as if he were looking at me, I scratched that tender dip beneath his chin, and his purr turned to a happy roar. When I lifted my head, Adam was staring at me in disbelief, as if I'd made roses grow out of a dirty ashtray. I chuckled inwardly. It was easy to woo the cat. I'm just glad it's not on my agenda to win his master's heart.

CHAPTER

5

Animals and small children, huh?

Adam pondered the notion as he scrubbed out his frying pan. He'd never in a million years expected Pepto to do an about-face and decide to actually *like* someone. He took a pad of steel wool and worked at a bit of egg yolk stubbornly clinging to the pan. Of course, loath as he might be to admit it, Adam had liked his new neighbor, too. Even without the bird-of-paradise, persimmons and improbable red hair, she'd still be charming and funny. She was a breath of fresh air for his very stale attitude, and having her here tonight had provided a moment of relief from the pressure mounting inside him.

He'd turned into the equivalent of a human pressure cooker lately, and Cassia Carr was an unexpected release valve. He'd been tempted to lecture her about the wisdom of being as open and trusting as she'd been in her little hometown, but decided instead that he'd just keep an eye on her. The inhabitants of this building were all good people—many had lived here twenty years or more. Cassia was obviously a quick study and would develop street smarts quickly enough without his advice.

The phone rang just as Adam put the frying pan in the dish rack to dry. He glanced at the caller ID. It was his agent and best friend, Terrance Becker.

"Adam, old man, you're back! Listen, buddy, are you all right? I heard you had a pretty rough time over there."

"No rougher than anyone else. At least I didn't starve to death." Sickening images shimmered in his mind like heat waves off the desert floor. Adam hadn't known until recently how painful death from malnutrition could be.

"You did tighten your belt a couple notches, though," Terrance said. "I talked to Frankie."

Frankie Wachter was the photographer who traveled with Adam. He hoped Frankie didn't have too big a mouth. Terrance didn't need to know every gory detail of their trip to Burundi. There were some things Adam would just as soon keep under wraps. The wrenching emotions both he and Frankie had experienced were private. His research and articles could speak for him, and nothing else need be said.

"The magazine loved your stuff, by the way. You sent them so much that they're serializing it. Frankie got some great pictures, too. Heart wrenching. Whenever you want to quit freelancing and write for just one publication, let me know, okay? I've got several offers for you."

Adam grunted a non-comment. Being tied down had never suited him. As a journalist whose career had centered primarily on human rights issues, Adam wanted to be free to go where circumstance and instinct took him. Ironically, this last time it had taken him to one of the poorest places he'd ever been—Burundi, a landlocked country about the size of Maryland whose population had an overall life expectancy of less than forty-seven years, and 12 percent of whom were infected with AIDS. The tension between the Tutsis and the Hutus left the people in constant turmoil. It was a difficult life, especially for the youngest, most helpless members of society, the children. When Adam had gone in to do a story on a small relief organization that was attempting to provide minimal life-sustaining provisions for the people, he'd had no idea that what he would see and experience could so utterly change him.

Knowing the statistics was nothing compared to seeing the reality. If 70 percent of all malnourished people in the world were children and forty thousand a day died of starvation, then where were the people who could help them? Vulnerable, helpless and defenseless, the children had greater nutritional demands than the adults and were utterly unable to forage for themselves. At night, when the camp was silent, Adam had lain on his cot staring into the blackness, wondering what he could do to put a thumb in a dike of this magnitude. Life was leaking out of these young ones, and he had no way to stop it.

"So what are you planning next?"

Adam felt himself flinch. He'd drifted light-years away from Terrance and the conversation about his career. "Not a thing."

"A little R & R? Good idea. A few days off and you'll feel like a new man." Terrance sounded worried. "That's what you meant, right?"

"Not really. I'm burned and I'm bummed. The last thing I feel like doing is working."

"You don't have to cover every tragedy in the world," Terrance told him. "Not everything you do has to be nominated for a Pulitzer. Lighten up. Do something not quite so heavy for a change, a little mind candy. How about a piece on baseball? Or music, like 'Adam Cavanaugh on Aging Rockers—The Dolls, the Dope and the Depends.' Boomers might eat it up."

"Good try, but no thanks. I'm tired in a way I've never been tired before." Wordsmith that he was, even Adam couldn't describe it. "It's in my bones this time. Watching children die and being absolutely helpless to stop it changes a person."

"But like you said in your article, those kids were past the point of no return before you ever got to them."

"That doesn't make it any easier. Or prettier. Sorry, Terrance. This writer is taking time off—a long time. I haven't got it in me anymore."

"Just for a while…"

"Maybe forever."

He heard Terrance's sharp intake of breath and knew what was coming next.

"Promise me this, Adam. Before you throw in the towel, give it some time. Find a story to write that isn't going to eat your heart out and see how that feels before you make any rash decisions."

"That's not going to help." Something had broken in him that needed to heal—his heart. No story he could think of was going to distract him enough for that to happen.

"Just promise."

"Only if something falls into my lap. I'm not going out to look for a fluff piece just to prove to you that I'm telling you the truth."

"Think this through, Adam…."

"Gotta go. I'll call you when that story comes knocking on my door."

Adam stared at the phone a long time after he'd hung up. He couldn't believe he'd just chopped away at the cable that had kept him connected to life for the past fifteen years, had brought him a Pulitzer and a myriad of other journalistic awards. But the import and meaning he'd always attributed to life, the idea of God, peace and goodwill on earth, humanity and brotherhood had all evaporated during his time in Burundi. Something was deeply wrong with a world in which a child could be born, live and die and leave no more impression than a raindrop in an ocean.

CHAPTER

6

Why people think city living is so great is beyond me.

Everyone says things are so convenient here. Maybe, but I think it's a little weird that I could order a pizza, a taxi and an ambulance at the same time and count on the pizza to come first. Of course, in Simms the rumor that you're sick can arrive before the illness does, so maybe it's, as Grandpa always said, "a horse apiece."

I rode the brakes as I nosed my way into the right lane on I-494 and made ready to pull onto the exit ramp that led to the "shortcut" I've devised to get to work. Shortcut…hah! There's no such thing. Not here, at least.

In Simms we talk in miles. If something is sixty miles away, it's probably sixty minutes away, too, give or take a few, depending on the weight of my foot on the accelerator. Here, miles have no meaning, as far as I can tell. It takes me thirty-five minutes to get to work if I time it right and three times that in rush-hour traffic. I don't know if I've driven five miles or fifty. I only know that it seems like a hundred.

I haven't got it fine-tuned yet, but I'm getting there. I haven't been late for work in a week and I've completely gotten over the urge to shriek every time I hit the gas and edge off an on-ramp into speeding traffic. I'll just say this—more than once I've been thankful that I'm right with God when I'm pulling onto the freeway.

My car was a hand-me-down from my father, who got it as a hand-me-down from a parishioner. Actually, it probably belonged to a few people before that, as well. As pedigreed cars go, mine's an elderly mutt, over eighty-four in dog years.

As I pulled into Parker Bennett's parking lot I heard a yell from behind me. "Hey, lady, your muffler just fell off!"

I slowed and looked through my rearview mirror. I assumed it was a joke, but with my car anything is possible. Then I saw who was standing in the middle of the parking lot grinning with that gap-toothed grin of his. I'd met Randy Mills at work first, but I also ran into him at the church I attended a couple Sundays ago. How great is that? God gave me a Christian friend right off the bat. He's a lean and lanky scarecrow kind of guy, with sandy hair and sandy freckles. I leaned out the window and waved before pulling into a parking space. By the time I'd gathered my purse and my lunch, Randy was standing arms akimbo, theatrically studying my tires.

"Sorry, I was mistaken. It wasn't your muffler at all. It was your whole transmission that dropped. Do you have tape and bubblegum in your tool kit, or do you want me to fix it for you? I've got a bale of twine in my trunk."

"Very funny, Randy. I don't make fun of *your* car." I tried my best to look indignant.

"Don't bother locking it, Cassia," Randy advised. "If you're lucky, somebody will come by and steal it."

"Not if I can help it. I put it in the garage every night."

"No kidding?" Randy sounded and looked amazed. "You actually protect that thing?"

"At least I'm not like some of my neighbors who leave their expensive cars out at night because there's too much useless junk in their garages."

"Right," Randy said with a grin. "You *drive* your useless junk."

We fell into step together as we walked toward the front doors of Parker Bennett's main office. I had to skip every few steps to keep up with the long-legged accountant.

"It's a good car," I said defensively. "Never a problem. I have it serviced regularly."

"I'm sure you do. Just don't wash it. It's only the rust that's holding it together."

"You're just jealous because your car doesn't have two hundred and thirty thousand miles on it."

"No kidding? Two thirty?" Randy whistled. "I didn't know they could get that high." Then his genial face sobered. "Seriously, Cassia, it's time to get something newer. It doesn't have to be expensive, but you shouldn't be driving city streets in that thing. You're going to end up stranded someplace." He eyed me up and down. "A lamb among the wolves."

"I can change a tire, check the oil, test the air in the tires and even make sure the alternator belt is tight."

"Maybe so, but rebuilding the whole chassis is probably beyond you, and that's what you'll need to do soon."

I skipped again to match my steps to Randy's long stride. "If it's any comfort, my sister agrees with you. She's suggested that I take her car this winter and she'll buy a new one."

"Why don't *you* get the new one?" Randy held the door for me.

"I don't need one."

"Sometimes life is about more than 'needing.' What if you *want* one?"

"But I don't."

"I can't believe that."

"For the last eighteen months, Randy, the closest thing I've come to a traffic jam is having to wait for a semi to come by in the other lane so that I can pass a tractor. Besides, I can use a pair of jumper cables just as well as the next girl."

"I'm sure you can." As he sighed and rolled his eyes, mine followed his gaze upward to the three-story waterfall and banks of glass elevators that glided whisper soft up and down. "No matter how long I work here, I don't think I'll get over all this wasted space. All of Simms could fit in here, with a floor left over."

"It's pretty impressive, though, don't you think?" he asked.

"But is it good for anything? That's the question."

Randy stopped to stare at me. I caught a glimpse of my hair in the polished chrome base of the elevator as we waited for the cab to return for us. It was particularly unruly today, framing my face in a boisterous cloud. Sometimes I think my hair has more personality than I do. It certainly has a mind of its own.

Sometimes Ken accuses me of looking like a fall maple in full color. That's one of his nicer compliments. Usually he compares me to something from his work orbit. "Cassia, you're pretty as a new power saw," "clever as a Swiss army knife" or "feisty as new sandpaper." When I've really pleased him, he always says, "I've never had or sold a model home quite as fine as you." When he and I don't agree, it's always, "Darlin,' quit talking like your attic's not finished yet." Quite a romantic, that Ken.

"Does everything have to be useful for you to enjoy it, Cassia?" Randy asked, bringing me back to the present.

"Of course not, but it helps."

"They must raise children differently where you come from."

"Simms? Maybe they do. I know people who still make their children apologize to telemarketers before they hang up on them." I paused to eyeball him for a change. "Tell me, Randy, what's your story? You don't get to hear mine without sharing a little of your own. I know you're an accountant and that you go to church just a few blocks from here, but other than that…'

He shrugged his wide but bony shoulders beneath his jacket. "Not much to tell. I was born and raised in a middle-class suburb of the Twin Cities. Had a good education, went to the university, became a CPA and here I am, at Parker Bennett."

"That's a little dull, don't you think? Surely there must be people in your life."

"A younger brother and sister, two parents who are teachers. And a pack of first and second cousins that I see on holidays. I'm single because the right girl just hasn't come along yet. And I have a cat named Franklin, after the stove in my parents' cabin."

"That's what I was talking about! The people in your life, what you do for fun! *That's* the best part of a person's life, not what they own."

"What is it with you, anyway? I've never met anyone as—" he searched for words "—as *content* as you are." He scratched his sandy head in puzzlement. "You've come here every day for nearly a month in your old junker of a car, carrying a sack lunch and humming like a canary. The execs drive BMWs or Jags and go out for power lunches to grouse about how hard they have it. What's your secret?"

He looked so sincere and cute and vulnerable standing there trying to puzzle me out that I wanted to give him a squeeze. I did, however, restrain my impulses.

"My secret? Randy, I'm the most transparent person on the planet. With me, what you see is what you get."

"That's what you say, but there's something…" Randy looked so puzzled that I had to laugh.

"So you want my secret? Okay, I'll give you my confidential formula. But it's one I'm sure you already know." I dug in my purse for a scrap of paper and came up with half a deposit slip from my checkbook. I scribbled down the information for which Randy was digging, then I slipped the scrap inside the little New Testament I always carry and pressed it into his palm. "Here you are."

"I've already got a Bible, Cassia."

I ignored him.

The elevator arrived as he looked at the packet in his hand. As we stepped inside, I asked. "What floor do you want? I'll drive."

"Sixth floor. I want to stop at the cafeteria and grab some coffee. I got up too late to make my own this morning." Then he opened the little Testament and read what I'd scratched on the bit of paper. Hebrews 13:5, one of my favorites.

Keep your lives free from the love of money and be content with what you have, because God has said, "Never will I leave you; never will I forsake you."

He slipped the Testament into his pocket and stepped off the elevator on the sixth floor shaking his head.

On the way down the hall to my office, I ran through the game I'd been playing every day since I joined Parker Bennett. It was one my mother always used to break the ice and help us kids remember each other's names at vacation Bible school. Children would introduce themselves by giving their first names and an adjective that described them. I was always

Curly Cassia and my sister Jolly Jane. Over the years our classes were filled with notables such as Mucky Matthew (something to do with the fact that he did barn chores before coming to church school), Blinking Bonnie, Running Ronnie, Silly Sarah and, my personal favorite, Daring Dan. The game got to be such a popular tradition that all the vacation Bible school classes used it, and it's been my memory tool ever since. It's come in particularly handy since I was hired at Parker Bennett. Every face is new, and I find myself applying adjectives to each person I meet. In my portion of the office alone are Stunning Stella, Paranoid Paula, Betting Bob, Thoughtful Thelma, Ego Ed, Jealous Jan and—even though it's not playing the game right—Petty Betty. The only one I didn't need to add a descriptive adjective to was someone with an already memorable name—Cricket.

Cricket is about my age, and while I'm tall and slender, she's short and round and always has a glorious smile that can light up a room. Cricket told me immediately how she came to have her unusual name. Her much-in-love parents—Jim and Mimi—tried to give her a name that was a combination of their own two names. Unfortunately, all they could come up with was Jimini. It wasn't long till everyone was calling the baby Jimini Cricket, and before long, Jimini had gone by the wayside and now she's just Cricket. She's forever fighting her weight, loves food, abhors exercise and thinks television reality shows are ridiculous. She also feels the need to watch every one of those shows just to make sure that someone doesn't slip something relevant or enlightening into one of them. Cricket has been a real blessing in the office, not to mention a huge dose of comic relief.

That's not to say my office mates aren't all wonderful people—they are, and I like them all very much. But each does have a quirk or two that stand out above all others—Ed, for example.

Ed's a nice guy. He's friendly, cheerful and generous. He's also got a mirror taped to the inside drawer of his desk so he can check his hair for a strand out of place and his teeth for an errant speck of spinach. If Ed lost his hair, he would run right out and buy a wardrobe of hairpieces—a rug for every room, so to speak. Paula and Betty (it figures) think Ed had something "done" around his eyes over his last vacation. Thelma says he just looked "rested," but apparently Paula counts crow's-feet and keeps a tally. Now they're trying to work up the nerve to ask who his plastic surgeon was. I've warned them against it. If Ed hasn't had a touch-up, he'll be as upset as a woman who is asked when her baby is due six months after she's delivered.

I hope they aren't counting my wrinkles. I didn't have many when I came to Parker Bennett, but they could be adding up quickly now. I'm not much for looking in the mirror. Just seeing myself full-length in a department-store window surprises me. Since all the mirrors in Simms are attached to dressers, I'd even forgotten how long my legs are. Now when I see them in a full-length mirror, I'm reminded of walking on stilts. Ken did tell me once, however, that his buddies thought I had great legs. It was one of the first and only times I'd wished that they'd stick to talking about trucks, power washers, construction materials and the like.

I'd had the most trouble finding an adjective for Thelma. I went back and forth between Thoughtful and Thrifty for a few days before I settled on Thoughtful. She's the dearest, kindest person in the office, always remembering to ask how Winslow is settling in, to compliment Stella on her new shoes or Jan on a different haircut. She also carries her lunch to work in the same paper bag all week, washes out Baggies so she can reuse them and insists that a teabag can be reused at least four or five times before it loses its punch.

I passed the office of my boss, Ned Lakestone, the man who's in charge of the many smaller offices that make up the customer service department. His door is rarely open and I don't think he likes people very much. Customer service is an odd place for a recluse to work, but Stella assures me that Ned's the best kind of boss to have—one who never interrupts his employees' workday with instructions or directives. According to Stella, that type is a real nuisance. Besides, if Mr. Lakestone got involved with us, she probably wouldn't have time to change her nail polish every day.

For some strange reason, as I neared the office, the fine hairs on the back of my neck began to tingle. It reminded me of Boosters, Ken's dog, when he senses some change in the air or nearly imperceptible hint that something's not quite as it should be. Then the fur on Boosters's neck stands up and he puts his nose to the ground because something is very suspicious.

Looking back, I realized that if I'd known what was coming, every hair on my head would have stood up and taken notice.

I pushed my way through the throng of people who'd crowded the hallway in front of the customer service department and wondered what on earth was going on in my office. If I hadn't known better, I'd have suspected they were having a rummage and bake sale inside and everyone was gathering for a first look at the merchandise. Now, *that* tells me I've spent far too much time in Simms.

So for the second time in not so very many days, I forged ahead. "Excuse me, sorry, I didn't mean to step on your foot, excuse me…" The door was shut, so, not knowing what I'd find on the other side, I opened it, slid in sideways through the crack and shut it again.

"What's going on here…?" My voice drifted away as I stared in wonderment at the sight before me. Ego Ed was standing on, of all places, the top of his desk. Everything on the desk had been swept to one side and he was poised there, foam coffee cup in one hand, holding his arms in the air in a victor's triumphant V. When I came in, he glanced at me and yelled, "Yee-haw!"

And he was the sanest one in the pack.

Petty Betty was going in circles—literally, as if one foot had been nailed to the floor and she kept circling around it, getting nowhere fast. Her hands were flapping like pathetic little bird wings and her eyes were wild.

Stella was dumping nail polish bottles into her purse and ignoring her telephone which rang incessantly.

Betting Bob was on the phone in loud conversation

with what sounded like his bookie. "Flytail in the second! Flytail in the second!" I'd been at work only three weeks, so I'm not fluent in what Stella calls Bob's "gamble speak," but I was pretty sure that was the language he was talking.

Cricket and Thelma were in intense conversation, and Paranoid Paula was blatantly eavesdropping. Paula had her purse clutched to her chest and kept muttering over and over to the other two, who were ignoring her, "Don't count your chickens before they're hatched. You might be sorry. Don't count your chickens before they're hatched!"

The filing cabinets appeared to have ruptured and hemorrhaged all over the floor, and the rest of the room was in equal disarray. It was as if someone had gleefully run through the place overturning garbage cans and pushing things off desks.

Stella, despite the fact that she was carrying on a private conversation with herself punctuated by words like "shoes," "diamonds" and "I'll show them," seemed to be one of the calmer of the lot.

I neared her desk cautiously, wary of flying emery boards and cuticle clippers. "Stella, what's going on in here?"

Her head shot up and she stared at me. "You don't *know?*"

"I realize that I didn't get in as early today as I usually do, but I'm still on time. What's everyone else doing here so early?"

"I called Thelma," she explained mysteriously. "And she called Paula and Jan. They were supposed to tell

Bob, Ed, Betty, Cricket and you. Maybe they didn't have your home phone number."

"Call me for what?" Alice, when she fell through the looking glass, had nothing on me.

"To tell you that *we won!*"

"'Wee one'? Who had a baby? I didn't realize anyone was due. It didn't say who was expecting on your collection envelope."

"No, we w-o-n. Us. These people here." Ed made a gesture around the room. "We. Us. You!"

Cricket tossed a pile of papers into the air like confetti and let them fall to the floor.

What was she, nuts?

"Won? Won what?" I couldn't think of any contests other than Parker Bennett's employee of the month award, and that wasn't all that big a deal. Most of the employee photos they hung on the lobby wall looked like mug shots anyway.

"The lottery, of course!"

"The lottery?" I echoed, feeling more stupid by the second.

By then Cricket was in a world of her own doing some sort of silly dance step around the perimeter of the room singing "New York, New York." Cricket is a terrible singer, but I did figure out that she was chirping about the Big Apple. She stopped long enough to grab my hands and twirl me around in a circle. "The Powerball! Cassia, haven't you been watching the billboards or listening to the radio?"

"I've been doing a lot around the apartment," I admitted. "Winslow and I have had a lot of walks...."

She finally stopped what she was doing and looked straight into my eyes. "Cassia, remember those tickets we bought? One of them was the winning number. We're all millionaires."

"I didn't buy any tickets!"

Grandpa would do backflips in his grave if he thought I'd been involved in any kind of gambling. Oh, Grandpa wouldn't have liked this at all.

"Of course you bought tickets. What do you think you put five dollars into the envelope in my desk for?"

"Somebody was having a baby or a birthday or…"

Stella's face registered astonishment. "You really don't know, do you?"

"About what?"

Cricket's eyes grew large. "She really doesn't know! Tell her about the pool, Stella."

"The last Friday of every month we all put five bucks into the pool, and I buy lottery tickets for the Powerball. We've been doing it for ages. It's been just for fun, but this weekend…" Stella could hardly continue. "We won!" Understanding dawned in Stella's beautiful blue eyes. "And you thought you were putting money toward a *baby gift?*"

I nodded dumbly. I had a very bad feeling rising in my chest.

"No one had a baby, Cassia. The money you put in the envelope on Friday was for lottery tickets."

"But it's always for someone's retirement or wedding or…"

"Except on the last Friday of every month."

"But I've never been here on a 'last Friday.'"

"That's why you didn't know. That's the day we buy lottery tickets."

"I wouldn't have put money in that envelope if I'd known it was for that." I could see Grandpa, at warp speed, spinning in his grave.

"Too late now," Stella said. "It's yours." She reached for a sheet of paper and thrust it into my hands. "On Saturday morning I pick up the money and buy the tickets. I photocopied all the tickets onto a sheet for you, just like I do for everyone else. I faxed them to you. Everyone knows to check on their numbers. And Saturday night we won!"

"But I didn't do anything," I protested. *Including hooking up the fax machine that annoys me so much.* "This is all a misunderstanding."

"Of course you did something. Everyone who puts money into the kitty shares equally in the win."

"Well, I can't take it. The rest of you can split it. Have a nice dinner, or something. On me." Cricket's eyes grew so round I thought they would pop right out of her head. Frantically she gave me the signal to zip my mouth.

"It isn't going to work that way."

"I don't want it. Give me my five dollars back and we'll pretend this never happened." I felt panic rising in my gut. I was an innocent babe where money was concerned. Grandpa had seen to that.

"Are you nuts?" Stella's ice-blue eyes were wide with astonishment. "This is the deal, Cassia. Anybody who puts money in the pot shares in the winnings. I suppose we never really thought anything big would come of this, but now that it has, rules are rules. You *have* to take it."

"She's in shock—pay no attention to her," Cricket babbled. "You can't expect to get anything sensible out of her right now. Give her some time to get used to this."

"I don't need time," I pleaded, my stomach sick. "You take it. Giving money to me is like shipping snow to Antarctica! I don't need it!"

"Where do you live, Cassia?" Stella demanded. "An apartment somewhere, right?"

"Yes, but…"

"How many bedrooms do you have? One or two?"

"One, but it's what I can afford…." I snapped my mouth shut, seeing the point Stella was trying to make and not wanting to help her make it.

"And what about that dog?"

"Winslow? What about him?"

"Does he get to be outside and play?"

"When I can take him. We go to the park."

"Wouldn't you like a fenced-in yard for him?"

"Of course, but…"

"And another bedroom or two so you could move around?"

"Yes, but…"

"And where do you give your money?"

"Tithing, mostly. The rest I live on."

"Tithing, huh? Isn't that like ten percent of your income? And didn't you say something about going back to school to finish a master's program?"

"Yes…" My suspicious meter was suddenly flailing.

"Here's a chance to give much more than the ten percent of the pittance you earn here."

"Of course, but I don't believe in the lottery. It's like, like…like ill-gotten gains. Do you know how many families are hurt by gambling?"

As I spoke, Bob yelled in the background, "Whaddayamean it's too late to place that bet? Do you know who you're talking to here?"

"Then I'm glad you did win a portion of this money," Cricket concluded earnestly. "Because you, at least, will handle it properly."

"I really don't know what I'd do with a million dollars, Stella. You're sure I can't give it back? I wish my grandfather were here…."

"A million dollars?"

Something in Stella's voice was so odd that I looked up at her. She was staring at me in amazement and the start of a smile played around her lips. "You aren't going to get a million dollars, Cassia."

"I'm not?" Good news at last. I wished Cricket would quit smirking at me. She was not helping my mental state.

"Cassia," Stella said gently, "the jackpot was almost one hundred and eighty-five million dollars. Your share is…" She held up a slip of paper on which she'd done her own math earlier. "This."

On the paper was written "$20,555,000.00." Over twenty million dollars.

A rushing filled my ears as blood raced to my head. I reached for the desk just as my kneecaps liquefied.

"You'll get used to the idea," Ed assured me as he

jumped down from his desk. "But I got used to the idea in a minute or two." He stabbed his fist into the air. "Vacation time. Look out, fishies! Lake cabin, here I come!" He came to his senses for a moment. "Oh, man, I'd better look at boats right away. Maybe a cabin cruiser." He darted for his phone.

"Who'd waste money on fishing when you can travel?" Betty said. "I'm going to go around the world. I wonder which direction I should go first—around the equator or over the poles?"

As we were talking, Paranoid Paula sat at her desk writing furiously while the others bounced frenetically from one dream to another.

"What are you doing?" I asked, shakiness in my voice. This was too surreal for me.

"Writing my will." Paula paused to lick the tip of her pencil and began to write again. "If I'm going to be a multimillionaire, I don't want that lazy, no-good son-in-law of mine to have a dime. Why, if I were hit by a bus in the parking lot on my way home today, he'd quit his job, put his feet up and never move again except to change the batteries in the remote."

I felt tremors running through my body, and my hands shook as I put them to my cheeks. My nerve endings were flailing like a downed electrical cable, blue fire shooting from the tips of the exposed wire.

"Well, we aren't going to get quite as much as we'd all like to think," Betty announced. "After all, a good share will go to taxes." Then she brightened. "But I think we can all manage on the few million that are left."

* * *

I didn't even realize I'd fainted until I woke up with Thelma's worried face next to mine and my office mates frantically waving pieces of paper near my face to give me more air. Ed unceremoniously helped me to sit up and propped me against the side of Stella's desk.

"I've called someone to take you home," Stella said briskly. "You need time to think this through. The rest of us have known since Sunday."

"I fainted, too," Betty chimed in. "Plop. Just like that. Right on the kitchen table. I barely missed a hot casserole. You'll snap out of it soon enough. I did."

"Who did you call?" I asked faintly. I'd never given anyone my sister's phone number, and Grandma didn't drive. Even Cricket didn't know much about me outside of work.

"Randy, that guy you always talk to in the parking lot. He's going to drive your car home and take a taxi back to work."

At that moment there was a loud rap on the door, and Bob opened it a crack to let Randy through. The din in the hallway was deafening.

"The media has arrived," Bob said breathlessly. "Randy, there's a back door. You'd better use that to get Cassia out of here. Otherwise she's going to be mobbed."

Randy nodded briskly. Thrusting his hands under my arms, he hoisted me to my feet. "Come on, Cassia, let's get you home. And one day we'll go shopping for a new car for you. I hear you came into enough money to buy it."

7

Apparently I fainted again when I saw the people clustered around my car. I didn't come to until we were nearing my apartment building.

I looked across the car at Randy, who was driving with grim determination on his face. When he heard me stir, he turned toward me.

"Are you okay? You didn't bump your head or anything, did you?"

I investigated the top of my head for lumps. "No, I don't think so. I've never fainted before," I admitted, "except the time I had stitches and the injection to kill pain hadn't started to work yet. I feel really silly."

"If you were going to faint again, this was as good a time as any. I probably would have fainted, too."

I studied his profile. "It isn't true, is it? Any of this, I mean. Did Cricket put you guys up to this? What a joker she is."

"No joke, Cassia. No prank. You and your office

mates won a hundred and eighty-five million dollars. Of course, after taxes, if you all decide to take a lump sum, that will be more like…"

I covered my ears like a small child. "I don't want to hear it. I don't want to know."

The accountant in Randy got the best of him. "You can't stick your head in the sand like an ostrich. It's something you've got to deal with."

All the things I'd ever learned about money from Proverbs began to tumble through my head like a bunch of rogue gymnasts.

Riches won't help on the day of judgment…. Trust in money and down you go! Don't weary yourself trying to get rich…. The person who wants to get rich quick will only get into trouble….

"Maybe I could give it away." A flutter of hope rose in me.

Randy swiveled his head to stare at me. "*Give* it away?"

"I could…" Then I felt as if I'd smacked myself in the face. "But I don't even know how to do that!"

"You couldn't just stand on the street corner and hand out money," Randy said, his voice thick with sarcasm. Then he looked at me and I could tell he regretted being sharp with me. "You wouldn't want that kind of money to go to just anyone, Cassia," he pleaded. "It would have to go to good causes, to bona fide charities…."

"All right. Name some. I'll call them." Didn't anyone understand how catastrophic this was? I'm the last person on earth who should be entrusted with this kind of money. I'm completely inexperienced with large sums of cash. Besides, Christians are squeamish about things like the lottery. Even though the Bible doesn't expressly say *don't do it,* there are many reasons not to. For me to take lottery money as my own was nearly unthinkable.

I sat back to consider my nonexistent options.

"I'm pretty clear on the fact that I can't take it, Randy. Proverbs 28:22 is the clincher, don't you think?"

The blank expression on his face told me he hadn't been thinking that at all.

"'Trying to get rich quick is evil and leads to poverty,'" I quoted. "I really can't afford to get any more poverty-stricken than I already am, you know. Except for that twenty million, I'm barely making it right now."

He gave me a very pained expression. "Listen to me, Cassia. I want you to go home and talk to your family and friends. Then call an attorney. He'll probably have you contact your banker or investment counselor and an accountant. Let those people help you decide." His look was pleading. "You'll do that, won't you?"

"I suppose it's a good idea. My sister is a loan officer in a bank. She could help me."

Randy looked relieved. I felt like hugging him for caring.

"She won't believe me. She'll say I've been dreaming."

"And in twenty-four hours, after you go to lottery headquarters, she won't be able to say that. The press will be there. You and your winnings will be front-page news."

"I don't know why everyone wants to rush in and get their money right away. Don't we have to wait for…for something? *Anything?*"

"There's probably not much sense in waiting. With so many of you involved, the news is out anyway."

Twenty-four hours. I have twenty-four hours to get used to the idea of being a millionaire. It's just not right. After all, I've had twenty-eight years practicing to be a pauper.

Randy pulled up in front of my building, hopped out of the car and ran around to my side to help me out. I guess I wasn't as steady as I thought, because I nearly pitched forward out the door and onto the sidewalk.

Fortunately Adam Cavanaugh came around the corner at that moment carrying a bag of groceries. When he saw Randy trying to prop me up, he set down the groceries and strode over.

"Cassia, are you okay?"

Well, do I look okay?

"She's had a shock. I offered to bring her home, but…"

"I can take her from here," Adam said briskly. "I live in the apartment below hers."

"Is that okay with you, Cassia?" Randy asked. He looked worried about turning me over to this big, rugged-looking stranger.

"Sure. Why not?" I was giddy and feeling light-headed. At the moment I wasn't sure I'd care if he handed me off to a boatful of tuna fishermen.

I'm not a little girl—I'm five feet eight inches tall—

but Adam somehow managed to scoop me up and carry me into the building.

"She can sit at my place until she's feeling better," he told Randy, who'd carried the groceries in behind us. "What happened to her?"

Randy sighed and shrugged. "It's pretty hard to explain. I think Cassia should tell you." He turned to me. "Are you okay?"

"Fine. Fit as a fiddle. Right as rain," I yammered.

He took his business card out of the silver card case in his pocket and scribbled on it. "I put my home number on the back. If you need anything, call me." Randy gave me a compassionate glance. "I'll say a prayer for you, Cassia."

"You're a saint, but I'm going to be fine. Really."

As soon as I figure out how to get rid of this money.

Reluctantly he backed out of the apartment. Adam gave him a reassuring nod and he disappeared.

Adam turned to me. "What happened?"

I opened my mouth and shut it again. How did I tell him that by tomorrow at this time I would own more money than any person in the world should have? It is obviously impossible to convince anyone that I don't want or need the money. I had to talk to someone who would understand.

"May I use your phone? I need to call my grandmother."

Adam looked a little annoyed, but didn't speak. Instead, he handed me the cordless phone and sat down in the chair across from mine. Pepto, cat-food breath and all, crawled up next to me, purring.

I dialed, hoping Mattie would pick up, but her phone rang until the answering machine clicked on and Mattie's message began. "Is this thing working? I can't hear anything...yes? Oh! Okay. Hello, this is Mattie Carr. I'm not here right now—do I have to say that? Of course they know I'm not here! Well, leave a message and your number and I'll call you back.... Unless you're calling long distance. Then *you* call me back, okay? There. How was that? Do I hang up now...?"

Grandma had refused to rerecord the message, and it sounded so like Mattie that Jane told me not even to attempt to get her to change it.

Jane didn't answer either. I was transferred into her voice mail at both home and work. I debated calling Ken. He still didn't accept the idea that I wasn't madly in love with him, and I didn't want to have him think that I wanted his advice about what to do with the money. Unless I'd underestimated him, I'd guess that Ken's idea of charity would probably be new four-wheelers for all his buddies.

That left me to talk to Winslow, Pepto or the man across from me staring at me as if I'd landed from outer space.

Although I didn't mean it to happen, tears started coursing down my face like little rivers. Some women cry pretty, but I'm not one of them. My nose gets red, my eyes bloodshot and my skin puffy.

Adam reached for a box of tissues and put it on the couch pillow next to me. Then he sat back, crossed his arms and waited for me to be done bawling.

I'd thought I was going to build up a real head of steam and cry for hours, but with Pepto purring beside me, kneading my thigh with his paws, and Adam patiently biding his time, I fizzled out midcry, although it took me a couple minutes to mop up and wish I'd had a pillowcase to put over my head to hide what were probably big red blotches, pale white skin and an unflattering starburst of freckles punctuating the mess.

"Want to talk about it?" Adam looked compassionate, nonjudgmental and mildly interested.

He was here, and Mattie and Jane weren't. "The most awful thing happened to me today!"

"Did you lose your job? Get mugged? Have your car stolen?"

His eyes widened each time I shook my head.

"You didn't get…you know…attacked by a man…."

"No!" And I collapsed again into a mess of tears. "I won the lottery!" As I was crying, I heard him get up, run water and put a teakettle on the stove. A few cupboard doors opened and closed. Shortly he returned carrying two mugs of steaming tea, spoons and a bowl of sugar on a tray.

He pressed a mug into my hands, and I took it gratefully. I watched him as he stoically waited for me to pull myself together. What an incredible-looking man, thought my wayward mind. Even in such dire straits, Adam could bully his way into my thoughts.

"I'm so sorry. I had no intention of falling apart. I'll just go back to my place…."

"I don't think I heard you right," he said, his full attention on me for the first time since we'd met. "I thought you said you'd won the lottery."

"I did. That's what's so awful!"

"Let me get this straight." Adam leaned forward, his dark eyes skewering me with intensity. "You won money and you're upset. I can't say I understand that. How much money did you win?"

I'd intentionally been blanking out the figure, so I said, "You know the big lottery? The one they drew for on Saturday night?"

"Yeah. There was an obscene amount of money in it—around a hundred and eighty-five million…." His voice trailed off and his eyes grew wide. Adam has lovely eyes. "You won that?"

I nodded miserably. "Not all of it. My office pool won it. Apparently nine of us participated and have to share it. It comes out to, oh, I don't know, something like twenty million. What am I going to do?" I felt the tears coming again.

He sat back, and I could tell he was stunned. He hesitated before answering, "Celebrate?"

"I can't celebrate."

"Why not?" His handsome face looked so puzzled I almost laughed.

"You don't know me very well," I began, "but I'm the daughter and granddaughter of preachers. For them, there's a whole lot wrong with winning the lottery—ill-gotten gains, potential addictions, deprivations of family and who knows what else? Gambling is frowned upon in our family."

"Then why did you buy the ticket?"

"I didn't know I was buying it. I thought I was putting five dollars into the office kitty for a gift for someone!"

His face began to clear, and amusement crept into his voice. "And though you didn't seek it or want it or even know you were a part of it, you won over twenty million dollars?"

My shoulders slumped. "Yes. Isn't it awful?"

He stared at me as if I'd lost my mind.

"I tried to give it back, but my office mates won't hear of it. Even Cricket, who I can usually count on to listen to me, insists the money is mine. I can't get my sister or grandmother on the phone. They'd understand my problem. I have to get rid of it somehow!"

His eyes narrowed. "So you'd be willing to put twenty million dollars back in the hands of the people who approve of the lottery?"

I opened my mouth to speak and snapped it shut again. I hadn't thought about it like that. I would be handing the money back to people who'd use it to sweeten another pot. Then which was worse? Keeping it or giving it back? Suddenly I didn't know. I started to cry again.

Pepto, who didn't like my tears, stood on my legs and tried to bat away the moisture with his paw.

"Do you want to go back to your apartment?" Adam asked gently.

Miserably I shook my head. I was terribly bad company right now and didn't want to be alone with myself. "Can I stay here for a bit? Just until I can find my sister or grandmother."

"I guess so," Adam said, obviously unsure what to do with me.

I heard the neighbor across the hall, our built-in decorum monitor, flutter by the door. A smile pulled at my lips, but I was too weary to do more than twitch the muscles in my face.

All this crying is exhausting. "If I could just lie down for a minute…" I sagged into the inviting softness of the couch. The leather felt cool and buttery against my fiery cheeks.

Pepto curled into my body as I put my head on a pillow. His thick body was solid and warm against me, and his purr rumbled softly in my ear. The last thing I felt was his tongue licking the inside of the arm I'd thrown around him.

CHAPTER

8

Adam paced the length of the galley kitchen like a lion in a small cage. He thought better when he was moving, and right now he needed all the help he could get. Cassia's bizarre predicament ricocheted around in his head until it began to hurt. Why on earth had this wacky woman and her off-the-wall story fallen into his lap now?

It was the ideal story, of course—Beautiful Young Woman Wins Lottery And Tries To Give It Back. Everyone and their uncle would want to read that. What would possess a woman like Cassia to return twenty million dollars? Why would the luckiest stroke in the world bring her to tears of dismay? Magazines and newspapers carrying the article would fly off the shelves. No doubt Cassia would be beating off talk radio chats, and daytime television would be vying for a first interview. The country needed a story like this to divert it from the murders at home and mayhem abroad. The story could be sweet and funny, much like Cassia herself. She was beautiful with her porcelain skin and fine, high cheekbones, and no doubt photogenic. He couldn't miss with this one.

But he wasn't writing anymore. He'd told his agent he was quitting. That he didn't want to write about more pain and loss.

Then he recalled what Terrance had said in return. *You don't have to cover every tragedy in the world... lighten up...do something not quite so heavy for a change, a little mind candy.*

Adam stuffed back a wry chuckle. He remembered very well his own final response. *I'll call you when that story comes knocking on my door.*

He looked over to his couch where Cassia and Pepto were snoozing. There she was, the story who'd come a-knocking.

Adam had rifled through her purse for a key, gone upstairs and let Winslow out for a run. He'd given the dog the bone he'd found still wrapped in plastic and left him happily gnawing on the delicacy. If Pepto was going to turn on him and abandon him for Cassia, Adam decided he might as well try to woo the big dog. So far, so good.

When he returned to the apartment and found the pair still sleeping, he wished he'd walked the dog longer. He wasn't happy about being alone with his thoughts. He'd stopped at the convenience store to glance at the headlines. Jackpot For One Winning Ticket. The story below said that the winner or winners would be claiming their money the next morning. He shook his head. One of the winners was sawing logs on his couch right now.

He didn't like what he was thinking, but he might as well admit it to himself. His energy for writing was back. He could feel adrenaline pulsing in his system and excitement coursing through him. This was nothing like the sad, hopelessly bleak stories about the children of Burundi.

If it had ended with her winning the money, it would have been easier to turn his back on the story, to ignore it and walk away. But there was also that remarkable hook, that amazing twist in the story. Cassia didn't want her share of the jackpot because her upbringing made her feel she'd gotten her hands on tainted money.

But, Adam mused, what that money could do….

He closed his eyes briefly, and behind his lids shimmered an image of his last day in Burundi. He'd said goodbye to Carl and John Austin, brothers and aid workers who had been distributing what little food and medicine they'd had available. He smiled and waved at the others he'd met and befriended in the brief time he and Frankie were there.

He was on his way to the truck that would take them to Bujumbura when he heard a heartrending sound somewhere nearby. It took only a moment to find the source of the sound. A mother, so thin she looked like a bony skeleton herself, was sitting on the ground holding a lifeless infant in her arms. She rocked and moaned, not even comprehending that Adam stood there watching helplessly, tears running down his own cheeks. The image evoked again the feelings that had made him retch before he got on the truck that would carry him back to the airport to catch a connection to the United States. While she grieved her child, he would return to more food than people knew what to do with, a place where obesity, not starvation, was a problem.

What could be done with millions of dollars? How many lives could it save?

But it was Cassia's money, not his. If only she could be convinced to give it to him for...

Get a grip, Cavanaugh. Adam ran his fingers through his hair. He didn't even know this woman, and he was trying to spend her money for her!

Slowly a lightbulb came on in his mind. He couldn't *touch* her money, but he could *write* about it. It would earn him some decent cash, seeing as he was an eye-witness. He was, literally, the only journalist in the world who could truthfully tell the story of this woman's struggle over the money. And every cent he made would go to aiding the children of Burundi. Adam felt the blood pounding in his ears. This story had to be a success. It was, Adam realized, a matter of life or death.

Maybe Cassia could even be persuaded to donate the money to help the Burundians, but it was too early. She hadn't talked with her family yet. He had an inkling from his own childhood in a churchgoing family, but didn't fully understand why this was so difficult for her. The religion stuff obviously meant more to her than it did to him.

He'd been a Christian, Adam thought. He'd believed in God and accepted Christ as his Savior. But then, as he'd begun to travel the world covering humanitarian stories and seeing so much suffering, he'd thought less and less about his faith and more and more about his insidious creeping doubt about why people suffer and children die needlessly. Now, after Burundi, the doubt had fully overtaken him. Raised in a family of believers—his cousin Chase, for example—he didn't like the conflicting feelings tugging at him, but how could a good God…

He gave himself a mental shake. There was no time for this now.

If he could convince Cassia to hang on until he could show her what kind of work she could do with that much money… Adam knew that if anyone could do it, he could, because he knew just how persistent and dogged he could be. Surely, with all the passion he felt for this cause, Cassia would consent. He would have to bide his time, however. He wouldn't rush her. But he could start looking for potential publishers now….

She slept two hours and woke up stretching like Pepto. A yawn, Adam noticed, showing the entire inside of her pink mouth and pearly teeth that was mirrored by his bad-tempered old cat. The cat that had become so enamored of this woman that he was now throwing himself on his back for her, begging for belly rubs. Astounding.

As Cassia stirred, it occurred to him that perhaps she wouldn't be as pleased with the idea of having her story written as he was. He would cross that bridge later. He was confident he could convince her how important this would be. He studied the lovely woman on his couch. Until she'd accepted the fact that she really was a multimillionaire, he'd keep the story he was writing to himself.

His mind went directly into writing mode.

Lottery Creates Reluctant Millionaire—Midas Moment
Turns Sour For Minneapolis Woman Who Doesn't Believe In Gambling

Ever dreamed of making it big the easy way by having your ship come in—winning the lottery or finding a valuable treasure in your attic? Do you know anyone who hasn't had that dream?

Then there is Cassia Carr, one of nine lottery winners sharing the recent $185-million jackpot. A series of misunderstandings led to one of the biggest wins in the history of the lottery, and a woman who's been trying to give her winnings away ever since....

CHAPTER

9

I paced the floor in front of my grandmother and sister as they sat on Mattie's couch staring at me.

"Over twenty million?" Jane echoed.

"Minus taxes," I said faintly, although it doesn't really matter. Having ten million is just as ridiculous as having twenty.

"Hoo-hoo-hoo," Jane said, sounding more like an owl than a banker. "Grandpa never prepared us for this!"

"Yes, he *did*. That's the problem, Jane! Proverbs 15:16!"

"'Better a little with reverence for God,'" Mattie murmured automatically, "'than great treasure and trouble with it.'"

I flung myself dramatically into a chair, but as usual, the theatrics were wasted on my family.

"I don't want to be rich!" I whined. "It's too much trouble! Matthew 6:24, and that's all I have to say about it." I shut my mouth.

No one can serve two masters. For you will hate one and love the other, or be devoted to one and despise the other. You cannot serve both God and money.

Grandma clapped her hands as she always did when it was time to get to work. "We have to pray. Cassia, don't make a decision or give away any of that money until we find out what God wants you to do with it."

"You mean I should go to Lottery Central and pick it up?" Even saying it aloud made me feel sick.

"Everyone else is. There's no way you can stop it from happening now, is there?"

If there was, I couldn't think what it might be.

"If she takes it, she could tithe it," Jane suggested tentatively. "Would that help?"

"Are you saying that it may be okay to put your trust in the luck of the draw as long as ten percent of anything you win goes to a church?" I asked.

"It's not that such games of chance are innately evil," Mattie said slowly. "The problem as I see it is that while to win might be a boon to one or two people, it can harm so many others."

"It's complex," Jane acknowledged. "Acts 1:21-26, you know. The disciples cast lots to decide who would replace Judas as a disciple."

Then they drew straws, and in this manner Matthias was chosen and became an apostle with the other eleven.

This whole thing was far more complicated than even I had realized.

"But why me? I just don't get it. Why couldn't some other more moneywise Christian have won it?"

Grandma chuckled. "You remind me of Moses, my dear. 'Here I am, Lord, send Aaron.'"

Okay, so Moses, *Moses,* didn't feel confident enough to talk to Pharaoh when God asked him to, so God let his brother Aaron take the job. Reading that part of Scripture always makes me want to yell, "Do it yourself, Moses! God's behind you. You don't need a mouthpiece." Yet here I am, doing the same thing.

Grandma looked at me intently, as if she were weighing what it was she had to say next. "You've been acting as though God abandoned you when you won the lottery. I think it is His will."

"That's pretty far-fetched, Mattie."

My grandmother beamed and her eyes danced with glee. "And that's one of the reasons I love Him so much, Cassia. Nothing is too 'far-fetched' for Him. On earth He traded in miracles. That's His business—a virgin birth, healing lepers, making the blind see, resurrecting people from the dead. I know this situation is mind-boggling for you, dear, but just set your concerns aside. Since this snowball has already turned into an avalanche, all you really can do is wait and see what He'll do with it."

"You're right, as usual." I sighed and glanced at my watch. "I hope He's in the mood to unveil His plan quickly."

"Follow His leading, Cassia. He'll pave the way."

That would be her last comment on the subject for a while, I knew. I have a sense that it's going to be a tangled path I travel before He gets me through this one.

* * *

I sat in the kitchen watching the hands of the clock laboriously inch toward the hour I was to meet my office mates outside lottery headquarters to pick up our money. When someone knocked on my door, I jumped up.

It was Mrs. Carver, the seventysomething from across the hall. When I opened the door, she bolted into my apartment before I could stop her. I hadn't met a neighbor other than Adam until someone got wind that there might be a lottery winner living in the building. Since then I'd been sought out, greeted, welcomed and offered everything from homemade cookies to a new plunger and warnings about the state of the pipes in the building. Maybe I have a wannabe chaperone living across the hall from me.

The media had sniffed out Ego Ed, who, of course, wanted to play big shot and talk about being a winner. One thing had led to another, and I'm now an item of special interest in my building.

Mrs. Carver, who'd brought me a crocheted doily and a package of peppermints last night, absently patted Winslow's head and focused her beady eyes on me. "I've been thinking about you all night. I hardly slept a wink."

That makes two of us.

She sized me up before sitting down on my couch uninvited. "I have only two words to say to you: cirrhosis of the liver."

Technically that was four words, but I didn't bother to point it out, since I had no clue what she was talking about anyway.

"My brother-in-law came into some money a few years back. Nothing like yours, of course, but more than he'd ever had before. Worst thing that could have happened to him." She shook her head mournfully. "My poor sister had her hands full. Wished a hundred times it had never happened."

"The liver disease?"

"No! The money! Turned him into a regular sort of idiot, it did. He started by buying an RV." She drawled out the letters, "Arrrr-veee," and shook her head sadly. "He went downhill from there. A fishing boat, a new gun and a snowmobile were next. And he turned to drink—all those new 'friends' he picked up along the way. It was the money, plain and simple, that caused that cirrhosis of the liver. My sister's always said so."

She looked at me pityingly as she stood up. "I just thought you should know."

As an afterthought, she turned back to me. "Oh, and by the way, again, welcome to the building."

When she opened the door to leave, Adam was standing on the other side, his hand raised to knock. He looked startled to see the elderly woman, but greeted her politely. After she disappeared into her apartment, he stepped into mine.

"What was that about?"

I told him and a grin spread across his face. "I think you'd better get used to receiving advice on how to handle this windfall of yours."

"It's not a windfall, it's a catastrophe. And it's not mine to keep. I just don't know what to do with it yet." *Give me a clue, Lord, soon!*

"So you've decided not to give it back to the lottery organization?"

"I'm waiting for an answer on that."

He looked confused. "From whom?"

I pointed upward. "Him."

"God?" He looked rather incredulous at something that made perfect sense to me.

"Of course. Who else?"

He nodded thoughtfully. "And in the meantime?"

"I take one small step at a time and pray for guidance with each and every one."

"So you *are* going to the lottery headquarters today?"

I sighed and felt tears welling in my eyes.

"Would you like me to drive you there?" His eyes were surprisingly compassionate considering that he obviously thought I'd lost my marbles.

"You'd do that?"

"Sure, if it would help."

"It would. Thank you. If we left now, maybe we could stop at Parker Bennett on the way. Today's payday and I'd like to pick up my check."

Adam did a double take and I realized how silly that statement must have sounded to him. But I'd earned those wages and planned to live on the money. I couldn't afford not to collect it.

"S-sure," he stammered. "Let's go."

Adam pulled up in front of the building in a battered-up Hummer that looked as if it had seen more ditches and cow paths than real roads. He tossed a computer case from the front seat to the back to make room for me. It still looked as if a ream of paper had exploded in the vehicle. There were pens, magazines, notebooks and used plastic coffee cups everywhere.

Not that I'm anyone to criticize, mind you. Jane refuses to ride in my car most of the time because I have to clear out the front seat in order to fit her into it. It makes perfect sense to me. I'm a single woman who usually doesn't have anyone in the front seat with me. Winslow is too big to fit in front. He sightsees and sleeps in the back. I clip coupons conscientiously because throwing them away unused makes me feel as though I'm throwing away money.

Whoa. The irony of that just hit me. I'm perfectly willing to hand over a few million to someone, but refuse to waste a dollar off on a brand of toothpaste I don't even like.

Anyway, the coupons, the stuff I need to mail, things to be returned, the library audio tapes I listen to when I drive, an extra sweater and pair of gloves take up most of the front seat. Basically, I think of my car as a large purse and treat it as such. Apparently Adam uses his Hummer as a briefcase.

"Sorry about the mess. I didn't know I'd be chauffeuring a pretty lady, or I would have cleaned it out."

"What is it you *do*, Adam? I don't think you've ever mentioned…" But before I could finish, I became distracted and began giving directions. "Do you know where I work? Parker Bennett? No? If you take this road…"

When we arrived, I guided him to a single door that I knew was open for employees during the day. It was near the desk at which I could pick up my payroll check and, thankfully, tucked away so I could scoot in and out without attracting too much attention.

"Wait here. I'll be right back."

I avoided everyone except Ellen at the payroll desk.

"Well, well, Cassia Carr, Customer Service, here to pick up your paycheck?"

"Yes, thank you."

Ellen handed me a white envelope with my name on it. "So, is the rumor true?" She snapped the large wad of gum in her mouth, put her hand on her hip and stared at me. "Must be, or you got hit by a truck in the hallway. You look like you don't know…and if you don't, who does?"

"There was a misunderstanding," I began.

"Well, I'm with you there. I wouldn't start spending before I had that check run through my account either. What a bummer it would be to think you'd won, get all worked up and then find out you'd made a mistake. I hear you're going to claim the big bucks today."

I stared at her and murmured weakly, "I don't want the money."

"No? You're going to take it in installments, huh? I'm not sure I'd want to take the payment all at once either. What if you messed around and lost it somehow? I've heard of people who've won the lottery, gone out and bought cars, houses, boats and ended up *owing* money! It's not easy being a lottery winner. I've heard that sometimes the money and attention are just too much to handle."

Ellen's mouth runneth over.

"You don't have any jealous relatives, do you? Nobody who'd put a contract with a hit man out on you to rub you out? I've heard of it, you know. Sometimes money creates as many problems as it solves…."

Don't I know.

Ellen gave a final earsplitting crack of her gum and turned around, leaving me with a view of her red polyester-clad backside.

If only I'd known this was going to happen, I never would have put money in that envelope…but how could I know?

As I turned to leave, Hank Henderson from the vice president's office strode by. I'd met him only once before, during my initial job orientation. At that time he'd left me with the distinct feeling that welcoming new employees was one of his more demeaning duties. Today, however, I had taken on a new importance.

"So, is the rumor true?" I didn't like the look in his eyes. Although they were a pale, anemic blue, they were also very green with envy. I felt a chill and realized that there were probably others as unhappy as I was about my winning the lottery—for entirely different reasons.

"I…ah…" Intuitively I sensed that Henderson was a heavy lottery player.

"Never mind. Ed couldn't keep his mouth closed if his life depended on it. Congratulations." He reached out and shook my limp hand. "The things I could do with that kind of money…" He looked at me so intently that I cringed. "Whatever you do, don't waste it."

I stared after him as he walked away. "Waste" ten

million or so dollars? A paroxysm of terror gripped me. How in the world was I, of all people, supposed to know what to do with that kind of money? The only thing I could even think of that I really needed was enough cash to pay the pet groomer. If Winslow was going to look like a million bucks, now I could actually pay for it.

Adam was waiting for me in the Hummer. He'd slunk down in his seat and seemed to be dozing. He opened one eye when I got into the vehicle. "Well?"

There should be a law against men as handsome as Adam Cavanaugh. I have enough to think about without feeling off-kilter every time I look at him. Usually I'm impervious to good-looking men—Ken really hates that about me, since he thinks he's the epitome of the breed—but Adam has an intriguing, rugged, world-weary air balanced with an almost palpable compassion in his eyes.

"Let's go," I said, sounding more determined than I felt.

I must have sighed, because Adam asked, "Scared?"

"Terrified. I don't know why this happened to me, of all people."

"I'm not much of a believer in coincidences," Adam murmured.

"My grandmother calls them 'God-incidences.'"

He looked at me sharply. "What if this is a 'God-incidence'? What if you're exactly the *right* person to receive this money?"

"I couldn't be!" We were closing in on lottery head-quarters and my palms were sweating buckets.

"Why not? You have faith in God. Maybe He meant you to have this."

"Don't confuse me. What kind of wisdom or power do I have to make the money work for something good?"

"If what I read is correct," Adam said slowly, "God prefers to work with people who don't have much power or influence. A teenaged mother for His Son, a couple ordinary fishermen, a little guy who had to climb a tree to get a glimpse of what was happening on the street…why *not* you?" An odd flicker crossed his features, as if he'd been reminded of something painful. Then he murmured softly, "You could do a lot of good in the world."

I don't know which startled me more—that Adam seemed very familiar with the Bible and how God worked, or that perhaps he was onto something. The question I'd been asking was "Why me, Lord?" I'd never even considered the other side of the question…. "Why not me?"

I recalled the phone conversation I'd had with my father last night. Dad has a way of summing things up so that they make sense. I had, he pointed out, come a long way from learning of the money and wanting to get it away from me as soon as possible. Simply "dumping" it and having others decide the money's fate was the cheap, irresponsible way out. "Cassia, to whom much is given, much is expected. It is a privilege to take this cross. This is discipleship. God has called you to do something worthwhile with this money. Will you follow His call?"

Why not me?

10

When we were two miles from lottery headquarters I tried to make Adam turn around and take me home, but he pretended not to hear me. I was yammering at the top of my lungs, but, like a father determined to take his unwilling child to the dentist, he set his jaw and drove on.

"Here we are. Do you see any of your friends?"

"Maybe they won't show up." I was really desperate now.

He parked, turned off the motor, crossed his arms and slumped in his seat as if settling for a long wait.

"I can't go in there alone. Will you come with me?" Somehow I'd made the leap from thinking of Adam not as a stranger but a bosom buddy.

He straightened sharply, looking interested—much more interested than I.

"Are you sure? I don't want to intrude."

"I can't do it alone." I felt an overwhelming sense of gratitude toward him. "Please?"

We were shown into a meeting room filled with long conference tables and metal chairs. Stella was there, looking lovely, as usual. The pale blue sweater set she wore was cashmere, and I had a hunch the diamond earrings were not from a sales cart in the hallways of the Mall of America. She smiled at me, but I could tell her mind was somewhere else—Harrods of London, probably.

Ed was combing his hair in the reflection from a large framed photo of a former lottery winner who was grinning and holding a check for a million dollars. If that was how big one smiled for one million dollars, what did one do for twenty? I doubted I'd smile at all, and entertained the faint hope that I could dodge behind Stella when it came time for picture taking. The last thing I wanted was for this to get back to Simms, where people knew me and my family. I didn't want to jeopardize the teachings or witness over which my grandfather had been so diligent.

My office mates glanced curiously at Adam but were so enmeshed in their own feelings that no one asked me who he was.

Paula was sitting grimly on the edge of a chair hugging her purse to her chest. Even now she seemed afraid her purse would be snatched.

"Hi, how are you doing?" I rubbed her shoulder and she jumped.

"I just want to get this over with. Once I see it in the bank with my name on the account, I'll feel better." She darted an uneasy glance my way. "There are lots of crooks and robbers out there, Cassia. Don't trust anyone." She gave Adam a once-over. "And don't let anyone tell you that they love you. Men will only love you for your money from now on."

I glanced at Adam.

He was trying to blend into the background, something virtually impossible for someone as physically prepossessing as he. It was as if he were a magnet— every single person in the room was drawn to him. I could tell by the looks, the stares and in Stella's case, the suggestive swivel in her hips.

The only ugly thing about Adam is his wristwatch, a complicated-looking affair that tells the date and time in every time zone around the world. He's the kind of guy whose face you'd expect to find on the cover of a magazine promoting "Sexiest Man of the Year." I'm attracted to him, there's no doubt, even though until yesterday he'd behaved as if I was a nuisance to be tolerated rather than a woman he found interesting.

Oh, well. Admiring Adam is a little like appreciating fine art—you understand the beauty even if you don't own it or can't touch it. I don't need the *Mona Lisa* in my living room to love her smile.

"Be careful, Thelma," Paula said. "Don't just hire the first fast talker who comes around to reroof your house. It could be a scam, you know. Why, I went right out and bought a paper shredder—identity theft is a growing problem...."

I can't listen to my office mate's obsessions. Just because Paranoid Paula thinks we can't trust anyone anymore doesn't mean it's true.

It hurts my heart to worry about that. When someone falls in love with me, I want it to be because I'm perfect for him, not because he thinks I come with an enormous dowry. James 5:1 was already coming true.

Look here, you rich people, weep and groan with anguish because of all the terrible troubles ahead of you.

Having money is a great deal of trouble.

The others were beside themselves with excitement, though. Everyone's cheeks were in high color, and Ego Ed was slowly beginning to resemble a rooster about to crow. Even Thelma, whom I'd found to be the rock of common sense around the office, was giddy with joy. She'd always had a good, practical head on her shoulders and could be counted on, I'd found, for wise advice. Today, however, she had nothing but stocks and bonds on her mind.

She grabbed my hands as I neared her. "Cassia, isn't this thrilling?"

I didn't want to be the one to break her bubble. "You have no idea."

"First thing I'm doing is taking my entire family on a cruise. And my grandson wants a pickup. His twin sisters are both graduating from high school next year, so I'll have to set up college funds…."

She was busily giving away the money she hadn't received yet, but who was I to criticize? At least she had a plan for hers, while I was behaving like Chicken Little, going in circles and peeping, "The sky is falling! The sky is falling!"

Is that really me? Where is God in that attitude?

"All I can do is turn this over to Him and let Him take care of the rest," I murmured.

Adam eyed me with the same look he might reserve for Pepto hanging from the top of a pair of shredded living-room curtains. "Just like that?" He snapped his fingers. Looking as though he'd just discovered a new species under the lens of his microscope, he muttered. "I've never run into anyone quite like you, Cassia Carr, not in all my travels."

"Then you aren't hanging out in the right groups, that's all." Feeling a million—or twenty million— pounds lighter, now that I'd shifted my problem off my shoulders and onto God's, I was able tolerate the rest of the morning, even the painful photo shoot. I did, however, manage to hide most of myself behind Stella's bodacious body.

The problem with me turning everything over to God is that, even though I know better and catch myself at it regularly, I always want to grab the problems back to tinker with them in my ineffectual, unproductive way. The lottery money is a perfect example. Although I knew He was the only one who could handle it, I kept putting my two cents' worth in where it wasn't needed.

Besides, I still have to deal with the mail, the telephone and the kazillions of people who suddenly know that I'm the recipient of millions of dollars. And it's been only two weeks today since we won the lottery. But apparently it didn't take much time to effect a total transformation in some people, as Cricket was quick to observe.

"Have you noticed that everyone from the office is getting a little weird on us, Cassia? Except you, of course."

"How so? I'm usually the one being considered weird, as in, 'There she is, that Christian with the weird ideas.'"

Cricket swished the ice in her Slurpee and took a sip before answering. "I thought so at first, too," she admitted. "But I've changed my mind." She stretched out in one of the wooden Adirondack chairs clustered around a fire pit not far from Lake Harriet. She and Stella had been shopping, a recurrent pastime for them, and Cricket had called me to join her as she rested up for another foray into retail.

"You're actually the only one whose personality hasn't changed. Everyone else is getting so...prima donna-ish. 'Why isn't the service faster?'" she mimicked. "'Why don't they make an SUV with three televisions?'" She locked eyes with me. "It's as if the money has made them impatient with life."

"It's like driving a new car," I said. I'd been mulling on this, as well. "They just want to see how much power is under the hood now that they have these ridiculous amounts of money. But they're all lovely people. It will pass."

"Is that why you didn't want the money, Cassia? Because it might change you?"

Sometimes I just want to hug Cricket. She, at least,

is trying to figure me out and not sweeping me into the loony bin without question.

"'If in doubt about a behavior,' Gramps always said, 'ask yourself what is true and good about it. Do good things come from it, or bad?'"

"Good for us, not so good for everyone else," Cricket commented. "I don't like to think about all the people who couldn't afford the tickets but bought them anyway."

"Me neither." We were silent, sobered by the idea.

"You know," I ventured, "none of it's really ours anyway."

Cricket looked at me as if I were speaking Greek. "It most certainly is. I work hard for my money—up until this, of course. I like to think I earn my paycheck."

"I don't doubt it for a minute. But everything we have is still a loaner. Remember when I dropped my clock radio on the floor and you lent me an alarm clock while mine was being fixed?"

"Yeah…" Her eyes narrowed suspiciously.

"Even though I was using the alarm clock, it wasn't mine, was it?"

"Of course not. I love that clock."

"In other words, you were happy to let me use it, but you didn't give it to me to keep forever."

"Right."

"Our lives are like that clock, Cricket. They're really not ours to begin with, so shouldn't we take care of them for the Owner?"

She mulled it over, her expressive face showing a dozen emotions. I could tell I'd hit a tender spot in her. "I've never thought about it like that…."

Finally Cricket brightened and announced, "I think only good should come from your money now that you have it. Make a list, Cassia. Who needs this money the most?"

"How's it going, Cassia?" Jane asked on Monday, knowing full well that if I were honest, I'd say, "dreadful."

"I'm gearing up for the postman."

"Still getting a lot of mail, huh?" Her rich, throaty voice was sympathetic across the phone line.

I eyed the baskets lined along my wall. Earlier in the day Winslow had knocked them over and had had a heyday slip-sliding around on the dozens of envelopes that had scattered across my hardwood floor. Now he was sleeping in the midst of them, a sunbeam shimmering through the window warming his coat and the envelopes making a papery bed beneath him. At least he could sleep with all that mail around him. I certainly hadn't been able to manage that.

"Do you want me to come over again tonight to go through it, or shall we meet at Grandma Mattie's?"

"Let me call you later. I'll work on it today. I also have to spend some time reading the classifieds."

"You're actually looking for another job? Tell me it isn't so."

"How am I going to pay my bills?" Everyone else resigned from Parker Bennett immediately. Maybe I'm silly, but I've continued to harbor the idea that I could take an unpaid leave, live on what I've saved for school and then go back to work. But my savings are dwindling more quickly than I thought they would. And returning to Parker Bennett doesn't seem very realistic anymore.

What's more, every charity, junk mail originator, schoolchild and incarcerated prisoner must have heard I'd come into money, because all were writing to explain why they, in particular, deserved a handout. And that was to say nothing of the suspect and scurrilous distant relatives I'd discovered in the past two weeks—ones my grandmother hadn't heard of.

She was quite sure I don't have a cousin George in Detroit who'd invented the diesel engine. (He spelled it "deesal engine.") I also didn't have a long-lost uncle Martin who had gone missing at sea, washed up on a shore off Miami and had just recovered from a twenty-year case of amnesia. I started to count the number of relatives we'd found for the family tree but quit when I realized that we were no longer working with a tree but with an entire forest—most of them scrubs and infected with oak wilt or Dutch elm disease.

And the sob stories! They broke my heart—until I realized that several had been written by the same hand but signed with different names and that an alarming number were coming in on expensive, heavy bond vellum paper from addresses that hinted at gated communities in the suburbs of Chicago.

"How, Lord? How will I know which of these are from hurting people and which are from frauds, swindlers and deceivers?" Sometimes it is said that money can burn a hole in your pocket. This money was burning a hole in my heart.

A heavy pounding at the door distracted me from the task at hand, but it was by no means an escape.

It was Freddy, the mailman. We're on a first-name basis since all these letters began pouring in. Today he looked like a pack animal carrying a heavy load. "Listen, Cassia, you'll have to come down to the post office to pick up your mail from now on. There's too much here to deliver to your little box, and my back is killing me."

"But Freddy, don't bring it all, just my bills. I can't handle the rest either!"

"That's not my decision to make. You'll have to deal with it yourself."

That's exactly what I've been afraid of—dealing with it myself. I'd already lost my light and phone bills in the mass of letters and feared threatening calls saying that if I didn't pay up they'd be shut off. How pathetic is that—a millionaire living in a walk-up apartment with no lights or phone?

CHAPTER

11

"If she'd only quit wearing that pink T-shirt with My Dog Can Lick Your Dog emblazoned across the chest...."

Who was he kidding? He was always thinking of her. He hadn't quit thinking about her in the three weeks since she'd won the money. She could wear an appliance carton with This Side Up written on it and he'd smile. Everything Cassia did these days tied him in knots.

"Terrance, she's so open and honest about her life and what's going on with this lottery business that I feel like I'm taking candy from a baby. She really doesn't want the money, which is a story in itself, but everything about her is interesting—her unusual point of view, her values, the way she lives her life, her beauty and the fact that she has no idea how stunning she is."

Adam paced the living room while his agent sat on the couch grinning like a Cheshire cat, gleefully taking the credit for suggesting Adam write a fluff story. Clearly Terrance was immensely enjoying the situation now unfolding. Adam, in faded jeans and a new white T-shirt, was a stark contrast to his agent's tailored suit coat and creased navy trousers. But they'd worked well together for many years, proving that sometimes opposites do attract.

"She even made me stop at work so she could pick up her paycheck," Adam marveled. "The woman could *buy* the business, and she's so determined not to take the money that she's worried she won't be able to pay the rent."

"Unbelievable!" Terrance chortled. "What'd I tell you, Adam, old boy? Now, isn't this fun? A story falls into your lap and brings a rich, beautiful woman with it? I told you it would take some brain candy to make you forget what you saw in Burundi."

Adam flinched and his eyes grew black and troubled. "Nothing in the world can make me forget that, Terry."

"Okay, okay," Terrance hurried to say. "Sorry I mentioned it. I know the wounds are too fresh."

Not too fresh, Adam thought, but too deep and too raw to nurse back to health. He knew in his heart that there would never be a time he'd be able to quit thinking of those insect-encrusted children starving to death and too weak to lift a hand to brush away the flies.

Nor did he want to forget. He didn't want to go back to his old, unconscious, self-centered thinking. Every time he'd ever come home from covering a war, an earthquake or some other sort of catastrophe, he'd refused to forget what war and raw nature could do. Otherwise it would be too easy to get comfortable and quit thinking about the millions of human beings out there who got less protein in a day than his bad-tempered, antisocial cat. And, of all he'd ever seen, Burundi was the worst of it. It was simply unfathomable to watch paper-thin children with malnourished and bloated bellies perishing before his eyes.

He eyed Terry speculatively. "How much money do you think you can get for me for this article?"

"First serial rights? With enough material to serialize it? I'm thinking we can hit several markets with this." The calculator in Terry's head was clacking away. "Good money." He threw out a figure. "How's that?"

Normally Adam would have nodded with pleasure at the amount, but tonight he knit his brows together. "That's it?"

"That's plenty! You aren't writing a screenplay, you know."

"Maybe I should."

"What are you talking about?"

"I know people over there who can make a dollar stretch a mile, and I'd trust them to do everything they could to help the children. I want every dime I can get."

"Then ask this Carr woman to donate to your good cause. She's got plenty. She could probably buy Burundi."

Although Adam had been thinking along the same lines, hearing Terry propose it gave him qualms. "That's not right, Terry. I'm already living a lie by writing a story about her and her unwanted millions and not letting her know what I'm doing. She's so open and accepting that she's as easy to take advantage of as anyone I've ever met. I can't take it upon myself to talk her into using her money for my pet project. I've crossed the line already, but I can't go any further."

"You make her sound—" Terry searched for the word "—naive and immature."

"I don't mean to. She may not have had a lot of experience with high rollers and business execs, but she's got life experience and knowledge that's priceless. She's difficult to explain, Terry. Besides, I'm just getting to know her myself. Give me some time and I'll put my finger on it. But for now, I'd be real scum to pressure her in that way."

"You're so ethical and clean living that you practically squeak," Terry replied. "Not that I think that's bad, mind you. You're a clear-eyed, plainspoken, tell-it-like-you-see-it kind of guy. But—" Terry sounded disappointed "—I suppose you're right about keeping Burundi out of it. You have your own reputation to uphold." He rubbed his hands together. "So how are you going to go about it? The story, I mean."

Adam flung himself into the big side chair. "The story? So far, I've got a stunning redhead who believes with all her heart that the millions she's won are 'ill-gotten gains' and has no idea what to do with it. She wants to wash her hands of it somehow. What's complicating this is her belief that God should be in charge of the funds and she's waiting to hear what He has to say. Several vultures, including faux relatives, nonexistent charities and opportunists, have started to surface and will no doubt keep multiplying. She's already learned a couple lessons the hard way."

"Go on," Terry encouraged him.

"They're beginning to circle in the hope that they can find the chink in her armor and she'll start handing the money out…." Adam paused. "And one snake in the grass, living in the apartment below hers, is trying to take advantage of her by skulking around, befriending her to compile a story and make money off her predicament."

"The plot thickens," Terry said as he pushed himself from the couch. "This is going to be good, Adam. I can feel it in my bones. A beautiful woman, money, faith, intrigue and greed—what magazine editor could ask for more?" He slapped Adam on the shoulder as he sauntered past him toward the door. "Let me know how it's going. And welcome back, man. Welcome back."

Adam stayed in his chair staring straight ahead until Terry closed the door and the sound of his footsteps receded.

Welcome back.

Only part of him had returned, Adam realized— much of his heart and mind were still in a desperate, dying country far away. The news told him that the situation in Burundi was deteriorating rapidly. Cassia's one-of-a-kind story held great potential for earning money fast. Would it be so bad to keep the good-neighbor charade up just a little longer? It wasn't as if he wanted anything for himself. Any money he made from this story would go to Burundi.

Lottery Creates Reluctant Millionaire—Midas Touch Turns Sour For Minneapolis Woman Who Doesn't Believe In Gambling
Cassia Carr, an early education instructor who has been working on her master's in child psychology, comes from a family of ministers who preach adamantly against compiling too many "worldly" possessions. Carr's worldly assets now include over ten million dollars after taxes, and the potential to buy most anything she chooses. While her office mates are apparently enjoying the fruits of their "nonlabor," Carr spends her time wishing she were, as she puts it, "broke and happy" again.

Part of her frustration stems from her seeming inability to trust the organizations lining up for a piece of the pie. A con man, known to the police by several aliases, represented himself to Carr as the director of a home for abused and battered women and their children. Carr was seriously considering a sizable donation to the organization when her sister, who is an investment banker, did some research and turned up no such organization. Police are now investigating. This may bring an end to a string of con games, scams and swindles perpetrated on the community over the past ten years.

The experience made the already skittish Carr even more gun shy....

The words were rolling from his fingertips. His heart was pumping with excitement. And he hated himself for it.

CHAPTER

12

"What are you doing hiding back here? Finding you was like finding a polar bear in a snowstorm." Jane flung her round and smiley self into the bench across from me. Though my sister probably doesn't realize it, we are celebrating a dubious anniversary— the day that was three weeks and a lifetime ago, the day I'd picked up my lottery winnings. I'd asked the hostess to give me the most private spot in the restaurant, and she'd done herself proud. We were stationed next to the kitchen and a cleanup station that had probably not seen its own cleanup since the business opened back in the nineties. No one would think to look back here.

"Ewww." Jane wrinkled her pert nose and shivered delicately. "You've always been cautious about over-spending, sis, but this is ridiculous."

"I think you can drink the coffee. I saw someone wash out an empty pot not long ago. Order the decaf."

The waitress came to take our orders and we both asked for sodas—in the can—unopened, no ice.

"Why did you tell me to come here instead of the place we usually eat, across the street?"

"I saw a guy from the press there and also a woman who's been following me for two days asking me for money. Ever since my picture was in the paper, people have been recognizing me."

"Ahh, the famous photo. The least you could have done was to stand up tall and smile for the photographer," Jane chided me. "You were probably more noticeable because you were peering out from behind Stella like you were a second head on her shoulders."

"I didn't mean to be seen. I was just peeking to see how much time I had before the photographer snapped the picture and…well, you know the rest."

"I certainly do. Now not only do I have to explain how my sister won the lottery, I have to tell people that when you were nine you caught your head in an electronic car window gone amok and haven't been the same since. I just say that in the family we call it 'The Big Squeeze' that made Cassia who she is today."

"Oh, you do not."

"No, but I'd like to. I need some way to explain how you, of all people, came to be a lottery-winning millionaire. The ones who know you can't believe you were playing the lottery and those who don't know you want to know how you're going to spend it. And," Jane continued breathlessly, "I heard from your friend Cricket that you made a bit of a fool of yourself at lottery headquarters."

More than once in the past three weeks I'd regretted introducing my sister to Cricket and Stella. They'd bonded immediately, and she'd taken to pumping them for the details she couldn't get out of me.

"How was I to know that every time they tried to come near me with that enormous check they wanted me to hold that I'd start crying and hyperventilating? I'm so confused. On one hand, by taking that check I feel like I've turned my back on everything I learned from our parents and grandparents…."

"And on the other?"

"Grandma Mattie says things happen for a reason and that I need to 'sit tight, pray and listen for Him.' I feel torn in half. That's the reason I've been researching charities and looking at all the petitions and proposals flooding in. At least it keeps me busy."

"Something else has happened, hasn't it?"

I hate it when she does that. What am I, transparent?

"I think my life is ruined."

"I'm glad you're not a drama queen," Jane said dryly. "I'd hate it if you were prone to exaggeration."

"You'd think your life was ruined, too, if you'd been scammed by a ten-year-old."

My sister did a double take. "What?"

"I can't believe how gullible I am. It's humiliating."

"So tell me about the kid."

"Convict in kid's clothing, you mean. The little felon was sitting on the steps of the apartment building when I went to work out at the gym this morning, and he was still there when I got back. He looked so forlorn that I asked if anything was wrong. His eyes welled up in tears and he looked so pathetic…."

Jane winced. "I'm not sure I want to hear the rest of this."

"He told me that his mom and dad were divorcing, that he had to move away from his friends into an apartment and leave his dog behind because they couldn't afford to keep him."

"You didn't…"

"I did. Fifty bucks for dog food."

"Awww, Cassia!"

"It would break my heart if I couldn't have Winslow." Still, that's a pretty weak defense for idiocy.

"So how did you figure out he didn't have a dog, wasn't moving and had a full set of parents?"

"It was purely by accident. I wanted to wash my gym clothes and needed change for the washer and dryer. I jogged to that game arcade a couple blocks from my place to get the coins. And there he was. The little bandit was acting like a big shot, buying sodas for everyone and popping money into machines so his friends could play."

Jane covered the lower portion of her face, and I knew she was laughing.

"It's not funny!"

"Being duped by a ten-year-old high roller? Cassia, it's hilarious. How gullible can you get?"

Pretty gullible.

"I'd report him to his mother if I were you," Jane said when she quit grinning. "That boy needs his creative energy channeled into something other than extortion. If I were his mom, he'd be on probation until he's eighteen." She eyed me speculatively. "Has this type of thing been happening to you a lot lately?"

I should never have made the mistake of allowing my shoulders to droop in front of Jane. Just as in the rest of the animal world, she saw my weak spot and went for it. Jugular Jane.

"You'd better tell me everything."

"Did you know Aunt Naomi has a dear friend in Seattle who's having brain surgery as soon as the family can collect money to pay for the surgery?"

"Jane, we don't *have* an 'Aunt Naomi.'"

I pulled a letter out of my purse and handed it to her. "We do now."

She looked on in horror as I withdrew a bundle of envelopes from the side pocket of my bag. "Here, you can look through these and decide what's worthy of attention. I had no idea we had so many kissing cousins in the family. I'm obviously incapable of separating the wheat from the chaff. I can't even identify the mini-mafia on my block."

"May I take these?" Jane asked, and without waiting for an answer she stuffed them into her own purse. "I'll deal with them."

"How?"

"I'll file them."

"Where?"

"In the circular file on the floor by my desk."

"You're going to just throw them away?" I felt both shocked and relieved. I'm too conscientious to throw them away and too upset to read them. I was relieved and thankful that Jane was willing to make the decision for me. "I'm in over my head, sis. I've been praying and praying, but I have no more idea what to do about this money than the day the winners were announced."

"How about the others? Have you heard from them?"

"Here and there. You know that Stella and Cricket are the only two I see regularly. Stella's father is an investment banker, so she's not too worried about being duped. She refuses to trust any men right now, however. She's afraid they'll all be after her money. She's obviously forgotten that with looks like hers, they'd be after her anyway, whether she were a princess or a pauper. Cricket's only investment so far has been shoes—and a new house to keep them in. I'm not sure that even they know what's going on with the others."

"Well, I'm compiling a list of people for you to interview to help you manage the money until you decide what's to be done with it. I want you to interview them so you find someone you know you can work with. I can pull together an entire team, if necessary, of people I know and trust."

"Can't it just sit where it is? In a bank?" I'd run the check immediately to Jane's bank and opened an account, hoping that was the last time I'd have to deal with it.

"Sis, I work in a bank and I wouldn't advise you to keep it there, not all of it. Balance your investments. Stocks, bonds…"

"Jane…" I wailed.

"Luke 16: 10-12. And I'm not going to say another word about it."

For unless you are honest in small matters, you won't be in large ones...and if you are untrustworthy about worldly wealth, who will trust you with the true riches of heaven? And if you are not faithful with other people's money, why should you be entrusted with money of your own?

I hate it when Jane's right.

"Now that we've got it settled that you'll ask for help with the money, who do you have to help you?" Jane asked.

"You, Mattie, Mom and Dad, Stella, Cricket..."

"I'm working, Mom and Dad are hours away, Mattie's elderly and doesn't need that kind of responsibility and Stella and Cricket have their own lives. You need help, Cassia."

"I just moved here. The only people I know are at my work—" unexpectedly Adam shimmered into my mind "—and at the apartment." I couldn't even say I knew people at church, though I had settled on the little community church less than a mile from my apartment as the place for me. Alive with faith and energy, it's a "church on the move," as my father would say. What's more, it's not so big that I'll get lost in the crowd. I like a smaller church just because I enjoy having someone miss me if I'm not at adult Sunday school or milling in the foyer between services.

"Good. Will you promise me that you'll ask for help from them, too?"

Ask help from Adam? I'm divided on that point. He's very nice and he's patient with me. In fact, he's been downright solicitous some days. Other days he's distant, as if his mind is a million miles away in an unhappy place. He seems as ambivalent about me as I am about him—that approach-avoidance thing. But to be honest, he at least improves the scenery around the apartment building.

"Maybe."

"Promise me, Cassia."

"Okay, okay. Anything to get you off my back."

"No matter how hard you try to ignore and deny it, the money is in your keeping. Until you know what you're doing about it, you need all the support you can get. So keep building the team, Cassia."

Keep building the team.

I was still considering Jane's advice after I stopped at the post office and picked up my mail. I've started sorting it while still at the post office and leaving a good share of it in the garbage there. I was pleased to see a letter postmarked Simms, SD, and none from long-lost Aunt Naomi.

Winslow was waiting for me at the front door when I returned to the apartment. I swear he smiles when he sees me.

"Come on, big guy. We've got a letter from Simms."

Winslow knows the routine. I get a bottle of water and an apple, he gets a bone and we clamber together onto my bed, adjust the comforter just so, plump a few pillows and read the mail. I always read it out loud, because Winslow seems interested.

If I don't read it aloud, he paws at my hand and whines until I break down and humor him. I've noticed that he loves letters from my parents but often dozes when I read something from Ken. I should probably take more of Winslow's opinions under advisement.

"Okay, buddy, here goes. This letter is from… whoa…the *mayor.*" I stared at the thick vellum stationery imprinted with the "Seal of Office" Mayor Ed Parker had designed for himself. It has a pheasant, a plow, Mount Rushmore, Wall Drug and a faint image of his wife all twined together in a gigantic knot.

Now, in some small towns being mayor is a part-time, little-respected position, but in Simms it's a big deal. There's usually more than one person running for office, and the competition can get hot and heavy. I once suggested the contest was so fierce because it was an excuse to use city money for ridiculous reasons, but Ken got all huffy and said there were "important city issues" involved. Apparently Ken and I also define "important" differently. It's not that big a deal to me whether the new city pickup truck is a Ford or a Chevy, although apparently it's a burning issue for some. They hold spur-of-the-moment, informal public debates in the coffee shop before the election so everyone is straight on the issues.

Money for chemicals for the water-processing plant is always on the agenda, as is a new car for the single policeman who patrols the streets. Ken recently told me the reason our local policeman never gets a new car. Apparently he's a little overenthusiastic, and the council is afraid if he has any more horsepower than his 1993 Ford he'll feel obligated to attempt high-speed chases.

Mayor Ed Parker is normally considered to be a practical and civic-minded fellow. The power went to his head a bit when he was first elected, and he tried to name a street after his family, but the family who had it before him protested. Finally they agreed that the new playground section of the city park should be called "Parker Park," and that seems to satisfy both him and his kin.

So to get a letter from the mayor of Simms is quite an honor. Winslow and I snuggled in to read. It was written just as Ed speaks. I could practically hear his voice in my head.

Dear Miss Carr,
Word has come to us of your remarkable windfall. Congratulations on securing such a large amount of money. With this win, you have become the talk of the town. You are now one of our Most Famous Citizens, right up there with Torvald Olleson, who invented the adjustable shoe scraper, which is making things so much easier for people in the community on muddy days. My wife swears by hers.

And we can't forget little Tommy Alfonso Rye, who is now an important doctor at the Mayo Clinic in either podiatry or proctology, I can't remember which. FYI, Dr. Tommy has been generous enough to give our fine little community money and designated it for upgrading the park in our town square. We plan to put in a fountain, which we'll call the Rye Fountain in his

honor. What's more, Torvald has donated shoe
scrapers for every public building in town, and we
are recognizing his contribution by honoring him
with a plaque to be hung at the school. This wonderful gesture was suggested by the school
janitor, who is having a lot less to clean up these
days.

I thought you'd want to know about the generosity of our successful citizens so that you
wouldn't be denied an opportunity to improve
life in Simms. Just so you know, we don't have
enough benches for the park yet, and the community band is protesting the bad condition of our
uniforms. I know how finely you were raised by
Pastor and Mrs. Carr and that you are the most
charitable of persons. A generous endowment
from you would no doubt result in a plaque such
as Torvald's or, if the gesture were large enough,
a portrait or bust in the city library. (The library
could use a few more books, too.)

I wouldn't have written, but I know how bad
you would feel being left out of these community
upgrades from our charitable givers. Far be it
from me to slight an important former community resident such as yourself.

The missus says "hi" and wants you to ask
Mattie for her piecrust recipe.
Yours truly,
The Honorable Edwin Willard Parker
Mayor of Simms

"Winslow!" I waved the paper in front of the dog's

face. "Can you believe this? Even the mayor of Simms!" Winslow snorted, wuffled, yawned sympathetically and shifted his big warm body closer to mine.

"Is this what money does to people? Makes them greedy for themselves and their pet charities? Not that there's anything wrong about giving money to Simms, of course, but shouldn't I, at least, be the one to initiate it? They don't even know if I'm keeping it or not."

I was as surprised as Winslow when tears began raining down my cheeks. Isn't there anyone I can trust anymore? Anyone I can be sure isn't looking at me and calculating just how much money they can get out of me for their good cause? It's easy for Jane to tell me I need a support group and people to talk to, but everyone here knows me only as a lottery winner, not as a person with tender feelings who loves Reuben sandwiches, open-toed shoes, merry-go-rounds and grape popsicles. To them, I'm money personified. I feel as though my personality and my life have been stripped away and replaced by a skin tattooed with images that say Rich. Gullible. Susceptible. Vulnerable. Loaded. Easy picking. Help Yourself. No-Interest Loans Available. Sucker.

"Do I look that stupid to you?" I waved the letter again in Winslow's face before realizing that I was asking—and planning to trust—the opinion of a dog.

"Oh, Winnie." I flopped on top of him and put my arms around him. "What am I going to do?"

He whined a bit and I realized that the button of my shirt was tangled in his fur and pulling his skin. I disentangled myself and rolled off the bed.

He looked at me, appeared to be relieved to be alone in the bed and went to sleep, leaving me even more alone with my problems and desperate to talk with someone who understood, preferably a human.

13

Adam Cavanaugh's door was open when I walked by, but neither he nor Pepto was in sight. I really hadn't expected to see him less than a half hour later when I returned from the store with the components for a major, professional-style pity party and sobfest. I'd purchased three pints of Ben & Jerry's—Half Baked, Peanut Butter Cup and Chocolate Chip Cookie Dough—a bag of fluffy orange Circus Peanuts, a jar of fudge ice cream topping to be eaten with a spoon, salsa, chips, Tums and Clearasil in case all the chocolate made my face break out. Even when I'm feeling sorry for myself, I like to plan ahead. I also rented three movies with sad endings—*Terms of Endearment*, *Where the Red Fern Grows* and *Black Beauty*—and bought a three-pack of tissues.

I even mourned the passing of some of my favorite ice cream flavors that are no longer in the freezer section. My sense of humor and my taste buds always enjoyed Peppermint Schtick, Entangled Mints, Hunka Burnin' Fudge and, oh yes, Economic Crunch. Some people are wine connoisseurs. I happen to know my ice cream.

Misery loves company, and I am my own best company.

I didn't even notice Pepto in the hallway until he stuck out a paw and snagged my pant leg with his claws. Persistence is Pepto's middle name. I shook my leg and tried to pull away. I would have kept on walking, but I'd have had to drag him with me, so I was forced to put down my packages and remove his claws one at a time.

How an animal can snarl and purr at the same time is beyond me.

I was so occupied with Pepto that I didn't even notice Adam come out of the apartment.

"Need help?"

"Oh!" I looked up. "I didn't see you standing there." I shook my freed pant leg. "Your animal accosted me."

"Smart animal. What are you up to? Grocery shopping *again?*"

I tried to close the open bag as I picked it up so he couldn't see what was inside. "A few specialty items, that's all."

I would have been fine if Pepto hadn't decided he wasn't finished with me yet and attempted to climb my leg. I yelped and dropped the bags.

"I don't know how you wooed that cat, but he won't leave you alone." Adam knelt and started to pick up my groceries while I surrendered and held Pepto, just as, in his own inimitable way, he'd been demanding all along.

"What's this?" Adam held up the Circus Peanuts and a bag of chips.

"I was a little low on groceries," I said haughtily, and tried to stop him from investigating further. Unfortunately it took two hands to hold Pepto, who had now interlocked himself with my jacket by weaving through the fabric with his claws. That animal is Velcro on steroids.

"And what have we here?"

Unmasked.

"Feeling sorry for yourself lately?"

"How did you know?" I gasped, realizing after I'd spoken that I'd given a full admission.

"I've seen the way you eat—I share the garbage can with you. When you're feeling good, everything there has been peeled off a fruit or vegetable. Then when I see you in the hall without a smile on your face, I can usually count on some sort of ice cream, doughnut or pizza container in the can the next day."

"You should be a detective!" I said, marveling. Then I got annoyed. "Are you spying on me?"

"Not intentionally. Force of habit. I have to keep my eyes open in my job."

"That reminds me. I've been going to ask you, what is your—"

The door opened and the elderly man across the hall from Adam glared out.

"Just going inside, George. Sorry about the noise."

Adam scooped up my groceries and beckoned me

in. I followed him inside only because he'd kidnapped both Ben and Jerry.

"Hey! It looks great in here. Have you been house-cleaning?" The counters and cupboards were polished, the floor gleamed and there was no dust in sight. Even the piles of magazines had been straightened.

"Not much else to do tonight. I didn't feel like going out."

"Yeah, me neither." I hoped it wasn't lying to say it like that. I simply didn't have anywhere to go.

"What's with all the food?"

"I was planning a party."

"For who? When?"

"Me. Tonight. A 'Poor Cassia Festival and Fashion Show.' I plan to eat and weep, try on all the clothes in my closet that don't fit and cry, watch movies and blubber. You know, just like most parties—I'll have a *bawl.*"

He didn't know if he should laugh at that or not. "If I could figure out how your mind works, I'd be the next Freud," he finally said helplessly. "Why does a beautiful woman, a multimillionaire, want to stay home and feel sorry for herself?"

"Because she's a multimillionaire, mostly." I gestured to my pocket. "Would you like to read the letter that I got from the mayor of my hometown?"

"Sure."

After finishing the letter and flinging himself backward onto the big leather couch, Adam laughed until he nearly cried.

"You can quit laughing any time, you know. This is

so not helpful." I tried to be stern, but hearing his in-fectious laughter and admitting the ridiculousness of Ed's letter made me chuckle, too.

"That is the funniest thing I've read in a long time, Cassia." He finally caught his breath and grinned lop-sidedly. Pepto snarled.

"To you, maybe." I sat beside him ramrod straight and crossed my arms primly. "It's as bad as getting letters from the AWOL 'Aunt' Naomi. Maybe worse. This is from someone I thought *cared* about me and my family!"

"Obviously they respect your grandmother's pie-crust."

He looked as if he was about to laugh again, so I poked his leg with the toe of my shoe. "I'm devastated. Haven't you noticed?"

Straightening and leaning forward, he looked into my eyes, then kissed me lightly in the center of my forehead. Unexpectedly I felt a trickle of emotion run through me like slow-moving electricity. It was cold and hot, spicy but sparkly. Thoughts of Jane's advice about team building flickered into my mind. Adam was suddenly on my short list of first picks.

Apparently he'd surprised even himself. "Sorry, that was probably too forward, but you looked so all-out miserable…"

I touched my forehead gently, vowing not to wash the spot for a week. "It's fine, really. The only other person who kisses me there is Winslow."

Adam's tongue popped out of his mouth, and I thought he was going to start spitting invisible dog hairs, but he gathered his self-control, crossed his own arms and stared at me.

"I meant to say—" I tried to recover "—that I'm in need of some human empathy and compassion." Abruptly I felt like a frustrated child. "Oh, why doesn't He hurry and tell me what to do with the money so I can get back to my life?"

"But what if this *is* your life now, Cassia?" Adam again looked into my eyes, and that sparkling sense of lightness bled through me.

"Proverbs 27:24."

"Sorry, but I don't speak Bible, Cassia. I can struggle through a little New Testament, but I'm not fluent in Old Testament. Not like you are, anyway."

"'Riches do not continue forever….'"

"Of course not, but God's got 'forever' planned, right? Looks like He wants you to have it in the here and now."

All right, I didn't want to do it, but I had to pull out the big guns.

"Habakkuk 2:9!"

Even my grandfather didn't quote Habakkuk all that much, because it was too difficult for the congregation to find, tucked as it was in the back of the Old Testament between Nahum and Zephaniah.

Adam looked at me dumbly until I quoted, "'How terrible it will be for you who get rich by unjust means!'"

I didn't even realize tears had formed in my eyes until I felt one skim my cheek.

When he held open his arms to gather me in, I didn't protest.

I babbled and blubbered into his shirt, making a general mess of both of us, until swirling emotions in me had worn themselves out. I blew my nose on the handkerchief he gave me and didn't object when he tucked me securely beneath his arm. We sat that way silently for a few minutes, Adam lost in his thoughts and I in mine. And when he spoke again, he knocked me right off my underpinnings.

"If your beliefs are so much a part of your life, why don't you trust Him?"

"Whaddayamean?" I demanded, both hurt and insulted.

He pushed himself off the couch and moved to the chair across from me. "It's clear that for you lottery money comes with a negative history—families hurt by gambling, money that could have been spent in everything from missions to medical research, a contributing factor in the breakups of relationships, the list goes on."

"So you *do* understand why I can't keep it."

"Then why do you have the money in the first place?"

"I didn't intentionally go out and buy tickets for it, if that's what you mean."

"I know that. It came to you through a misunderstanding, lack of familiarity with the habits of your office, crazy timing and who knows what else. Would you agree?"

I nodded mutely, wondering where he was going with this.

"If it was so unlikely that you, of all people, could

actually win the lottery—because you don't believe in it, don't participate in it and are, from what I've observed, money phobic…"

The man was reading me like a book.

"Try to imagine that you are exactly the *right* person to have the money. Then it's not about getting the money out of your care as quickly as possible, but about discovering what you're supposed to do with it."

And how would I discover that?

On Sunday I literally ran toward the Answer.

The community church looked like something from a Currier & Ives Christmas card—without the snow, of course. Now, in May, bright green ivy clung to the ancient red-brown bricks and gigantic elms shadowed the building. The shake-clad steeple stabbed into the sky and the stained glass windows looked spectacular even from the outside.

Growing up, I'd never really appreciated the faithful of the past. Like most kids, I believed that I was discovering everything for the very first time, that somehow my breakthroughs were more wonderful than anyone else's, that God was whispering just to me of the miraculous things He'd done. Then I'd opened a hymnbook.

Grandpa Ben often regaled us with what he called "the story behind the story" of the hymns. "Do you know," he would ask, lowering his voice until my eyes would widen and Jane would scuttle a bit closer to me on the couch, "that the man who wrote 'Amazing Grace' was a slave trader before he came to Christ?"

I once was lost, but now am found; Was blind, but now I see. That was an understatement.

How many things am I blind to right now?

"Help," I murmured to the only One listening, "please?"

CHAPTER

14

Carr's wish is to fund small, struggling Christian charities that often fly below public radar and are overlooked by larger charitable givers. Though it's a worthy goal, Carr is discovering the path to charity is paved with not only the genuine and the heartfelt, but also frauds, hoaxes and rip-off artists.

Nowhere is this more apparent than within her fast-growing extended family. Letters arrive daily from long-lost cousins, aunts and uncles asking for cash, assistance and even a college education....

Adam had begun talking briefly to Cassia about his work, that he traveled out of the country so much because he worked on assignment doing research for articles he wrote. She hadn't seemed interested in the articles, but immediately wanted to know which countries he'd visited and if riding a camel was really as uncomfortable as rumor had it. Totally guileless herself, she rarely seemed to consider that others would be less than honest in return.

Adam stared at his computer screen with warring emotions battling in his gut.

What am I? Pond scum or humanitarian? Conniving, deceitful lowlife or do-gooder? Don Quixote jousting at windmills?

Conflicting thoughts raced through his head like marathon sprinters when he recalled the expression on Cassia's face. Guilt—a relatively rare emotion in him—ran rampant.

He'd just attempted to manipulate her perspective for his own objectives. This woman could put his brain in a snarl like no one else. He'd interviewed belligerent radicals, intractable dictators of small countries, rebel leaders and, worst of all, politicians. None of them had flummoxed him like Cassia. Still, he was working her like a fine instrument, making her play the tune he wanted to hear and influencing her for his own purposes.

Definitely pond scum.

Wasn't he?

Clearly, the more he knew about her and the longer he could help Cassia to hang on to that money, the better his story would be. And maybe he'd been overscrupulous in rejecting Terry's suggestion. Of course it wouldn't be right to talk to Cassia about Burundi now, but if she should decide to look into various charities, perhaps in time he'd have the opportunity to make her see that his pet charity was more deserving than all the others.

But he had no business telling her that this money was "God's will" for her life when he knew full well that he was hoping to talk her into keeping it so that he could write an attention-grabbing story that would sell papers, magazines, or even a book, and maybe even determine where the money would go. He and God hadn't been on speaking terms since he'd returned from Burundi. It was ironic that now he was invoking "God's will" for someone else.

But what's a poor little rich girl to do? Even individuals in her own hometown are calculating their fair share of the city's daughter's bounty. Whom to trust, Carr has discovered, is as difficult as deciding what to do with the money itself….

Adam stared at his computer screen. This girl had to be protected not only from herself but from every other person with dollar signs instead of pupils in their eyes. And he was one of them. But he didn't want to hurt her. He had her best interests at heart.

So that makes me the big shot good guy, right?

Adam prowled the room like a caged animal, not noticing that Pepto, snaggle-toothed, disreputable and obviously relishing his master's pacing and discomfort, was stalking right along behind him. When he sat down, he pulled up a second story he was writing.

Central Africa, light-years away from most
people's minds and hearts, is Burundi, a landlocked, mountainous country, not much larger
than Maryland. It is populated by the Tutsis, the
Hutus and the country's original Twa pygmies.
The tension between the Tutsis, originally from
Ethiopia and Uganda, and the Hutus is decades
old and has erupted in conflict many times over
the past forty years.

Life is hard there, with the potential for
drought, flooding and landslides. That is not to
mention the toll of AIDS, which affects more
than 11 percent of the Burundians and has
ravaged population growth with lowered life
expectancy, reduced numbers of live births and
elevated death rates. Less than 3 percent of the
population will make it to sixty-five years of age.
The average life expectancy is approximately
forty-six years....

And so many won't make it for more than a few
months or years, he mused. The words on the screen
haunted him. The average fertility among Burundians
was over six births per woman. How many in each
family lived to adulthood? He didn't want to consider
it.

Burundi, Cassia and her unwanted money whirled
in his mind. How could it be bad to want so much for
those little ones whose pathetic lives could be counted
in months rather than years? He broke out in a sweat
just remembering.

He'd visited the home of a woman who, he'd been told, cared for orphans and castoffs. Her job was exacerbated by AIDS, as young parents could no longer take care of their children. It was another of the many images that he'd been unable to shake upon his return to this land of plenty. Open fires, ragged blankets, or parts of them, food for one or two being spread between six or seven—it was a pitiable sight. But it was the children's eyes that had gotten to him. They were like black holes burned in a blanket—ashy eyelashes, empty-appearing sockets, eyes that stared out of gaunt faces toward the bleak future. They had reminded Adam of miniature men and women waiting to die. The hopelessness of the children had hit him like an invisible wave, an icy miasma that cast a pall on his soul. It was a place no one would *want* to visit. Even those who were not dead were not actually living either. They were simply waiting out their time. The sporadic rations some received almost cruelly prolonged the inevitable.

He remembered dropping to his knees inside the hut as if someone had taken a swing at the backs of his legs with a club.

Frankie, his photographer, had taken it hard, as well.

"I can't shake the images," he'd told Adam when they'd spoken the week before. "Concentration is impossible. I can't think straight. Instead, all I can see is a slow-motion replay of the kids in that hut. Something's happening to me, Adam. I can't detach myself from this story. I watch people buy too much, eat too much, whine too much, and I want to yell at them. Don't they know how fortunate they are?"

More than once Adam had found Frankie out of sight with tears streaming down his cheeks. They'd both emptied their pockets of change and most of their cash, put it into a basket and given it to the children's caretaker. Her response had pierced their hearts.

"For the next ones," she had said. "For the next ones."

It was perfectly clear she didn't expect this group of children to be around long enough for it to actually help them or that the tide of homeless, helpless children had been stemmed. There would be more starving, hurting children to follow.

Adam's jaw tightened and a tiny nerve jumped in his cheek. He regretted starting Cassia's story, but the die was cast—the publishers and magazine editors were waiting. It was a bitter pill, but he was willing to take it. He hoped with all his heart that if Cassia had seen what he had seen and walked in his shoes, she would understand why it was important to give every dime he could to ease those suffering people's pain. But at this moment she had no idea what drove him. She literally didn't know Adam from…well, Adam.

His plan had now taken on a life of its own. He could sell her story, and if there was a God—a pretty big "if" for him these days—maybe she'd be willing to give that money to the children, as well.

But if she gave the money away too soon, who knew where it might end up? What was his part in this? Traitor or knight in shining armor? Perhaps a little of both. He'd do or say whatever it took to ensure that "his" children benefited from Cassia's money. Here, in the apartment beneath her own, Adam had an edge over the others. She trusted him. She was open and garrulous, naive and sweet, innocent and untouched by much of the world. Cassia was a bit of a miracle in this day and age. And she was real. She would talk to him, share her thoughts as willingly as she shared flowers, fruit salad and her faith. Getting a page-turning story from her would be like taking candy from a baby.

Adam froze for a moment before correcting himself. Like taking candy *for* a baby. He had to remember. What he was doing was *for* the babies.

He glanced at his watch. He had to get away from his own thoughts. He picked up his keys and left the apartment.

"Hey, old man, what's with you? You've hardly said a word all night." Dick Aimes clapped Adam on the shoulder. Dick, another journalist and longtime friend, had started writing about the same time Adam had first published. "Something wrong?"

"Decompressing, that's all."

He'd joined his buddies on one of their traditional Wednesday-night gatherings and, theoretically, at least, was supposed to be having fun.

One of the others at the table, a news reporter, added, "Stay home for a while. I've been assigned to court reporting. Take my job…please."

"Dick said you've been researching a new story and you won't say what it is. What's the big secret?"

Adam opened his mouth to respond and closed it again. The big story was the ethical conundrum in which he'd found himself. He was already on a slow, slippery side from the high road to the low. He didn't want to say anything to complicate his life further.

For the first time since he'd returned from Burundi he realized that he missed God. There was a time he could have discussed this with Him and gotten some advice. Unfortunately, God didn't exist for him anymore. Burundi had seen to that.

CHAPTER

15

I let the doorbell ring three times before I decided to answer it.

Jane and my grandmother always call before dropping in for a visit, and I can identify Adam's distinctive shave-and-a-haircut-six-bits knock. Not only that, Winslow, by some odd animal instinct, knows whenever Adam is at the door. He stands up and whines until I let Adam into the apartment. If I don't come immediately, Winslow gives me the evil eye. I *think* it's an evil eye, anyway. Who knows what a hairy, half-sheepdog's eyes are actually doing?

For some odd reason, Winslow is enamored of Adam, and Pepto is besotted with me. We've never dared put the two of *them* together in the same room for fear of World War III. It's Winslow we're most afraid for, since Pepto has been known to fearlessly take on everything from the refrigerator to the UPS man.

Adam has since switched to FedEx.

I was surprised and pleased to see my friend Randy on the other side of the peephole. I love it when he stops over after work.

"Hi, stranger!" I threw open the door and waved him in. "How are things at Parker Bennett?"

"Pretty dull." He looked like a deflated balloon. "I suppose you've changed your mind by now and realized that you don't have to go back to the drudgery of the working world."

"I haven't decided that at all. All I know is that I won't go back to Parker Bennett. I have to make a living somewhere. Want something to drink? Raspberry iced tea? Chai?"

"Whatever you're having will be fine." He pulled out a chair at the kitchen table and sank into it heavily.

"What's wrong?" I poured the tea over ice cubes and joined him at the table. I hadn't realized how much I'd missed our morning talks until I no longer had them to depend upon.

"Everyone is obsessed with you guys who won the lottery."

I suppose I shouldn't be surprised. Stella and Cricket had been traveling for the past few days, and they're my only source of information about Parker Bennett. Stella went to Europe on the *QE2* and is flying home after it docks. Cricket spent the weekend at a "fat farm." She's researched every spa in the nation, chosen her top ten and is going to try them out one by one. Her hope is that not only will she get a great vacation but she'll come back looking lean and svelte. Unfortunately, so far she's discovered only that she is severely allergic to exercise or anything that makes her sweat, and that she *loves* granola and soy milk ice cream. I think it will be considered a win if she comes home not having *gained* any weight. The only improvement she's reported to me so far is that she now owns and carries a "Buns of Steel" video with her everywhere she goes "just in case." She never tells me "just in case" what, but if she runs across a renegade pack of women dying to exercise and conveniently standing in an empty school gymnasium, she'll be the woman of the hour.

"Let me guess. They're all wishing it had been one of them who won."

"Pretty much."

"Tell me more," I encouraged. "I haven't heard anything about work in ages." I hadn't known my office mates long, but I missed them. Besides, if Randy were to ask what I've been doing, he'd die of boredom listening to the answer.

"You know about Bob, of course."

"Betting Bob? Nice guy. He's been on my mind a lot lately. What about him?"

Randy's jaw dropped. "You haven't heard? It's been in the papers and all over television."

"My television isn't even hooked up yet," I confessed, "and I'm finding I like it that way. The library is just down the street and I've been reading the books I said I'd get around to someday." I felt myself blush. "As for newspapers, well, I've been doing a little writing of my own. I've been working on this sweet little story about a golden retriever sheepdog cross and a thuggish hooligan of a cat…. I just never got a news-paper subscription started."

"Then you don't know that Bob's in jail?"

That stopped me right between the egg noodles and the cream of mushroom soup. "Bob? In jail?"

"If not yet, he will be soon." Randy shook his head soulfully. "Man, oh, man, Cassia, I never believed money could do something like that to a guy."

"What did money have to do with it?"

"He got the idea that his new money made him invincible, I guess. The way I heard it, Bob was at a casino for three days and nights, lost a lot of money and was pretty peeved about it. Apparently he drove home angry and exhausted. He got stopped by a cop and was pretty argumentative and confrontational. Then the policeman told him that he was obstructing justice and that he was going to take him in."

"Oh, no."

"But that's not the end of it. Apparently, even though he'd been losing, Bob still had a lot of money in his pocket, so he tried to bribe the policeman into letting him go."

I felt my heart sink. "He didn't."

"He did. Bribing a police officer. All that money and this is the mess he's in. Word is that he's already gambled away so much and is incurring so many legal bills and fines that he's not going to be all that much of a millionaire by the time he's done."

Pain welled up in my chest. "He was so kind to me the first days I worked at Parker Bennett," I murmured. "The first time I ran into serious difficulty with a customer, Bob was right there to help me out. I met his wife and son when they came to the office to pick him up. Great people. She's invited me over for coffee."

"Maybe it's a good thing she did, Cassia. She's going to need a lot of support. The legal system frowns on bribing police officers."

"I don't get it." I propped both elbows on the table, rested my chin in my palms and stared at Randy. "Why did he do it? He had everything he wanted or needed."

"Because he has an addiction, Cassia. We've known it around the company for years. You were only there three weeks and you saw it. The money just gave him permission to go wild. Bob's always wanted to be a high roller." Randy looked troubled. "Sorry I'm the bearer of bad news. I just meant to stop in, say hello and ask how things are for you."

I'm even cautious about Randy—and I'm really fond of him. Although I'm not suspicious by nature, I've become so skittish that I don't trust anyone any further than I can throw them. It's not my nature and I don't like it.

Randy must have sensed my thoughts, because he added, "I'm not here to spy on you, Cassia." He looked so dismayed I almost chuckled when he added, "Brother, do I have bad timing. I've been kicking myself every day since you won the money. Remember going upstairs together in the elevator that morning before you won the lottery?"

"I do."

"And how I kept razzing you about getting a new car?"

"Yes."

"I was going to ask you to go out with me that night. I saw you drive into the lot in that junker of yours and made up my mind I'd use the car as an excuse for us to get together. I'd thought we could drive to some used car lots and then go out for coffee. Then," he continued, "you got to your office and found out about the money. I knew immediately that there was no way I could try to date you without looking like I was after something."

He ran his long fingers through his straight sandy hair. "I can see that I've missed my chance. The look in your eyes says it all."

"Oh, Randy. It would have been so sweet."

"It *is* past tense, then? 'Would have been'?"

"For now, at least," I said regretfully. "This breaks my heart. I'm so sorry, but I'm overwhelmed. You're right about one thing. People are not always what I hope they'll be." I told him about the letter from the mayor, about being scammed by a little boy, the bizarre charities haunting me and half a dozen other tales of woe. By the time I was done, we were both laughing.

"Just so you know, Cassia, I understand completely. If it isn't too much to ask, could I just stop over sometimes and tell you what's happening at the office?"

His reluctance to give up was flattering. "I'd like that." I wonder if the FBI has a division that works exclusively on background checks for potential dates. Somebody could earn a lot of money with a service like that. Stella's business alone could probably keep them in the black.

"I promise. No money talk." He pushed away from the table. "Listen, I'd better run. Thanks for the visit." He took my hand in his, and I felt the soft warmth of his palm. "I've missed you, Cassia."

"And thanks—sort of—for the news about Bob." I withdrew my hand. "Maybe I will call his wife."

Winslow romped playfully between us as we walked to the door. To our surprise Adam stood in the hall just about to knock. Adam's expression slid from ease to wariness to ease again, all in the blink of an eye. I sensed in that split second that Adam had sized up Randy and filed him away as someone to watch. How curious.

I walked Randy to the stairway, and when I returned to the apartment, Adam had Winslow by the collar, their faces only inches apart. Adam talked some sort of gibberish to the dog, which Winslow seemed to understand perfectly. Winslow often looks at Adam with that smitten look young lovers have.

Maybe I'm jealous.

I pushed aside the embarrassing thought that I, a grown woman, was jealous because my dog likes Adam as much as he likes me. I smiled brightly. "What are you up to?"

"Not much." Adam looked at me innocently. "And you?"

"That was a friend from work." I walked into the living room as Adam followed. Because we're both home much of the day, we've fallen into the neighborly habit of stopping to chat. When his door is open I know it's a signal that company is welcome. He doesn't seem to need an invitation to drop by my place. Thanks to our proximity, we're both neighbors and friends, but we still don't introduce Winslow and Pepto.

"So what does your friend do at Parker Bennett?"

"He's an accountant. A 'numbers cruncher,' he says. He's always teasing me about my car, telling me I need a new one."

"Yeah, what is the story on that car? It's bringing down the property values in the neighborhood." He yawned and stretched the way Pepto does after an hour in the sun, his muscles rippling beneath his gray T-shirt. Those abs were a result of hours of crunches, no doubt. Adam could easily appear in an ad for joining your neighborhood gym.

"I keep it in the garage."

"Yeah, and my Hummer doesn't like looking at it in there either. It's an eyesore, Cassia." He sat down on the couch and patted the cushion next to him.

I joined him. "It gets the job done." *Hmm, new cologne.*

"Maybe some day you'll want to go more than fifteen miles before the radiator overheats, the wire holding the muffler in place drops off and you want to open the windows, which, I believe are all stuck in the closed position."

"I have an appointment to get it fixed, okay?"

What is it with men and cars, anyway? It's as if an old car—okay, a clunker like mine—is a personal insult to them, an intentional assault on their sensibilities.

"It's budgeted for this week and I'm taking it in on Thursday."

"Budgeted? Cassia, you're a multimillionaire. Go buy a new car. A *brand-new* car." He looked at my expression and threw his hands into the air. "I don't get it. What is a new car to you now? You could pay for it and a dozen others with the interest you've earned on it already."

My stomach sank and my eyes widened. "Interest? You mean there's going to be *more*? I forgot all about interest!"

"You don't have to sound so miserable about it. Most people like having their investments work for them."

"Not me. Can't I ever get this money train stopped?"

Adam stared at me so hard that I thought his gaze was going to slice right through me. He had something on his mind and was weighing the decision whether to say it or not.

"Spit it out," I ordered. "You're thinking so hard it's getting noisy in here." I nestled deeper into the couch. Winslow walked over to lick my hand.

"Do you want to go out for lunch on Wednesday?"

Well, knock me over with a feather! Adam Cavanaugh asking me out? I wanted to smack the side of my head and see if my ears and brain were still connected or if something had shorted out.

"That would be great," I heard myself say. No playing hard to get for me. Food is food and fun is fun. I don't pass either up if I can help it.

Feeling pleased and flattered, I had to immediately

harness my eager little mind. I was the one with a date on the brain. He'd asked me out—not on a date, but just out. To eat. Like regular folks do. I've been without a social life so long that I'm beginning to imagine things. No attachments, pleasant conversation, a toothpick and a mint, that's all. I'm feeling a little desperate for company of the opposite sex.

I even talked to Ken for half an hour last night.

"What's happening in the big city, hon? Gunfights? Car chases? Fraud? Corruption? Are you locking your doors and windows?" I heard Ken's gum snapping as he waited for an answer.

"You have the most skewed idea of city life I've ever heard. It's lovely here."

"Yeah, right. Whatever. Do you miss me?"

"Like a Minnesotan misses mosquitoes."

I did feel a little guilty saying that when I was actually glad to hear my phone ring and pleased to see a number on caller ID that, for once, wasn't a relative of mine. Fortunately, nothing ever offends Ken and my comment rolled off him as if he was wearing Teflon.

"Still got your sense of humor at least. When are you coming home?"

"I don't know."

"Why don't you come here? You've got your grand-mother's house to live in. I got us a couple new Sea-Doos so we can play at a lake somewhere. I'm also thinking about four-wheelers or dirt bikes. Or maybe you'd like a pair of riding horses better. I know how crazy you are about animals, especially Winslow. Say, how's that big old dust mop anyway? I kinda miss him, riding with me in the pickup, hanging his big ole' head out the window...."

Much as I resisted, I teared up at Ken's attempt at sweetness. He really is one of the most generous guys on the planet. Thickheaded, but generous. He is also, as my friends in Simms tend to point out, charming, easygoing, funny, handsome, rich, enthusiastic and absolutely crazy about me. Ken himself once told me I was as precious to him as his dog, Boosters. Loving Winslow as I do, I understand. I think it's the sweetest thing he's ever said to me.

Okay, so maybe I like him better than I let on....

We talked about a lot of things—our mutual friends, the remodeling of the old cinema, the new sign installed at the park and the antics of Ken's friends—and if anyone had been listening in, they would have sworn we were talking about twelve-year-olds and not grown men.

"Your friend Greta has been bugging me something awful. She wants to have a hen party when you come. She thinks you'll have a lot to talk about now that you're a millionaire."

"I'm sure."

"Aw, Cassia, don't sound so down about it. I know you aren't materialistic and you're practically allergic to wasting money, but I've been a millionaire for a couple years now and I like it."

I couldn't help bursting into laughter. Only Ken would equate being a millionaire with some other pleasant pastime like bowling or having a picnic.

That's probably why I have genuine fondness for the

guy. Money isn't an issue with him. He loves to work because he enjoys what he does. He likes the challenge of putting beautiful homes together and watching his clients' responses. Though he won't admit it even under penalty of death, he is artistic. It shows in the homes Ken builds. The details are always just right, the work flawless and those small touches that mean so much are always present.

When someone moves into one of Ken's homes, there are already flowers there to welcome them, a box of chocolates and a thank-you note for purchasing one of Ken's custom homes. And both crazy and thoughtful, Ken's signature in his new homes has become bathroom cabinets stocked with soap, toilet paper and toothbrushes. There's always a loaf of bread and a quart of milk in the refrigerator for the new home owners. If he knows there are children in the family, there's usually a box of ice cream treats in the freezer, too. When the movers leave and the family is standing alone in the mess, there are at least some basics they don't have to dig out of boxes. Simple, thoughtful and unusual as this practice is, Ken's trademark gesture is forever being written up in local newspapers, real estate brochures and even statewide papers. Each time a story is published, the article sells half a dozen homes. Ken, in his cheerful, practical way, lives the golden rule by treating others as he would have them treat him. Now he's thinking of adding a pound of coffee and a basket of fruit to his welcome gift, as well.

Even Ken is beginning to look like the one for me. Long story short, I need to get out of the house.

* * *

Out of the house turned out to be a trip with Mattie to the community church I'd attended on Sunday.

"There's a quilt show near you this week," Grandma Mattie said. "I saw it in the newspaper. Would you like to attend on Tuesday? Tomorrow?"

Translated, that meant Mattie would like to attend. Far be it from me to turn down a diversion. Shopping wasn't any fun. I looked at things knowing I could afford to buy them and then reminded myself of the promise I'd made to myself not to spend a dime of the lottery money until I was sure what to do with it. Poor little rich girl, that's me.

I drove my wreck of a car to Mattie's and waited for her by the door. She came out looking like a spill from a paint box in a bright purple pantsuit and a feather hat that would put a cardinal to shame.

Oh, no, they'd gotten to her, too, that gang of ladies who roamed her complex wearing purple clothes and red hats. The group is a cultural phenomenon—older women throwing caution to the winds and having fun just for, well, for the fun of it.

"You look…f-festive," I stammered. Her hat looked, other than having red feathers, like a derby or something Sherlock Holmes might wear or a blob of red jelly. Anyway, feathers drooped off the odd little brim like wilted leaves.

"Agnes, my next-door neighbor, loaned it to me. I'm thinking of joining their club, so she suggested I take her hat for a test run."

Great. People used to cruise the streets in cars

wanting to see how many admiring glances they got. Now my grandmother is taking a hat for a dry run. It's a funny world we live in.

"So this is the church you've attended," Grandma Mattie commented as we pulled into the parking lot of the rustic stone church. "How pretty."

"And growing." Traffic directors were waving flags and giving directions so as to make use of every inch of parking space in the lot. It reminded me of what they do in airplanes—add another row of seats into the same crowded real estate on the plane. Next thing I know, they'll be forcing a couple more rows of seats and asking the passengers to "Please hold your breath for the next two hours so that you do not disturb the person in the seat next to yours."

I helped Mattie out of the car and into the church. The main room of the education wing was now transformed into a quilter's wonderland. Just seeing all this bedding in one place made me want to curl up and take a nap. Mattie immediately wandered off in a blissful haze, muttering something about samplers, log cabins and flying geese, to begin a conversation with a woman who had threaded needles poked into her lapels. She must have been an officer in the quilting brigade. I headed for the coffee shop set up in the church kitchen at the far end of the room, smiling at the people standing proudly by their quilts wanting to share their sewing techniques or fabric choices or whatever.

I sewed once. I made an apron, a pot holder and a set of napkins in 4-H because I'd heard people won prizes at the county fair. My mother attributes all the gray hair at her temples to that one sewing project. She's still overly dramatic when she talks about it. After all, the doctor in the emergency room told her it hadn't been necessary to bring both me *and* the sewing machine into the E.R. Of course, my finger was still attached, impaled between the needle and the foot feed. My screams must have been loud, because I remember Jane tagging along holding her hands over her ears. If I'm a bit of a drama queen, I know I come by it naturally.

"Ms. Carr?"

I looked up to see Pastor Carl Osgood smiling down upon me. "We met briefly at church last Sunday, I believe."

Waves of recollection washed over me. Grandpa Ben always remembered all the new people in church, too.

"Yes. I'm new to the Cities. I've enjoyed visiting your church very much."

"Good. You are most welcome. We have a lively, growing community here. The Lord's working in big ways. And if you have any questions or I could be of service—spiritual or otherwise—please call me or come into the office at any time."

Hmm. A twinkle of an idea lit a corner of my mind.

"Pastor Osgood, I'm wondering if you can tell me something about some of the worthy charities that are low on funds right now…."

By the time Mattie found us, I'd extracted a promise that he would do some research for me, "make a few calls" and see if he and someone in need could help me with my "money problem." I'd never realized quite how many Christian efforts, missions, hospitals and schools were struggling around the world. I felt glimmers of hope. With Osgood working with me, I should be able to give my money away in no time at all.

CHAPTER

16

Adam was outside when I got home from the quilt show, the keys to his Hummer hanging rakishly from his back pocket, a cola in his hand. I parked—Randy prefers to say "hid"—my car in the garage and joined him out front.

Sometimes I long for a cherry cola like the ones Wilber Hanson makes—extra cherry syrup and a handful of maraschino cherries tossed in upon request. Mr. Hanson originally wanted to modernize his drugstore in the seventies by taking out the ornate old fountain, but since it was too big to move without great effort, he left it in place. Now it's become the most booming part of his business. He's even thrown up a few signs along the highway just as Wall Drug does. Instead of advertising cold water, he promises the best cherry cola in South Dakota. I guess if you wait long enough everything will come back into fashion eventually.

My grandfather believed that, and he never threw anything away. Grandma did, however, smuggle out that polyester leisure suit he bought on a wild and crazy whim, and gave it a nice burial. It was the only thing I ever remember him buying that was out of character. Grandpa in a leisure suit was like Grandma in stilettos and a boa....

"What have you been up to?"

"I was in church. How about you, Adam? Where do you go to church?"

He didn't look up. "I'm out of town a lot, you know."

Well, that had gone swimmingly. *Not.*

After we parted, it occurred to me that perhaps the reason Adam and I were neighbors had something to do with his lack of faith. Maybe I was here to be a part of his spiritual growth somehow. Possibly I'd be the one who'd lead him to the Lord.... I should have been a missionary. I certainly have it in my heart to collect lost souls.

"You give me the sign, Lord, if that's what this is about," I prayed silently. I've been praying for signs a lot lately. I hope I haven't missed any.

Thursday evening as I walked past Adam's door I impulsively asked him if he needed groceries.

Groceries to Adam are cat food, eggs, bacon and most anything with "instant" on the label. Apparently he was out of cat food, because Pepto was hissing and spitting at his cat dish as if it had better produce this instant *or else.* Pepto has been decimating light cords, drapery pulls and all his stuffed toys. Little headless catnip mice are lying all over Adam's place. It's disquieting to step on one when you're least expecting it.

"Sure. I'll go with you," he said, and we set off companionably for a local market with a restaurant attached.

Five minutes into shopping, I heard a familiar voice. "Cassia!"

To my surprise, Petty Betty and Paranoid Paula were coming down the aisle toward us.

"Hello, it's good to see you both. You look wonderful!"

Adam eyed Betty and Paula as intently as they were perusing him. I could sense their news-collecting antennae go up and begin to twitch. Paula also held her designer bag even closer to her chest. They might be millionaires, but juicy gossip is something money can't always buy.

"Adam, these are my friends and office mates from Parker Bennett. Maybe you remember them from lottery headquarters—Paula and Betty." I felt him stiffen for a mere second and then relax into such blinding charm that even I felt the heat.

Betty and Paula thawed immediately as he lingered over their handshakes, seemingly reluctant to pull away.

Whoa, is he good. My question is…why? What makes Betty and Paula so interesting other than the fact that they're millionaires? I watched them succumb to his charm. Betty's eyelashes fluttered so rapidly that I was surprised she didn't go airborne.

Adam should be used to the moneyed crowd by now. After all, he's got me. Except, of course, I don't spend mine.

Jealous, Cassia?

I glanced at Adam. He *is* a breathtaking man. He's rugged, intimidating, funny, mysterious and too handsome for his own good, as far as I'm concerned.

I turned to Betty. "So how are you…really, I mean?"

I'd expected any answer but tears.

Betty dabbed at her eyes as Paula ineffectively patted her on the shoulder. Finally she gathered herself together enough to speak.

"I'm sorry. I've been having some trouble with my children."

"No one is sick, I hope." Betty has three high school and college-age children.

"I had no idea how my winning the money would affect them. It never occurred to me that it would be a problem for them."

The way it was a problem for me? I wondered.

"They've changed," Betty said. "We were never rich when they were growing up, but weren't exactly poor either. The kids didn't seem to mind occasional hand-me-downs or sharing a single secondhand car. And now…"

Paula picked up the story. "She's having a problem with them fighting and arguing. Everyone is afraid that Betty is going to give one of the kids more money than she does the others. I told her to do it my way," Paula continued. "Remember that will I was writing? Well, I cut all the lazy ones right out of it. You should see my son-in-law now! He cleans up and goes to work. Gave up television and has started to exercise. And he's polite as a choirboy."

"What changed?"

"He wants to get back into my good graces, of course. Right now I've got my daughter's money tied up so tight that he couldn't get to it with a hacksaw." Paula smiled stiffly, satisfied. "I'll keep him dancing to my tune for a few years, and hopefully, because my daughter loves the bum, he'll learn some good habits. Maybe I'll even *want* to give him money one day." She smiled nastily. "And until then, I don't have to watch him lie on the couch with one hand in the chips and the other on the remote."

Adam, whom I'd almost forgotten was beside me, slipped in a question. "So the money hasn't exactly been a benefit for your family?"

"I can now say for sure that money doesn't buy happiness." Betty sighed. "But I never dreamed that money would make my children so greedy."

"Why don't you give it away?" I asked, knowing full well the kind of response I'd receive. "There are lots of good causes that can use the money."

Both women looked at me as if I were a crayon short of a box. "Give it away?" they chimed in unison.

"If it's making you and your family miserable…"

"Not *that* miserable," Paula protested.

"We're just venting, Cassia. You know that. You're one of the few people we can talk to these days who understands…." She looked shyly from beneath her eyelashes. "I thought you were crazy to be unhappy

when you won that share of the money, but I'm beginning to understand. It's not as easy as I thought it would
be."

"We'll work it out, though," Paula blurted. "So don't
worry about us."

"Even so, may I pray for you?"

Paula looked up doubtfully, as if God were hanging
from the ceiling tile above her. "I suppose it wouldn't
hurt." Then her eyes narrowed. "But not here, in
public."

"At home, then." I reached out with both hands to
hold Paula's right hand and Betty's left. "And if there's
any time you want to 'vent,' I'm around, okay?"

Adam didn't speak until we were halfway to the
apartment house.

"So you believe Paula and Betty should trust God
for what they need and use the money they have for the
good of others, sharing with the ones in most need?"

Finally I was making sense to someone.

"So why isn't that good advice for you? What makes
you think that you're so different from anyone else,
Cassia? Practice what you preach. The money came to
you. It's your responsibility to be a steward, whether
you like it or not."

"I've come to that conclusion myself," I admitted,
and told him about my conversation with Pastor
Osgood. I thought he'd respond enthusiastically, but he
only nodded, his expression thoughtful.

"Adam?"

"Hmm?" He hadn't shaved today, and the dusky
shadow of stubble against his tanned skin made his

visage dark and shadowy. His eyelashes, so thick and black that I know women who'd trade a molar for them, fluttered over his high cheekbones and hooded his eyes. Sometimes he looked so soulful and distant that I felt this man, despite all the time I'd spent with him, was an utter stranger.

"Do you have a phone book in your car? Or can we stop someplace that does?"

He eyed me cautiously. "I have the white pages in the back. I make a lot of calls from my car."

I found the book, turned around and slid back into my own seat. "You have phone books, atlases and what looks like a geography library back there. What is it you do with that stuff anyway? Are we anywhere close to…" I put my finger on the tiny line in the middle of the pages and read the address of my grandmother's apartment building. I've been getting there by my own method that has nothing to do with street signs. I take a right at McDonald's, a left at Kentucky Fried, another left at the Dairy Queen. It's the fast-food mapping technique.

Adam had told me he was "between jobs" and did some writing, but I hadn't pressed further. Every time I decided to try he got this aggrieved expression in his eyes that told me he didn't want to talk about it. I don't want to talk about Ken all the time either, so I understand. There are places that a person just isn't ready to go on a moment's notice. I wonder if Adam was fired from his last job. Every time he even alludes to it, he looks as though he wants to cry.

"Any other personal errands before the chauffeur

turns into a white rat and the Hummer into a pumpkin?" Adam asked.

"Would you like to meet my sister and my grandmother? Jane is helping Gram do some baking."

Sometimes I amaze myself. What am I doing? I've been very careful not to talk much about my handsome neighbor. I know that once Jane and Grandma get wind of a new male friend in my life, I'll never get any peace from them. At least perhaps Grandma will quit asking when I last washed clothes. She still thinks the Laundromat is the primo place to get a date. As if I'd ever go out with a guy too cheap or broke to own a washing machine and dryer.

Funny, but Ken is beginning to look better and better. Money didn't change him. His friends have told me so. Maybe the toys he buys are bigger—Harleys rather than crotch-rockets and pickups with dualies and extended cabs instead of the cheaper models—but he wouldn't curl up and die if all his money were gone tomorrow. He'd discuss it with Boosters and his buddies, reminisce about the good old days and get back to work. There's something there to be learned, I think.

Maybe absence does make the heart grow fonder.... Then I glanced at Adam and finished the rest of the phrase in my head. *Or give you serious competition.*

An odd expression flitted across Adam's features— guilt, remorse, regret, shame—before he nodded. "Sure. Why not?"

I can't really read him. The people in my life have always been very straightforward. The mysterious male has been limited to fiction and fantasy for me. For the first time ever, I'm attracted to an enigma. He occasionally speaks of Christianity in his life in the past tense, but that's not enough. The idea of reintroducing Adam to his faith warms my soul. Once God has him firmly in His grip of grace, then maybe…

No wonder Ken was so reluctant to let me come to the city. What-You-See-Is-What-You-Get Ken didn't want me to meet the competition.

17

I smelled cookies baking as we got off the elevator. Oatmeal raisin. Chocolate chip. Macaroons. And banana bread. Yum.

We followed our noses to Grandma's apartment door. I knocked once and walked inside.

"Hi, Cassia, did you come to help? We're doing molasses cookies next, and you make the best frosting… oh, hello, there…" Jane's voice slid the continuum from drill sergeant to restaurant hostess to enamored groupie in a matter of seconds. Adam has that kind of effect on women, I've noticed.

I'd barely made introductions before Jane hustled Adam into the kitchen and Grandma started loading a plate with freshly baked delicacies. Before I even got a civil greeting, he had a glass of milk in his hand.

It is one thing for Jane or Grandma to run into my neighbors when visiting my place. It is quite another to have me bring someone into Family Central.

I knew exactly what was going on in their heads.

Jane: "Well, well, something serious must be happening. He's gorgeous."

Grandma: "He's a nice-looking young man. I wonder if she met him in the Laundromat?"

Jane: "Does Ken know about this?"

Grandma: "I wonder if his grandparents are still living."

Jane: "Does he know about Cassia's money? If so, how do we know we can trust him?"

Grandma: "He has honest eyes. Such a beautiful color. I wonder if he knows the Lord? Cassia wouldn't be interested in someone who doesn't."

Jane: "I don't trust him. He's after my sister's money, no doubt about it."

Grandma: "I'm so glad she has a new friend."

Jane: "What on earth is she thinking?"

Grandma: "I'll pray about it."

Jane watched him with the eyes of a hawk. Adam was a field mouse of dubious origins that she would obviously have loved to swoop down upon to nip off his head. Grandma, on the other hand, was smiling happily, thinking how nice it was that her little Cassia wasn't alone in the city anymore.

Fortunately, I'm somewhere between unadulterated distrust and benign benevolence, and find the whole thing quite amusing. I could tell by Adam's expression that he knew he'd walked into something potentially combustible, but he didn't know quite what to make of it.

"So, Adam," Jane said as nonchalantly as a loaded

semi barreling down the highway, "tell me about yourself. I'd love to know *everything* about you."

"Oh, please do," Grandma said happily. "We love to meet Cassia's friends."

Wait a minute.

Jane wasn't usually this high-pressure, nor was Grandma a fluffy, clueless old lady. They were playing good cop/bad cop. They'd been waiting for the opportunity to find out more about my neighbor, and I'd trotted him right into their trap.

It was all I could do to keep from laughing out loud.

My poor family. They've been worried sick about me, about how I reacted to the money and now about not wanting me hurt by someone who had their eyes on my bank account and not my heart. But this! I gave them a big grin and, to Adam's surprise, tucked my arm into the crook of his and gave it a squeeze. He looked down at me, startled, and then a slow, wide grin spread across his face. I smiled right back.

Let them think about that for a while.

By the time I'd told Jane and Grandma about our meeting with Betty and Paula, they'd given up their inquisition of Adam. My sister and grandmother, I'm afraid, have begun to live vicariously through me. Jane's husband, Dave, travels for his work, often for three or four days at a time, giving Jane plenty of time to meddle in my business. And I could tell they already liked Adam.

"This is my husband and me when we were first married. Isn't he handsome?" Grandma had trapped Adam on the couch. He had an open photo album on his lap, and she was regaling him with stories. They both looked perfectly happy.

"Now I see where Cassia got her smile," Adam said. "Look at that grin."

White head and dark touched as they leaned together over the old black-and-white images.

"Oh, my, there's our first house. Needed a good coat of paint, didn't it? At that time we were lucky to have walls and a roof at all. Those were good times."

"Good times?" Adam echoed. "When you couldn't even afford a gallon of paint?"

"It doesn't matter what's on the outside of the house if the inside is happy. And we were very happy."

"So the hardship was okay with you?"

"Second Corinthians, 4:17, you know."

He looked at her puzzled, but didn't ask. He must be growing accustomed to our biblical shorthand.

"'These troubles and sufferings of ours are, after all, quite small and won't last very long. Yet this short time of distress will result in God's richest blessings upon us forever and ever!'"

Grandma gave me an elfin grin. "Frankly, in the past when I've thought of getting almost more than I can handle, I've assumed it would be troubles of some sort. But until this happened to Cassia, I'd really never thought of trouble being too *much* money."

"God works in mysterious ways," I muttered. That statement is fast becoming my new mantra. Every time I turn a corner lately, there's something new I didn't expect.

Grandma Mattie sent us home with tins of cookies, a

sack of old magazines and some new flour-sacking dish-cloths on which she'd embroidered roosters. As we walked away from her apartment, she gave me a thumbs-up sign.

Now where had she learned to do that?

It was the magazines that puzzled Adam.

"What are these for?"

"To read."

"But they're all out of date."

"Of course they are. I'm third on the list."

"Huh?"

"It's something that's been going on in our family for years. Someone orders a magazine they like and tells everyone they're getting it. Jane, for instance, likes *Good Housekeeping*. She gets and reads it, marks the interesting spots and gives the magazine to Mattie. Then Mattie reads it, responds to Jane's comments and makes a few of her own. After that, she gives it to me."

"And you read them?"

"Of course. This way we really get our money's worth out of that magazine. It was something Grandpa thought up."

"Even if the news is two or three months old?"

"If it's new, it's news. If it's old, it's history. Either way, I learn something. And best of all, I get to read Jane's and Mattie's comments, so I know what they're thinking about a subject, as well."

As seems to happen a lot with Adam and me, he looked completely mystified by my ways.

"Then, if they are still in decent shape, I give them to Mattie's friends at the nursing home."

He threw up his hands. "Cassia, I used to think you were exceptional. Now I think you and your entire family are extraordinary."

"We like saving money, remember? To us it's a game. But we aren't idiots, either. I do have a pension fund, you know."

The ride home was quiet. Adam seemed to be slipping slowly but inexorably into a quagmire of moroseness.

Sometimes there's a murky darkness about him that borders on despondency. I don't know where or what it comes from, but I've seen it more and more lately. It's as if he has a tumor growing inside him, taking him over and shutting him down. It's when these moods come on that I am so clearly reminded that, no matter how much time I've spent with him, Adam Cavanaugh is still very much a stranger to me.

CHAPTER

18

Friday evening Adam stood staring out the window watching Cassia's retreating figure. Winslow, glad to be on a walk, was pulling so hard on his leash that her long slender legs churned to keep up with the exuberant pet. Though he couldn't hear her, Adam had a good idea that Cassia was laughing. He hadn't quit thinking of her in the five weeks since she'd won the lottery, and every day he loathed himself a little more.

Like taking candy from a baby. Kicking crutches out from beneath old ladies on the street. Shooting someone in the back. Robbing a nursing home. Putting salt in the sugar bowl. Juvenile, self-indulgent, despicable, low, sneaky, untrustworthy, infantile, underhanded, devious, contemptible, loathsome, repugnant, abhorrent, vile...

Adam had never needed a thesaurus before and he didn't need one now. Rat, pond scum, leech...

"Well, I'm glad to see you, too," Terrance Becker

said as he lounged on the big leather couch in Adam's apartment drinking stiff black coffee that tasted like chicory. He took a swig and shuddered. "How you can drink this stuff so black is beyond me. How do you get to sleep at night with all the caffeine in your system?"

"Practice," Adam said grimly. "Occasionally staying awake has saved my life."

Terrance knew Adam meant that literally and nodded. "Good point." He eyed his client as Adam stared blankly out the window, not even noticing that Pepto was trying to sharpen his claws on the leg of his jeans. "Do you mind that brute clawing you like that?"

Adam looked down and saw Pepto embedded in his pant leg and shook him off. The feline said something unseemly in cat language and stalked off, probably to destroy a curtain in the bedroom in an act of revenge.

"What is eating at you anyway, man? I've never seen you like this." Then Terrance perked up. "Of course, it is a pleasant change from that disheartened, defeated attitude you had when you got off the plane from Burundi."

"Very funny."

"This is supposed to be an entertaining story you're working on, remember? Mind candy? Fluff? Easy inconsequential reading for your hungry public, right? What's gone wrong?"

"Nothing. Everything. Aw, I don't know." Adam scraped his hair away from his forehead to reveal the profile that usually made women weak in the knees.

Terrance, oblivious to that, continued. "Which is it? Nothing or everything?"

"The research is great. Cassia has made me her confidant, a friend. She thinks of me as her sounding board in this struggle she's having over the money. And she's already introduced me to some of the other winners, so I've got their stories, as well."

"And?"

"And she and her family are the most quotable people I've ever met. I could take off in a million directions on the things they say—God's testing Cassia with too much money, the outside of a house not needing paint if the inside is a happy home, the shtick with those out-of-date magazines. The family alone is worth a book."

"What could be better?" Terrance sat up straight.

"It's all a lie, that's why. She trusts me. She believes I'm holding her secrets confidential. Worst of all, she thinks I'm her friend."

"Well, aren't you? Every time you talk about her I can see the light in your eyes. Light I haven't seen for some time, by the way. When you walked off the plane from Burundi, I thought it was gone forever."

"I am her friend. At least, I want to be. She's like a breath of spring after a long winter. She's funny, smart, quirky…and she has a soul that seems to—" Adam searched for a word "—a soul that shines."

Terrance arched an eyebrow but didn't comment.

"And preying on her for information with the intention of spreading her personal thoughts all over the media makes me sick to my stomach." Adam spat out each word with such force that it seemed to hurt. He sank into the cat-claw chair across from Terrance. "I should have told her from the beginning what I was up to. Then she could have said yes or no. Now when I break it to her, she's going to be furious." He looked at Terrance meaningfully. "Redheaded, claws-out, fangs-sharpened furious."

"So we have some guilt and remorse going on."

"I've been a straight shooter all my life. I call it like I see it. Now I know why. Being deceptive goes against every fiber of my being."

"So quit."

Adam looked up sharply. "What?"

"Quit. Stop. End it. Cease and desist. Put an end to the charade."

Adam contemplated his agent. "Do you mean that?"

Terrance locked gazes with him and stared back.

"Because you have no idea how many times I've decided to do just that."

"What changes your mind?"

As if he were folding in on himself, Adam sank deeper in the chair. "I've even been at Cassia's door with my hand raised to knock. I was this close." He made a gesture with his hand to show Terrance how near he'd come to spilling it all.

"Why'd you stop?"

"Because the FedEx man walked through the front door of the building."

"I've never seen anyone stop you from doing anything you wanted to do. Why him?"

"Because he brought me these." Adam reached for a large padded manila envelope that appeared battered and worn from its journey. Adam's address and the return address were written in a pinched hand that looked out of place on the large folder. He handed it to Terrance without explanation.

Terrance opened it, drew out a stack of eight-by-ten photos and stifled a gasp.

"Frankie sent them," Adam said, referring to his photographer on the Burundi trip. "He told me there were some he didn't want published, but he'd send them to me because he knew I'd understand."

Frankie Wachter was as good at his job as Adam was at his. The photos, though no doubt taken in a quick series, were crisp and detailed, the angles and lighting flawless. That perhaps was what made the photos so awful.

A mother sobbing over the dead body of a child who could have been as young as three or as old as ten. When children were malnourished, one never quite knew. A father scraping a shallow grave with his bare hands for the tiny body that lay in the dirt beside him. And Adam, doubled over and weeping, holding the leaf-thin shell of a baby in his arms.

Terrance drew a breath and dropped the pictures. "I never knew...I thought I did, but...is this what you saw over there?"

"Starving children are very quiet. Did you know that? They have no energy to struggle. You hold them, knowing death is going to come, but still you're surprised to realize they've slipped away without your knowing. Terrance, I saw dozens of people—mostly children—slipping away." He couldn't even bring himself to verbalize the pain—from rashes, open wounds, blindness or blood that won't clot—in which some of those people must have been.

Adam stood and prowled the room like a miserable jungle cat. "That's why I've kept going with this story and hating myself all the while. I've been studying what it costs to keep a child alive. Terrance, if I worked the rest of my life for this and gave everything I earned to the rescue efforts there, I still couldn't do all that needs to be done. But I have to try anyway. I've had this idea that with the stories I'm writing about Burundi and the money I could make on this lottery story, I could actually *do* something." He looked at Terrance until his agent squirmed. "But I feel like I'm selling my soul to make it happen."

Terrance paled. "I didn't mean for this…Adam, I have no idea what to say."

"Either way, it's killing me." Adam's eyes hardened. "The only thing that's kept me moving forward is that I know Cassia will recover from my deception. The children, well, that's a matter of life and death."

"And your friendship with Cassia?"

"It can't survive this fraud I've been perpetrating on her. I know that. She is loyal, honest and sincere as they come. She's a Christian, Terrance. She refuses to mess with the truth."

"Aren't Christians supposed to be forgiving, too? 'Turn the other cheek,' and all that?"

It was odd, Adam thought. He and Terrance had never had a talk about faith when Adam had actually thought he believed in God. Now, after Burundi, when he wasn't so sure anymore, it came up.

"Yeah, that's true." He wished he had Cassia's ability to rattle off Bible quotations, chapter and verse, but he had to settle for, "It's in the Gospels somewhere." Something bubbled up from long ago, a memory of his mother standing in the middle of their bright yellow kitchen. There were avocado-green appliances, the ones she was so proud of, and countertops in matching green. He remembered flowers from the garden on her table in a milk-glass vase and even the smell of the casserole in the oven. It was as real as though he could touch it.

"'Love your enemies, Adam,'" she was saying. "'Do good to those who hate you. Pray for the happiness of those who curse you. Implore God's blessing on those who hurt you. If someone slaps you on one cheek, let him slap the other, too! If someone demands your coat, give him your shirt besides. Give what you have to anyone who asks you for it….'" And then the memory faded. His mother was a Christian, and as beautiful and loving as Cassia.

He sighed. "But even Christians have limits, don't they?"

"You've got me there, buddy." Terrance stood up and put his arm on Adam's shoulder. "Listen, I just want you to know that now I understand this turmoil you're going through. If nothing else, do a generic bit on lottery winners and we'll really try to make something happen with the Burundi thing. There's probably a chapter for a book in that, too. Maybe you could get your message out that way. You're going to have to follow your heart on this one."

My soul is being ripped in two. Though he'd been careful not to let Cassia know the depth of his feelings for her, she had burrowed her way into his spirit. He'd set up his own heartbreak by lying to her in the beginning. But what he'd seen in Burundi was about more than just himself and Cassia. Adam stared after Terrance as he left the building. He'd remembered the last part of what his mother had said to him that day.

Treat others as you want them to treat you.

Was this how he wanted to be treated? Lied to, deceived, used? The ache in his gut throbbed. He was selling out on his own values, he knew, but it was for a good cause, the best he could think of. Did that make it right? Cassia's sweet face shimmered in his mind. Doing what he was doing would ensure that their relationship would be over soon, that he'd never know if the feelings he was developing for her could ever turn into something more permanent.

This was a decision he'd possibly regret for the rest of his life, but at least he had a life to live. No matter what it cost him personally, he had to give those children a chance. Wearily he returned to his computer.

Starvation has many faces. It also manifests itself in many ways. Children who have a single non-protein staple in their diets often suffer from kwashiorkor, a disease whose symptoms include enlarged liver, edema, swelling and growth retardation. Niacin deficiency will produce pellagra and its accompanying diarrhea, rashes and tissue irritation, while a thiamine deficiency produces beriberi and heart disease or brain and nerve disease. Lack of the vitamins and minerals that many Americans automatically pop into their mouths with a glass of morning orange juice results in scurvy, bleeding, gum disease, convulsions, fever, loss of blood pressure or death. Malnutrition can result in blindness, rickets, anemia, shrinkage of vital organs, retardation and a host of unspeakable suffering. Is this the torment to which we choose to consign many of the world's children?

The helpless feelings that are generated by these massive problems often lead to an attitude of hopelessness, but there is good news. Remarkably, children can recover from severe starvation. An orphanage in Bujumbura, Burundi, can accept another one hundred children into its program for less than seventy dollars per child, per month.

Seventy dollars a month—a little over two dollars a day, a latte at the drive through, a soda and candy bar at break time, the money wasted by not clipping that restaurant coupon from the newspaper—the difference between life and death?

It is time for us to wake up, to realize that one person can make a difference.

CHAPTER

19

"Are you happy, Cassia?" Cricket sat on my couch eating from a plate of Mattie's gingersnaps.

It's Tuesday evening and Cricket is back from her latest spa. Her eyebrows are nicely shaped and she has a fresh manicure and pedicure. Otherwise, she looks exactly the same as when she left. Apparently this spa didn't have the magic potion she was looking for either—the one that makes a cute, short woman into a ravishingly beautiful, leggy, six-foot-tall model. At least with spas, the hunt is almost as much fun as finding the pot of gold at the end of the rainbow.

She has a milk mustache on her upper lip and a perplexed expression on her pleasant features. "Really happy?"

"Sure. Aren't you?" I sat down on the couch beside her. "Why do you ask?"

"Because if you *are* happy, then I think you're the only one who actually is."

"What's wrong, Cricket? Have you had bad news?"

"No. Not that. I just expected something when we won the lottery. Something…more."

"What did you imagine would happen?"

Cricket breathed a dramatic, Cricket-like sigh. "I expected it to be more fun. I've always been broke because I love to shop."

Cricket wasn't saying anything I didn't already know.

"And shopping's not as much fun anymore!"

"Really?" Now, that surprised me. "Why?"

"It used to be an adventure, a hunt. For the best buys, the biggest sales, the most shoes for the least amount of money. Now it's like going on a photo safari and having the animals walk up and circle the Jeep, waiting for me to take their pictures."

I must have looked blank.

"No more thrill of adventure! No more danger of succumbing to something I can't afford in the high-end department! Because," Cricket said morosely, "I can afford it all. I always thought buying things made me happy. Now I realize that it was the search that was fun, not the buying. Now if I want a designer dress, I go out and buy one. What's the fun in that?"

"When you had to work for it, it was more fun?"

"Yes." She looked at me beseechingly. "Am I losing my mind?"

"Hardly. Maybe you're just getting it back." I curled my feet under me and settled in for a visit.

"What's that supposed to mean?"

"When I work hard for something—clothing,

artwork for my living room, school tuition—I see its value. I know that this sweater cost me a half day of work at Parker Bennett, for example. But with all the money in the world, you value things differently when you can buy anything you want. The pleasure is gone. You aren't working toward a goal anymore. You forget the difference between what you want and what you need."

Cricket bobbed her head. "That's me, all right. I'm feeling cheated because I have it all."

"What's wrong with you?" Jane peered at me over the tops of her reading glasses as I stormed into her house the next afternoon. She was sitting at her dining-room table with papers, flow sheets and investment brochures spread around her. I'd said hello to my brother-in-law—or as I lovingly called him, *bother*-in-law; we both knew it is Jane who is the biggest bother—outside where he was trimming hedges.

I eyed the papers gloomily, knowing that they were all about me and my money. The only thing that kept me going was a single exasperating and pointed verse that had etched itself inside my head—1 Corinthians 9:16.

If I were volunteering my services of my own free will, then the Lord would give me a special reward; but that is not the situation, for God has picked me out and given me this sacred trust and I have no choice.

I don't have a choice. I can't heedlessly give the money away, even though it's my heartfelt desire. Much as I've fought it, I do have to be conscientious about it. Unfortunately, other than Ken, my only role model in the millionaire category I'd found in the funny papers. Scrooge McDuck never mentions a problem like this.

But now that I have it and I'm responsible for it, I'm getting the message. If nothing else, it's coming with the postman every morning.

"Look at this." I opened the bag I was carrying and dumped it onto the only clear spot on the table. There were investment brochures and pleas from charities spanning Save the Whales (a good idea) to Save the Spotted Itchy Five-Legged Biting Monkey Beetle (probably not such a good idea). There were flyers for every cruise ship in existence, real estate agents wanting to sell me mansions in the Deep South and yurts in Nepal. I had been blessed with the opportunity to join AARP and Mensa. If I'd been courted by a group called NUISANCE, for Newly Unhappy Individuals Suffering Abundance of Nasty Cash Evils, I would have signed on in a heartbeat.

I'm still being wooed by unidentifiable new friends and relatives. Someone in Scotland had seen my red hair, done a search of the name Carr and deduced they were long-distant relatives from clan Carr. Now the entire clan is petitioning me for money so that they can all come to the United States to visit "fortunate Cousin Cassia." Mysteriously, however, the name in the return address on all the envelopes is a man named Howie Earl Crispin who, according to the postmark, lives in Yuma, Arizona. It's amazing how far a clan can travel. Besides, my ancestors are from Wales and Ireland.

"Where are all these people getting my name?"

"Newspapers, the Internet, mailing lists, talking to neighbors and maybe even a detective or two."

"No way." I felt a cold chill.

"I just added the detectives to scare you," Jane said in her evil-sister way. "Sit down. I've been consulting with investment persons I know and the people at my bank. I think we've figured out a way to get this money working for you more efficiently and keep it safe at the same time. Then you can take as long as you want to decide what to do with it."

"Working more efficiently? Aren't my millions pretty efficient on their own?"

Jane looked at me with exasperated patience. "Cassia, if you ever intend to set up foundations or work as a philanthropist, you'll have the money renewing itself so that you can continue to fund those concerns."

"Concerns?" Oh, I have concerns, all right. I closed my eyes and recalled the discouraging conversation I'd had with Pastor Osgood only two days ago.

"I took your offer of financial gifts for those charities our church supports to the weekly business meeting and…" He'd sounded worried, and before I heard another word out of his mouth my heart took a nosedive into the soles of my feet. "It's not that they don't want it, exactly. It's just that some on the board are a little uneasy about distributing *gambling* money through our church coffers. They're afraid of what kind of witness it might be."

"But I didn't gamble to get it!" I wailed. "I thought I was buying a baby gift!"

"I know that, you know that and the board knows that. But still…"

Even though I'd done nothing wrong, the board didn't want to take the money because that would suggest approval of how it had been obtained.

"Charities and nonprofits, you goose." Jane interrupted my rambling.

"Do you mean this will go on for the rest of my life? I'll never be poor again?" My nightmares were coming true.

"Snap out of it, sis! Quit whining and start working. You've been given this money for a reason. You," she emphasized, "not anyone else. I've contacted two major ministries in the past two weeks, both of which have grappled with accepting money that was won at gambling and turned it down. So now it's time to set the wheels in motion for fiscal responsibility." Jane studied me with something more akin to compassion. "So you'll quit resisting and roll with it?"

That doesn't mean I have to be comfortable with it.

"There have to be organizations that will—"

"But this isn't about *them*. What does God want *you* to do?"

"Hi, Pepto, is your boss at home?" The big cat lay in the doorway waiting, I presume, for the Federal Express man. Pepto doesn't like failure, and so far the FedEx guy had pretty much ignored him. There's nothing a cat hates more than being ignored.

Pepto sees that as his job in the world. Cats are the ones who should be aloof and distant. How dare someone with only two legs take away his thunder? The FedEx guy is definitely a hard nut for Pepto to crack but, much to his feline satisfaction, the postman now carries kitty treats in his pockets just to keep Pepto off his case.

"You're talking to the boss. I'm just the cook and litter-box custodian, didn't you know?" Adam was at his laptop computer, but he quickly saved and backed out of the document he was working on as I entered. "What's up?"

"I've surrendered."

"What do you mean?" As usual, Adam wore the softest, most comfortable looking chamois shirt and washed-out jeans. His shirt was a pale blue and open at the neck to reveal a pleasant thicket of dark chest hair. He was barefoot, and I observed that even his feet were chiseled and beautiful. Had the man no flaws whatsoever?

"Capitulated. Waved the white flag." I flopped down on his couch. "God conked me over the head with my grandmother."

"That must have hurt."

"Not literally, of course."

"What a relief. My next thought was for Grandma." He smiled indulgently, and I immediately felt better. Pouring my thoughts out to Adam is so natural and easy. He never seems to take me too seriously, which I like. I don't feel pressured by him the way I do by Ken. Of course, Ken is itching to marry me, and Adam doesn't have any designs on me whatsoever.

"My sister has gathered a team of financial wizards

to manage the money." I noticed Adam straighten slightly, as if interested.

"Oh? I thought your pastor was helping you give it away."

I told him where that had gone. "So I'm still the steward. And not only is the money safe, it's drawing interest, which is rolled back into the initial sum and making more interest. It reminds me of a snowball rolling downhill and becoming an avalanche."

"You started with a pretty big snowball. And then what?"

"To wait for doors to open. To see God on the other side of them beckoning me on. To let it all hang out, so to speak. No more fussing. No more fretting. Instead, I'm asking myself who Jesus would give it to—widows, prisoners…" I looked at his laptop. "What are you doing? You're always on that thing."

"Just an assignment I took on. It's turning into an entire series of articles," Adam said vaguely before jumping to his feet. "By the way, I bought some Godiva ice cream. Interested?"

Weak willed and famished, I took the bait. Yum.

My answering machine was flashing when I got back to my apartment. I rarely pick up the phone anymore unless I recognize the name on the caller ID. This was one I hadn't seen for a few days. Randy. I punched in his number and waited for him to answer.

"Hi, this is Randy. May I help you?"

"I don't know. You called me."

"Cassia?" His voice brightened. "How are you? I've

missed you around the old workhouse. Did you ever get a new car?"

"Not yet."

"Really? I thought…with the money and all…well, it's none of my business." He cleared his throat and changed the subject. "I was wondering if you were ready for coffee with an old workmate yet."

I hate being suspicious—and lonesome—so I followed my gut. "What did you have in mind?"

"A coffee shop somewhere? Tomorrow after work? I'll drive you. I don't want to be responsible for causing that car's last gasp of breath before dying."

After we hung up, I sat on the couch stroking Winslow and thinking about the people in my life I know for certain I can trust.

Mattie and Jane, of course, my parents—but they are far away. The other winners, I suppose, who don't need more money—except poor Bob, who is now probably even more sorry than I that we won. There is Ken, who has his own money and isn't interested in material things unless there's a picture of a hunting dog engraved on it.

And Adam. It feels so easy and right to trust Adam. He never demands anything of me, yet is always there for me when I need him. It's almost as if he reads my mind sometimes. Occasionally he acts a little strange when I start talking about the money, but who wouldn't? He's also very protective of Winslow, who would be bumped off by Pepto if the cat ever got the chance, a hundred and some pounds difference in weight notwithstanding. For the moment, that's it. I have to tread carefully. Now that I've accepted God's assignment, still murky and undefined as it might be, I have to do all I can to carry out His will. Part of that is not allowing into my circle any deceivers who might steer me in the wrong direction.

CHAPTER

20

Randy was waiting for me at the coffee shop on the corner two blocks from my apartment. I saw him through the window and stopped just out of his line of sight to study him.

His height is similar to Ken's, but that's where the resemblance stops. Ken is brash, Randy is shy. Ken is forward and confident, Randy is often tentative and unsure. In both cases, I'm glad Ken and Randy know and respect my feelings about sexual intimacy. Ken knows I'm a virgin and accepts it as, he says, part of my "charm." He has high regard for my standards and I really believe he likes me better for it. Despite his "good old boy" bluster, Ken is a man of principles and faith.

Randy's sweetness attracted me to him in my first days at Parker Bennett Manufacturing, and once I discovered he was a Christian, it made our relationship so much better. In other times and on other terms, perhaps Randy and I...

The kind of man I want in my life is steady, solid and daring, all in one package. Someone who, while able to balance inequities, can see problems and fix them. Someone who can't be easily swayed by circumstance.

I looked at Randy again and felt a yearning in my chest. Sweet Randy…and Adam.

But I'm very aware of the importance of not being "unequally yoked." Grandpa sometimes said, tongue in cheek, that a Christian marrying a non-Christian was a little like "hooking up a cow and a cornstalk and hoping they'll pull in the same direction."

It's disheartening to think of it that way, but I'm an optimist and refuse to lose hope. Just because Adam has misplaced his faith for the time being, it doesn't mean he'll never find it again. How thrilling and satisfying it would be to be a part of his coming back to the Lord.

But for now, Adam isn't showing much interest. I shook myself like a wet dog and headed toward the coffee-shop door, disgusted with myself for having developed the equivalent of a grade-school crush on my neighbor.

"Puppy love," I muttered as I went to greet Randy. "Just puppy love."

It didn't occur to me until later that Winslow had been a puppy once and he'd completely taken over my life and my heart.

Randy jumped to his feet so quickly that his chair tipped backward and nearly toppled to the floor. He tried to grab it and greet me at the same time.

"Hey, how's it going?"

"Good as can be expected for a poor little rich girl."
As I sat down across from him, he pushed toward me
a cookie the size of a Frisbee dotted with chunks of
chocolate and macadamia nuts.

"I hope we're sharing this thing."

"If you want. What can I get you to drink?"

It took some moments of awkward juggling on
Randy's part to get the beverages. It took some time,
too, for either of us to think of something more to say.
While I feel comfortable with Randy, I don't really
know him. A twinge of suspicion raced through my
nervous system and I doused it with a swig of cap-
puccino. I can't go through the rest of my life paranoid.
Then I'd be like Paula, and that just won't do.

Cricket kept me up-to-date on Paula's current obsessions. Paula had decided that if something so wonderful could happen to her, then the reverse could be equally
true.

"She's been waiting for the other shoe to drop,"
Cricket told me. "If something amazing and completely unexpected can happen one day, then what
about the next? She's jumpy as butter on a hot pan,
Cassia. Paula has never trusted the world, and now it's
even more uncertain. Since something so good happened, she's now waiting for the bad that will balance
it out. I think she's more anxious than ever."

No, Paula was not who I wanted to be.

"Cassia." Randy nervously turned the coffee mug in
tiny circles. "I need to say something to you and I
don't want you to take it wrong." He hesitated.

"Although I'm not sure there is actually a way for you to take it right."

I tipped my head to one side and listened.

"Much as I've been trying, I can't quit thinking about you. I'm not a forward kind of guy. When I meet someone I really like, it takes me a while to get up the nerve to say it out loud. Well, I like you. A lot. I knew it from the first day you came to Parker Bennett and so did you, I think." He blushed until his skin was darker than the roots of his sandy hair. "I still want to get to know you better."

He looked at me with stricken eyes. "But now I know that no matter what I do or say, you'll wonder if I'm telling the truth or if I just want to get closer to all that money. I still have to say this, Cassia. I *do* like you. I may even love you."

Oh, what a mess this money is making of my life.

"Wa…well…oh, my…" I'm always at my most brilliant verbally under such conditions.

"I just wanted to say it, Cassia. You don't need to respond. I'm not expecting anything from you." His hair flopped over one eye and I had an urge to brush it away from his forehead.

His skin felt warm and he stared at me, startled by my touch.

"You're right, Randy. Things aren't the same as when I couldn't afford anything but baling wire, duct tape and chewing gum to keep my car together. I still have the same car, but everything else has changed. God's got me in a headlock here, Randy. He's calling all the shots and I'm glad to let Him do it. That doesn't just mean about the money, but personal things, as well. Relationships. The future. Everything."

"I'm the king of bad timing." He looked so despondent that it was almost comical. Ken was never downcast, and although I'm sure Adam has some very dark times, he doesn't show them so fully in his features. Randy's thoughts and emotions spread all the way from his head to his toes.

I put my hand on his arm. "You're my friend."

"That's a start."

Pretty soon I'll have to install a revolving door in my apartment to facilitate these men coming and going in my life. Ken wants to marry me, Randy wants a relationship and, though I'm just beginning to admit it, even to myself, I think I'm falling in love with Adam. And that's the poorest choice of all, considering we don't share the same beliefs. It's either feast or famine in the men department for me.

"So what exactly does 'friends' mean?" Stella asked the next day. Once she'd finished grilling me about Randy she started an inquisition about Adam. Cricket, who doesn't have the ability to turn into an ice princess, looked pleased for me.

It feels good to be with these, my…if not soul mates…money mates. We meet for lunch every few days to debrief and download. It's good to hear how my friends are managing.

"Friends friends. Coffee and conversation. An occasional movie. Shopping. Renting a video and making popcorn…"

"Wait a minute. At your *house?*"

"I suppose. Where else do you watch a video?" I eyed her speculatively. "Why?"

"Sounds a little too friendly to me." Stella stirred her iced tea and dumped another packet of low-calorie sweetener into the brew. She was wearing a pale blue cashmere sweater and white pants. On her feet were either Manolo Blahnik or Jimmy Choo sandals that revealed her exquisitely painted toenails. The nails were the same blue as her sweater and had a tiny white motif painted on each one. There was a minuscule pearl somehow attached to the design on the nail of her big toe. Stella obviously didn't plan to go hiking any time soon. She also wore diamond earrings that looked too large to be real but were anyway—diamonds so large that in the right light they could start bonfires.

"Stella, you've never trusted men. Don't tell me it's gotten worse."

She pulled a card from the front of her purse and handed it to me.

Confidential and Accurate
Helen Cross, Private Investigator
Contact at 888-555-1212

I stared at the business card until Cricket grabbed it from my hand and gasped, "You aren't actually checking men out before you date them, are you?"

Stella raised a cool eyebrow.

That eyebrow thing is a move I envy. When I was younger I often tried to do that, but managed only to make myself look as if I suffered from serious and in-operable tics.

"Aren't you?"

Poor Cricket's face crumpled. When Stella was called away to the telephone, Cricket leaned closer and said, "I know she's probably right, but I enjoy the attention I'm getting from guys. No matter what I do to myself, I'll never look as good as Stella does right out of the shower. I might as well take advantage of the opportunities I have."

"The only thing that needs improving is your self-esteem. You look perfectly wonderful, Cricket." And I meant it. Her dark curly hair, upturned nose and the extra pounds she refers to as "baby fat" make her about as cozy and appealing as a human can be.

Cricket leaned close to me with an air of confiden-tiality. "So how is it for you? With guys, I mean. And intimacy?" She flushed so red she looked as though her cheeks had been painted on with crayon. "Like do you…" She held up her hands helplessly, as if she couldn't find the words.

"Do we kiss, hug, make love, you mean?" I smiled at her gently, hoping to ease her discomfort. "I'm a virgin, Cricket."

The cheeks I thought couldn't get any redder did. "You don't have to tell me…."

"Actually, I want to. You aren't the only one who's wondered how we Christians manage that."

"So…" She urged me on.

"I'm—all Christians—are created the same way as anyone else, Cricket. We're built with natural desires. Not being intimate is a choice Christians make. No one 'forces' us. We save intimacy for marriage because we want to." My friend looked so puzzled that I wanted to smile. "And we want to because it's what God wants for us."

"And He wants it for you because…" Cricket was intent on our conversation.

"Because He designed us. He put us here on earth and gave us the ability to love. And He gave us a sequence for getting the most out of that love. Marriage and intimacy are the ultimate steps in His divine sequence."

"I'm not sure what you mean," Cricket admitted.

"Just that intimacy should be the culmination of the sequence of meeting, getting acquainted, falling in love and marrying. He's right, you know. How many couples rush into intimacy before they know enough about each other, and the relationship fails? How many devalue one of the most loving, giving acts a couple can have together?"

"When you put it that way…" Cricket mused.

"Besides, as my grandmother Mattie puts it, it's 'a gift you can only give once.'"

Cricket grinned. "Now I get it." She paused and her brow furrowed. "It makes sense."

Curiosity satisfied, Cricket picked up the other conversation just where we'd left off. "Frankly, I think Stella is getting a little weird about the security thing. You and Thelma have the right idea, actually," Cricket concluded.

"What's that?"

"Thelma went out and bought a new side-by-side refrigerator freezer, a minivan and a treadmill. She says she wouldn't have bought the treadmill, but she feels obligated to stay healthy and live long enough to enjoy putting her grandchildren through college. She's putting the rest away for a rainy day."

It would have to be a *very* rainy day for Thelma to use up all her money. I had visions of Noah and his ark floating by her own personal floodworthy yacht.

Cricket looked around to see if Stella was returning before she whispered, "What are you going to do about the men in your life, Cassia? I don't want to live my life with mistrust and suspicion."

"Ken, back in Simms, has already got all the money he needs. Adam, my neighbor, doesn't seem the least bit interested in my money. And Randy and I are just friends. Besides, I plan to give it away as soon as I can figure out how. So far not only has it been difficult to find the right place for it, but it keeps multiplying. It's driving me nuts!"

"Well," Cricket said, reaching for a handful of goldfish crackers from the bowl on the table, "we're a fine threesome. Instead of Larry, Moe and Curly, we're Chary, Woe and Surly. This crazy lottery has made us into a very wealthy version of the Three Stooges."

When Stella returned, we got down to the business of eating lunch. Stella ordered the vegetable plate, no dressing. Cricket ordered a side salad and a cup of broth. I ordered a large cheeseburger, fries, a mug of hot chocolate, fried mushrooms for an appetizer and a piece of Death by Fudge cake for dessert.

"I've heard that expression that a person can't be too rich or too thin, but I don't agree," I told them as they stared at me. "I'm already too rich. No use losing weight, too."

We had almost finished eating when Stella choked on her final radish. Her eyes grew big and she stared at the door of the restaurant. "Is that who I think it is?"

"Who?" Cricket and I chimed in unison.

"Is that incredible, handsome, breathtaking man who's walking toward the table the guy you had at lottery headquarters?"

"Now, there's a man I'd willingly go out with, investigated or not," Cricket said.

I turned to look at this vision of manliness who had my friends melting and saw Adam striding across the room.

He reached us and put his hand on my shoulder. "I just picked up Winslow. He smells like a perfumery and looks like an overstuffed poodle with blue bows in his hair. You've got to find another dog groomer, Cassia. Winslow and I had a talk. He's beginning to question his masculinity. Are you ready to go?"

Adam, who had taken Winslow for a trim and bath, pulled up a chair and straddled it backward. I felt more than saw Stella shift from her normal ice-princess mode to watchful, demure but sensuous hunter. Man hunter. I knew a girl in high school who could morph from a normal human into a flirtatious creature when the opposite sex appeared. She could also bat her eyelashes and emit a megawatt smile that could lead a ship through fog. It had fascinated me then, and it fascinated me now.

Adam, however, was oblivious to Stella's flirtation. He has a way of keeping people at bay when he chooses. When he lets his guard down, he shows his funny, charming and even playful side. Then something happens—as if a thought or reminder of something bad hits him—and he disappears, leaving only a shadow of himself in his place. When that happens, he grows distant and quiet, as though something is breaking inside him. Adam can build a barrier around himself with the speed of light. Stella didn't even have a chance.

But Adam was all there again as we walked back to the building—it was I who was in a bit of a fog. And without my quite knowing how it came about, we arranged that Adam would come over to my apartment at five that evening for a supper of burgers, salad and the homemade pie my grandmother and sister had dropped off last night.

"How many dishes does it take to cook a burger?" Adam asked after dinner, holding a dish towel and eyeing the growing rack of clean dishes.

"Too many. Let's sit down and watch a movie."

Adam took one end of the couch and I the other. Then Winslow, jealous for "his" spot on the couch— the one in which I was sitting—started nudging me over with his nose. When he'd managed to edge me to midcouch, he scrambled aboard, packing us like three large sardines in a very small tin.

As the movie played, Winslow yawned and stretched, cramming me more tightly into Adam's side until I curled comfortably into the crook of his arm. Relaxed, I drifted in a drowsy haze as I heard Adam switch off the DVD player and begin to channel surf. The last thing I remembered as I fell asleep was his hand gently stroking my hair.

I awoke gradually, in tiny increments, experiencing pins and needles prickling in my sleeping foot, hearing Winslow's snuffly snore and feeling Adam's hand in my hair, winding a curly strand around his finger.

I looked up drowsily into his face.

"Sleeping Beauty awakes."

"How long was I out?"

"Not long. Maybe an hour."

I struggled to sit up, but he held me firmly in place.

"You don't have to. I like it."

"I'm squashing you."

"Like Tinker Bell and Captain Hook. I can hardly feel you." His hand tightened around my shoulder.

I probably should have jumped to my feet, but my body was engulfed in lassitude and I liked the warm, firm feel of his chest against my shoulder.

We sat that way through the ten-o'clock news, Leno, a rerun of *Star Trek* and three passes through the hall by the neighbors. Finally, about midnight, I squirmed again and rose from my nesting place. "I'd better walk Winslow."

Adam stood, too, and eyed the dog, now on the floor, unconscious and snoring at my feet. "Yeah, he really looks desperate to get out. Or is it just me you want out the door?"

"Of course not you! This has been a fantastic

evening, just the kind I like. No noisy restaurants or crowds. Cozy. Like me."

"You certainly are."

And before I realized exactly what he had in mind, Adam took my face in his hands.

I stepped backward and nearly toppled over Winslow. "I can't… I shouldn't…"

"Don't kiss on first dates?" He looked amused. "Sorry, Cassia. I know how seriously you take the Bible's admonitions about getting involved with a guy like me." With the back of his knuckles he stroked my cheek. He smiled sadly and turned to leave.

My fingertips rested on the skin his touch had branded, and I sighed.

A guy like me. Who exactly is a guy like Adam? A believer who has lost his faith? A seeker who will find it again? Perhaps I'm to be a part of his rediscovery process! Whether I ever date him or not is nothing compared to his experiencing God again…yet I couldn't help hoping the former would follow that latter. This evening had shown me just how comfortable I could be with Adam, if only there were no barriers to prevent our growing closer.

CHAPTER

21

"I can't do it anymore, Terrance." Adam paced the soft carpeted floors of his agent's office.

Only for Adam would Terrance give up his Saturday morning.

At first glance, the office looked like that of a successful CEO, but behind those wood-paneled walls were floor-to-ceiling bookshelves housing more manuscripts and tomes than some small libraries, all in tidy, organized rows. Terrance was as painstaking and cautious as Adam was adventurous. They'd maintained their relationship for the past ten years by balancing each other's personalities. Terrance was one of the few who fully knew the depth of Adam's passion and commitment.

Although Adam was now wearing a path in the newly laid cream carpet, Terrance let him pace.

"I can't lie to her for another day. Every time she trusts me with another thought about her post-lottery experiences, I feel like it's a blade in my heart. Deceit has never been my style and I won't do it anymore, not even for the sake of a story."

"Do you have enough to write it?"

Adam glared at his agent. "I do. It's started, but I won't let you get your hands on it. She'd never trust me again. That's what hurts. I've spent my life trying to be trustworthy, and now…"

Terrance leaned back in his leather chair and folded his arms over his chest. "So when did you actually realize that you were in love with her?"

Adam nearly tripped on a nonexistent lump in the carpet. "In love with her? Get real, Terrance. I never mix work and pleasure. Work is work and, well, everything else is…everything else," he finished lamely.

"Is that how you stayed so detached from your experience in Burundi?"

"Come on, Terry, you know that would take a heart of stone."

"And your heart is hardly stone." Terrance smiled in a knowing way that had always driven Adam crazy. "Your heart is as soft and sentimental as any I've seen."

"And that's our little secret." Adam scraped his fingers through his hair. "It would ruin my reputation if people knew I was actually human."

"It would certainly be awful if it got out that you're not a robotic wunderkind who can write award-winning pieces on Ebola, the economy of third-world countries and the ravages of terrorism in his sleep. You've covered a lot of human rights issues, come away despairing and never let it show. But think of this,

Adam. You're doing a story on a woman who won the lottery and doesn't even want the money. Compare it to your past stories, and it's not worthy of all this angst…unless you're in love."

Adam flung himself into a leather wing chair. "I don't know. Maybe you're right."

Terrance's eyebrows rose toward his hairline, as if he hadn't expected Adam to fess up quite so quickly.

"I think it's that red hair…or the freckles…or that wacky view she has of the world. Maybe it's the way she keeps pretending the money's not there and pinches pennies till they scream just for the fun of it. She can put herself together better with fifty bucks' worth of clothes from a discount store than any runway model wearing thousands of dollars' worth of designer garments."

Terrance nodded his encouragement.

"It's as if every day when she opens her eyes, the world is brand-new. She's so grateful to God and happy to be alive. And that big dumb dog…he adores her. She just sits down with him and talks to him face-to-face and he listens. I can't even imagine how wonderful she'd be with children." Adam made a grunting sound. "Even *Pepto* listens to her!"

Terrance seemed to understand perfectly. "So you're *really* in love with her."

"How did I let it happen?" Adam growled, although he already knew. It had been so gradual that he was in love before he realized it. That bizarre mix of flowers, that crazy salad that looked like swamp sludge and tasted delicious, the way Pepto trusted her—no, adored her—

her goodness, that wild red hair, her goofy habit of spouting Scripture as if everyone had the whole Book memorized…

He'd been sunk from the beginning, he realized now. He just hadn't realized how deeply he'd fallen.

It wasn't until he'd almost kissed her that he'd known for sure. She looked and smelled like cotton candy and catnip, fresh soap and spring air, like peaches. He was so hooked. Adam felt like a trout flopping on the shore. There would be no catch and release with this one.

"You let down your famous Cavanaugh guard. For once you didn't think about time demands or emotional commitments draining the energy you try to save for your work. You told me you were going to quit writing, remember? You walked in, but left your armor outside." Terrance's eyes twinkled merrily. "And you got caught. Bing. Cupid's arrow sailed right through your heart."

"Cut it out, Terry. You aren't helping. I can't believe I let this happen. Now I *care*. I'm going to break her heart when I tell her what I've been up to."

"Then why tell her?"

Adam looked at Terrance, his eyes anguished. "You don't know her like I do. I can't *not* tell her, even though she'll be devastated. She's trusted me at a time when she hasn't let many into her inner circle. She's afraid of being pulled this way and that by people who want her to line their pockets or fund their charities." He raked his fingers through his hair until it stood in dark spikes. "She's afraid of people exactly like me."

"Why hasn't she already given the dough away? What is she waiting for?"

"God. She's waiting for Him to show her what she's supposed to do with it. Until she thinks He's given the okay, she'll hang back."

"And He's not talking?"

"Apparently not yet, but she's patient. She's convinced that there's a heavenly design on that money and it's her job to carry it out."

"If you give up the story, you aren't going to be able to do what you want in Burundi," Terrance pointed out. "It's not as if you aren't trying to do something charitable. Maybe she could give you—"

"Terrance, the best I can hope to come out of this after I tell her the truth is that we're still on speaking terms. Cassia will forgive, but it's going to be harder to forget. She says that 'as far as the east is from the west' stuff is God's forte."

Terrance looked even more befuddled.

"Psalms 103:12. 'He has removed our sins as far away from us as the east is from the west.' God not only forgives sins, but then, once you ask forgiveness for them, He forgets them, too."

Suddenly Adam let out a growl that reverberated throughout the room and made Terrance jump.

Adam put his hands over his eyes and groaned. "It's worse than I thought, Terry. Now she's got *me* spouting Scripture verses and expecting you to understand!"

CHAPTER

22

"What's wrong with you?" I carefully picked a ripe black cherry from the bowl my sister set in front of me. "You look like the dog ate your homework."

Jane made sure that Mattie was still involved in the kitchen with Dave. They were conspiring over a surprise dessert for dinner. "I need to talk to you. I've been putting it off, but it can't wait any longer."

"So talk." I gazed at my sister benevolently. I've been looking at everything through magnanimous pink glasses all week and am practically dizzy with happiness. Floating on bubbles of hope, I've been praying about and planning how it will be when Adam sees what's missing in his life. Preoccupied as I am with what part God wants me to play in bringing Adam back into the family—the family of God—it's consumed much of my prayer time.

It makes sense. Adam knows what belief in God is about and sees it lived in his own family. And he cares for me, I know he does. I've been living the "happily ever after" part all week, the part after God taps Adam on the shoulder and shows him what's been missing, so even Jane's creased forehead and downturned lips don't faze me.

I can't help it that Jane isn't the one in love. I almost giggled, but that would only have upset her more. Finally it's my turn at romance. I had no idea how glorious it could be.

"You've been floating around here like a rubber ducky in a bathtub, oblivious to the fact that you're in danger of being sucked down the drain at any moment."

"Oooh, scary." I took another cherry and nibbled at it. "I hate it when that happens."

"Sis! Wake up!"

She looked like a grumpy old cloud, and I didn't want her raining on my parade. "Jane, I'm not in the mood."

"Well, *get* into it. This is important."

"You're making me tired, sis. Just tell me, what's so important that you can't allow me to enjoy being happy?"

For a moment my sister looked hurt and scared. "Jane, are you all right?"

Obviously not. She looked as though she were about to cry. Then she wailed, "No, I'm not all right, and you aren't either!"

My pink hazy fog dissipated. "You're scaring me. What's wrong? Is it something to do with Mom or Dad? They're okay, aren't they? I should call…"

Before I could jump to my feet, Jane grabbed me. "Mom and Dad are fine. Everyone is fine…sort of. Everyone but Adam Cavanaugh, that is. I have to tell you something, Cassia."

My heart banged in my chest so hard it hurt my ears.

"Stella came to see me yesterday. She's a smart, savvy woman, Cassia, and more suspicious than most."

"That's not a news flash, Jane. I suppose beautiful women like her have to be cautious. I wouldn't know."

"Because you aren't beautiful? Cassia, you are absolutely stunning, and you don't even know it!"

"Thanks, I think. But what has this got to do with Stella?"

Jane reached into her pocket, drew out a business card and handed it to me.

Confidential and Accurate
Helen Cross, Private Investigator
Contact at 888-555-1212

"So?" I handed the card back.

"You know the name, then?"

"Sure. Stella has told me about her. They're acquaintances, even friends. Stella says she's been using Ms. Cross regularly since the lottery winnings. She checks out everything from charitable organizations to first dates. Ridiculous, huh?"

"Maybe it's smarter than you think."

"To spy on people? Hardly." I lowered my voice. "Frankly, I'm afraid Stella is pretty full of herself, and the money hasn't helped. I love her and all…"

"Cassia, Stella had a bad feeling about your neighbor."

"And Randy, and everyone on the planet walking on two legs." I didn't tell her that Stella had flirted with Adam and been ignored. No wonder she was suspicious. That had probably never happened to her before.

"So she asked this Ms. Cross to run Adam's name through a search."

A chill raced through me. My intestines did an acrobatic flip and the taste in my mouth grew metallic. "She spied on Adam?"

"She called it 'checking' on him."

"Spying, pure and simple!" I don't believe I've ever felt so indignant or outraged. I looked around for my jacket and purse. "I have to talk to Stella."

"She was right, Cassia. I don't think your friend Adam is completely aboveboard."

"What do you mean?" I sat down again. I had to. My legs were collapsing.

"Do you know what Adam Cavanaugh does for a living?"

"Vaguely. He travels with his job and is a writer or editor. I didn't ask for details." I went all woozy again, thinking about all the not-so-serious things we laughed about. "We have so many other things to discuss...."

"He's a journalist." Jane opened a magazine and pushed it toward me. There was Adam, a casual sports jacket thrown over his traditional chamois shirt and faded jeans, smiling and shaking hands with an important-looking man.

*Adam Cavanaugh, Pulitzer Prize-winning jour-
nalist, meets with the head of the prize commit-
tee, which had praised him for his fine work and
humanitarian efforts. Cavanaugh, when asked
how long he would continue his rigorous and
emotionally taxing schedule, was quoted as
saying, "One of these days I'm going to find a
less gut-wrenching story to do, but until then, I
feel this is the place I need to be and can do the
most good." Cavanaugh, whose next assignment
is Burundi, will travel with the Red Cross and
several humanitarian groups in the area."*

A journalist? Like the many reporters who had been
stalking me since the lottery winners were announced?
They'd all returned again, full force, when Bob's
gambling blunders had come to light—no doubt
hoping one of the other winners would have an equally
juicy story and rapid fall into poverty. Was Adam like
the others who were jockeying to get my "story?"

"You didn't get that close to him, did you, sis? I
know you're neighbors and all, but you haven't known
him that long…."

I felt as though my body were imploding as my heart
and feelings crumbled to dust. I'd trusted him. I was
willing to love him. I've never felt such devastation and
betrayal.

No wonder he was so attentive and listened so closely
to my words. This was why he was so solicitous, patient
and friendly. I thought I was avoiding the den of media
vipers, and I'd had one virtually in my nest all along!

Involuntarily, my hand went to my face where Adam had touched me. How could someone so loving, gentle and precious be so…insincere?

I knew in that moment I'd never been in love before, not until Adam. And how did I know? Because I had never, ever felt so brokenhearted.

And then I did what has become my default reaction to shock. I fainted.

I scared Jane badly. As I came to, I heard panic in her voice and wished I'd stayed out longer. Much as I know logically that it is better to find out that Adam is a liar and a hypocrite now rather than later, I resent both her and Stella for meddling in my life. I kept my eyes closed and lay very still, not wanting to face her just yet.

Then my grandmother rushed into the room and waved something, a dish towel, probably, in my face. Meanwhile Jane spilled out the story of what had just happened.

Smart man that he is, Dave announced that he was taking Winslow for a walk. A very long walk.

It took everything in my power not to smile when Mattie said, "Jane, you meddled in this just as much as Stella did. If Stella thought it was so important that your sister know these things, why didn't she tell Cassia herself?"

"I didn't do it because I was snoopy, Grandma. I love Cassia. I don't want her hurt."

"But she's hurt anyway."

"Stella came to me wondering what she should do. I thought it might be easier for her to take coming from me…." Jane was on the verge of tears, and although I knew it wasn't right, I didn't feel like rescuing her, so I continued to lie perfectly still.

"You wouldn't want her to get mixed up with someone who was trying to trick her, would you?" Jane sounded righteous and a little huffy.

My grandmother's voice was patient and long-suffering. "Cassia's a smart girl and a cautious one. If the man isn't what he says he is, she would have found out in due time. It's her life—let her live it and learn from it."

"But she's crazy about him! We couldn't let that go on…."

"We?"

"Grandma! You aren't saying I should have just let her fall in love and have her heart broken?" Jane quit fluttering around me and turned her focus to our grandmother.

"I remember a time when you were worried that she was going to fall in love with Ken and not see his 'imperfections,' either."

"I stayed out of that…mostly. We don't always have to learn the hard way, do we?"

"Sometimes that's the *only* way we learn, dear. Besides, Cassia is in close contact with the Lord at all times. Don't you think they've been talking about Adam, too?"

"Yes, but…"

"There's no 'yes, butting' God, Janie. Now, quit staring at me and rouse your sister. You have some apologizing to do."

In spite of Mattie's little lecture, my sister was not nearly as repentant as I wanted her to be, but I was getting sore lying on the floor. I made a great show of coming to gradually—eye flutters, little groans and all. I might have felt more guilty about it if my sister— as soon as she knew I wasn't brain damaged or anything—hadn't started in on me again.

"You'll thank Stella and me one day, Cassia. She cares about you. *I* care about you."

"And that gives you permission to interfere in my life?"

"I'm your sister. It's my job." She crossed her arms across her chest and jutted her jaw forward, reminding me of Pepi, a little bull terrier we owned when we were children. When he was trying to be fierce, he would tuck his head into his shoulders, growl and make a yappy little scene. And when we were finished being amused by him, one of us would pick him up, scratch him under the chin and do something ridiculous to him like make him ride around in our doll buggy and love him out of his snit. I wasn't ready to pick up Jane and scratch her under the chin just yet.

"This is between Adam and me," I insisted.

"Then why didn't he tell you that he was a journalist?"

"He said something about writing, but I never pursued it."

"You just didn't want to know, did you?"

"How do you know he's writing a story about me anyway?" But I knew better. Why else would he be so interested in my thoughts, my family, my friends? He'd be a fool not to take advantage of a sucker like me.

My sister's pitying look was more than I could stand.

"Jane, I understand that you were trying to protect me, but what you and Stella did was underhanded."

"It's not as if we were trying to hurt you."

I knew she was convinced that she'd done the right thing. She's also incorrigible.

"What are you going to do now?" she ventured.

"To clean up your mess, you mean?"

"It's not *my* mess if Adam Cavanaugh is the one who made it."

If only I felt as calm as I sounded. My guts felt as though they were in a blender. Why had Adam done this? He obviously has plenty of awards and enough money to be content. This felt hurtful, intrusive, even cruel. I thought we were friends… and more.

"You're going to face him, aren't you? And make him explain?" Jane persisted.

I sighed. How, I wondered, could even a wordsmith like Adam Cavanaugh explain this?

I crept home after dinner feeling used and abused. Though Mattie tried to cheer me up, it didn't work. If I hadn't been a lottery winner, would Adam have even given me the time of day? Probably not. All around me people were holding their hands out, begging for a slice of me—the money, the notoriety, my story.

How, I wondered, did God feel? People were always asking Him for things, trying to make bargains with Him, using His name for their own purposes, wanting success, health and wealth.

He must feel like a heavenly ATM machine where people come to take, take, take and never give back. I could relate.

CHAPTER

23

One of the more intriguing aspects of this Million Dollar Dilemma is that Carr, a professing Christian, was raised to believe that gambling is not acceptable.

While gambling is not specifically forbidden or much mentioned in the Bible—except for the fact that the Roman soldiers cast lots for Jesus' robe after the Crucifixion—Carr believes it is inappropriate for her to do anything that might make her an unsuitable role model for others....

Adam threw the article he'd been writing to the table as Terrance watched.

"I'm quitting."

"Quitting what, exactly?" Terrance shifted in his chair.

"Quitting writing this article about the lottery winners. Quitting betraying Cassia. Quitting being a hypocrite. Quitting journalism maybe." He picked up the paper and threw it into the trash.

"Your life's work?" Terrance asked pointedly.

"If I have to. Terry, I've always lived my life as ethically and aboveboard as possible. I chose to focus on human rights issues because it was a way I could contribute to the world, let others know how much need there is out there and provoke them to action. Doing this story behind Cassia's back feels so wrong. I'm walking in quicksand and pulling her in with me. We're both going to suffocate under this lie."

"But now there's a book deal—" Terrance's mouth snapped shut as Adam stared at him.

"'Book deal?'"

"I ran it by an acquiring editor at lunch yesterday. I had no intention of bringing you up, but it just sort of…happened. He loves the idea. Said there were a few books around, some of them a few years old, about lottery winners, but none about someone trying to give it all away. He'd like you to research all the big lottery winners in the last five years or so and see where the people are now. He said your reputation as a writer would give it lots of credibility and—"

"I thought you were the one who told me I could quit."

Terrance flushed and looked a little ashamed of himself. "I didn't *really* know we could get a book deal when I said it."

"'We' aren't getting anything. This whole subject breeds corruption in everyone involved." Adam paused. "Except Cassia, who seems to be supernaturally protected from greed."

"It weirds me out when you say stuff like that, Adam. I know she's very religious and all, but you seem to be catching it."

Adam scowled even more deeply and his eyes flashed. "There was a time in my life when I was religious, too," he told the agent.

"No kidding?" Terrance leaned forward.

"Don't look so surprised. You know I grew up with a Christian grandmother who made sure my brothers and I knew what the Bible was about. We were sent to church-affiliated schools. My family always went to church on Sundays. Grandma never missed an opportunity to talk about being a Christian and the power of prayer. I even said yes to Christ."

"So what happened?"

Adam put his head in his hands and runneled his fingers through his dark hair. He'd let it grow longer on the sides of late. Cassia liked it that way.

"Too many horror stories. Wars, famine, pestilence, innocent women and children plagued by conflicts in which they were completely innocent. I started writing those stories because I thought I could raise awareness in the world. Instead, I lost my own faith. How could a gracious God allow these things to happen? My grandmother said that God wasn't the cause of evil, that sin was, but I always wondered why He couldn't just *stop* it. I was sure I'd never believe again when I came home from Burundi."

"And then Cassia showed up," Terrance concluded.

"She sure did. Invoking all those Bible passages, forgetting that no one other than her family could convey entire philosophical thoughts and opinions with a verse-and-chapter citation," Adam said softly. It had driven him crazy and he'd loved it. She was funny and smart, and he never minded that she set herself up to explain time after time.

He'd also fallen for her convoluted logic, which meandered this way and that, only to end up right on target. He admired and envied her absolute trust in God to provide and her determination to do what He wanted her to do. She allowed no one else to influence that.

"I hadn't seen faith like that for a very long time, probably since my own grandmother died. I'd begun to think faith and religion were all a charade." Adam sighed. "But there's nothing sham about Cassia. Nothing."

"So you'll just quit?" Terrance asked, incredulous.

"Yes. And I'll have to tell Cassia."

"Is that really necessary?"

"If we're to go on as friends…"

"Or more?" Terrance inquired.

"It's too big to sit between us." Eyes unfocused, Adam stared at an invisible point on the wall. "Maybe, if I give it a little time and distance, we could even learn to laugh about it."

"Right. Laugh." Terrance looked at him sympathetically. "You've got it bad, haven't you, buddy? The uncommitted, detached, stoic Adam Cavanaugh has found the woman who can tame him."

After Terrance left, Adam attempted to busy himself reading the stacks of mail he'd received that morning, but he couldn't focus. Everything reminded him of Cassia. Cruise ships, mortgage offerings, credit cards, life insurance policies—he wasn't interested in any of them unless he could share them with Cassia. That realization was devastating. Adam had made up his mind years ago that he was not—and never would be—the marrying kind.

Cassia, on the other hand, wouldn't be interested in a relationship with a man that didn't involve marriage.

Nothing was turning out as he had planned.

Absorbed as he was in untangling this conundrum, Adam responded automatically to the knock at his door, not checking to see who it might be.

It was, he was quick to discover, a spitfire so hot under the collar he could have sworn he saw smoke coming out of her ears. Cassia Carr was a heat-seeking missile and, radar in place, she was headed right for him, ready to blow him out of the water.

"You…you…" She looked like a lovely, fluffy red Guinea hen protecting her nest. It was obvious that she couldn't come up with any names to call him—none that she'd allow to slip past her lips.

"You…thug! Robber! Thief! How dare you skulk around pretending you're my friend when all along you're pilfering snippets of my life to use for your stories! You're nothing but a low-down, stealing…"

"Bandit?" Adam offered gloomily.

"Yes, and…"

"Crook?"

The outrage and disappointment on her face speared his heart. He'd taken something from her that was so personal—her friendship, her confidences and the intimate moments she didn't share with just anyone. She'd even allowed him to be the one who took her to the lottery offices to get the money! She couldn't have handed him this story any more completely if she'd tried!

"Gullible fool," she muttered. "Henrietta Hick, right off the farm, that's me. Trust everyone you meet. It's a miracle I didn't just leave my doors open at night with a 'Help yourself' note on the kitchen table."

"It's my fault entirely, Cassia. Not yours. It wasn't supposed to turn out like this…." He scraped his hands through his hair knowing nothing he could do or say was going to calm her down now…or maybe ever.

CHAPTER
24

It's been two days now, and I'm still weeping like a willow. If I cry any more, I'll have to rehydrate.

Jane, seeming to read my mind, handed me a liter of water and another box of tissues.

"How could he?" I asked for the hundredth time, still expecting Jane or Mattie to have an answer. For the hundredth time they looked at me helplessly, as if I'd asked them to explain the theory behind quantum physics.

Men and quantum physics aren't that different, I guess. Both are incomprehensible, problematical and virtually unintelligible to the ordinary person like me. I'm sure I've considered quantum physics more often than falling head over heels for a scoundrel like Adam.

Winslow, who hates it when I cry, looks as though he's about to have a nervous breakdown. He's licked tears off my cheeks until they're red and raw. His pink tongue hangs out of his mouth in a way that suggests that it is so exhausted it couldn't roll itself back into his gaping maw. Jane, too, has been crying. Her nose looks like Bozo the Clown's. Mattie is the only one who hasn't shed any tears, but her eyes have been squeezed tightly shut, her lips moving and her fingers clasped in an attitude of prayer.

We'd explored every avenue of excuses for Adam and come up with none that would mitigate his treachery. From there we—Jane, actually—moved on to bashing the entire male population.

"Animals, all of them," she muttered.

"Be nice. Don't say bad things about animals. Animals have good qualities. They don't have to shave their legs."

"Barbarians."

"They can do seventy-four different functions with a pocket knife and a match."

"Uncivilized…uncouth…."

"They can wear the same pair of shoes for an entire year without anyone thinking they have no fashion sense."

"Whose side are you on, anyway?"

"You'd better eat something, dear," Grandma said. "You haven't put a thing in your mouth in almost two days."

"I just can't, Mattie. My stomach turns over every time I think of the lies Adam has perpetrated on me," I told her.

"Toast and tea," Mattie decided, ignoring me. She'd fed us toast and tea for almost every childhood trauma. "And a little chocolate."

I felt a quiver of life in my taste buds. "Maybe just a sip of tea…" *And a jar of fudge ice cream topping and a spoon.*

"Praise God," Mattie said. "I think you're beginning to snap out of it."

"'Snap' isn't exactly the word," I said, sipping at the highly sugared tea she handed me. "Right now there's no 'snap' left in me. But my red hair is kicking in."

Anger is normally a stranger to me, but according to my family, when I finally do reach boiling point, I'm quite a sight to behold. Fortunately for me, my grandfather, who'd learned to control his own temper, had taught me two things about anger. First, it's a fine motivator. Second, being angry is a miserable way to live. I learned early that the best way to settle a score is to take the high road and to rise above the conflict.

Grandma spoke. "There's some good that will come out of this, just you wait and see."

"But what?" I wailed.

"That, you'll have to ask God about." She gave me an enigmatic smile.

The only time I ever consider the benefits of a king-size bed is when Winslow sleeps with me. I made the mistake of allowing him into my bed when he was a puppy and his piteous yowls in the middle of the night made me weak with sympathy. I've been breaking him of the habit every since.

Since the Cavanaugh debacle, Winslow has found that if he lays his enormous head on the side of the bed and stares up at me through wispy bangs, I'll eventually say, "Oh, come on, then. It's all right."

He scrambles up—no easy feat—and lays his head on the pillow next to mine, promptly falls asleep and begins to snore. In the night he twitches in his dreams. I wonder who or what he's chasing. Pepto, probably, who fascinates him even though they have yet to meet. Winslow is well acquainted with Pepto's scent and perks up every time he catches it. I should tell him that sometimes the dream is simply better than the reality. I certainly discovered that with Adam.

The phone rang as we were dozing off. I almost ignored it, but my curiosity usually wins out over my common sense, so I answered it.

"Cassia?"

For a moment I didn't recognize the voice. It was low, grave and seriously masculine. "Ken?"

"How are you, honey? I heard about the jerk in your building."

I closed my eyes and stifled a groan. *Oh, no. Jane, you blabbermouth!* "Ken—"

"I'll be up in the morning."

"Ken, you don't have to—"

"Of course I do. I don't want anyone messing with you, Cassia. Do you want me to pound him flat for you?" He sounded cheered by the idea. "I could rearrange his face, remove a few teeth and make his nose point in the opposite direction…."

"Oh, quit it. I'm okay."

"And I'm coming, so don't try to argue. I told you that building was a lousy place for you, honey. But no, you wouldn't listen to me—you had to find out for yourself...."

"G'night, Ken." I gently hung up the receiver and breathed a deep sigh. It was completely unnecessary for him to come to the Cities and comfort me. Still, I thought as I drifted off to sleep, it was very, very sweet....

Winslow growled so deep in his chest that I could feel his body vibrate. I sat straight up in bed and listened. Nothing.

It was 6:00 a.m., three hours before I'd planned to get up. Winslow made a clumsy slide and noisy crash off the bed and onto the floor and trotted woofing toward the front door. I pulled on some jeans and threw a sweatshirt over the oversize T-shirt I'd worn to bed and followed him.

I heard a scrambling sound outside, as if someone had fallen on the floor and was trying to get up. Then I heard the old shave-and-a-haircut-six-bits knock and my heart sank. Not Adam!

"Honey, are you in there?"

Ken. I threw open the door and let him in.

"Hey, babe!"

Before I knew what was happening, Ken scooped me into his arms and spun me around. I gasped and hung on.

He gave me a smack on the lips that made me recall that his nickname in high school had been Hoover, according to the grapevine, for the suction.

"What time did you get here?" I managed as he settled me onto the floor.

"I left right after I talked to you. I didn't want to wake you when I got here, so I just slept outside your door."

"On the floor?"

"Sure. I'd do anything for you." He looked around. "This isn't the Ritz, is it? Kinda cozy, though. Hey, dawg, come 'ere." Winslow, who'd been impatiently waiting his turn for attention, shook his wagging end so hard that his ears quivered.

Ken dropped to one knee, scratched him behind his ears and did that dog-whisperer thing he did. Before long, Winslow licked his face, sighed happily and dropped to the floor with a thud.

"This wasn't necessary, you know. I'm fine."

He took in my bird's-nest hair, bleary eyes and pale skin studded with freckles. "You don't look so fine. You're beautiful, of course, but not fine." He looked around. "Have you got any coffee in this joint or do we have to go out?"

"There's a coffee shop down the street that has blueberry crunch coffee cake that's even better than Mattie's. And I want a whole milk latte with three shots of espresso."

Ken grinned, and his white teeth gleamed in his tanned face. "That's my Cassia. I love a woman who doesn't diet."

Ken often says I'm a little on the scrawny side for his taste, "like a half-grown chicken, half down and half feathers."

Translation: There's not enough meat on my bones and I'm mostly squawk and noise.

I surely do attract romantic men.

* * *

The coffee shop was busy but it felt good to be away from my apartment and distracted from the doldrums I'd been steeped in there. Ken didn't hurt my mood either. He was as solicitous as I've ever seen him, bringing me candy-coated spoons to stir my coffee, chocolate-covered coffee beans and a tin of after-coffee mints. He loped to the counter for refills on both lattes and coffee cake and hovered over me as if I was a delicate flower. I hadn't known he had it in him.

"Settle down," I said finally. "I'm disappointed, not dying."

"I'd love to get my hands on this guy." He clenched and unclenched his fists menacingly. Then he blinked slowly and a guarded expression settled on his features. "Is there anything else I should know about this fellow?"

Like, was I in love with him?

Ken's no dummy, but there was no use confessing to an unreciprocated infatuation.

"He's just a guy that I thought was a friend and neighbor. I'm apparently not as good a judge of character as I thought. I'm going to be fine, Ken. And you know perfectly well that I *do not* want you punching anybody. Exodus 21:12."

Anyone who hits a man so hard that he dies shall surely be put to death.

"I'm not going to kill the guy, you know!"

I had to smile. Ken, at least, has begun to catch on to our family's abridged form of speech. He's a quiet Christian, on a journey of his own. Relatively new to faith in Christ, he's always listening, sorting out what he calls "the God stuff." He's fascinated by our family's biblical shorthand and it made me smile that, even though he doesn't speak it, it was a language he's learned to understand.

"Well, I don't want you to talk that way. I have to take some responsibility, too. I should have been more careful."

Careful about falling in love. What an odd concept. Who *plans* to fall in love? No one ever says, "I'm going to fall in love today. I have time to fall in love with the guy at the coffee shop if it doesn't take more than an hour."

"Okay, I'm here for you, babe. Whatever you want."

I felt a stirring of appreciation and affection within me. In a pinch, Ken is really coming through. Maybe I'd underestimated him.

"My friend Cricket is having some people over for a cookout. Want to go?" I wiggled my toes as we sat on benches in the art gallery looking at a piece of important contemporary art Ken had dubbed "worm tracks." I was happy to be out of my shoes for the first time since we'd left my place this morning.

We'd been to the sculpture garden, the zoo and the Science Museum, and it was still only four o'clock in the afternoon. Ken is an efficient sightseer. He scans the place, heads for what interests him and moves on. He took his time in the zoo but managed the sculpture garden in just a few minutes.

"What kind of name is Cricket?"

"A rich one. She's one of those who won the lottery."

Ken shrugged. "May as well go, unless there's somewhere else you'd rather eat."

At least, I realized, I felt like eating again.

Cricket's house is a tribute to all things feminine, from the soft pastel colors of the stucco to the over-abundance of potted flowers scattered everywhere. Her first purchase since the lottery, the house has been like a big playhouse for Cricket, who's been buying, moving, returning, buying furniture again and again. I could tell from the way Ken whistled under his breath that he approved of the soundness of the structure, if not the soft pink and pale turquoise exterior.

Cricket came to the door in a grass skirt and wearing leis around her neck. I could hear hula music and laughter in the background. "You came!" She flung her arms around me and gave me a hug. In my ear she whispered, "Stella told me what happened."

Then her gaze shifted to Ken. "But you seem to have recovered nicely. Where *do* you find these hunky men?"

I looked over at Ken, who was studying an appetizer platter. He picked up a skewer of teriyaki chicken and pineapple before turning to beam that devastatingly charming grin of his at me.

Cricket put her hand to her chest. "Be still, my heart," she murmured as she drifted off, grass skirt rustling.

All my money mates—what else can I call them?—were present except for Bob. Bob is avoiding the public for the time being. Probably a wise decision.

Thelma was sitting by the pool in a wheelchair, her leg in a cast.

I introduced her to Ken and asked, "What happened to you?"

Thelma used the cane in her lap to tap her cast. "Just the craziest thing, I tell you. I was on my way to the basement to pack boxes for the Veterans of Foreign Wars pickup, and a step gave way. Whoosh. Just like that, a broken leg."

"Sorry about that," Ken said solicitously.

Thelma beamed at him. "It's fine. Frankly, I believe I'm fortunate not to have been hurt more seriously." She tapped her cast again. "Yes, sir, this has been my lucky day."

"It's all in the perspective, isn't it?" Ken commented as we moved away from Thelma. "Whether we're lucky or not, I mean."

I felt a spot melting in my heart. I'd never given him credit for being introspective—shame on me. "What's your take on things, Ken?"

He stopped and turned to look me full in the face. "That no matter what, I'm very lucky to know you, Cassia. You are—" he grinned "—a 'treasure beyond measure' to me."

"Ken, you're a poet!" I grabbed his hands and we both laughed.

And I didn't want to let go. Obviously neither did Ken. We walked hand in hand to the big spit, where someone Cricket had hired was cooking pork roasts.

It wasn't as if Ken and I hadn't dated or held hands or laughed together over private jokes before, but this time it was different. This time I really wanted it to happen again—soon.

Ego Ed was less talkative than usual. He had an expensive toupee on his head and a sad expression on his face. While Ken was whacking his way to a croquet victory on the lawn, I sat down by Ed near the pool.

"You're quiet today."

"Just haven't got much to say."

"Cricket told me your daughter is getting married soon. Congratulations. You'll be a proud father walking her down the aisle."

To my surprise, Ed gave a rather ungentlemanly snort. "Hah! Wedding's been called off."

"Oh, I'm sorry. I didn't realize…"

"It's okay. It might feel good to talk about it." He eyed me speculatively. "I've always thought you were easy to talk to, nonjudgmental. You know what I mean?"

"I think so."

"Well, my daughter really loved this guy—and she thought he loved her. Then I won the lottery. They were looking at a house to buy, something with a nice yard and a couple extra bedrooms for the kids they were planning to have…then all of a sudden he started driving her by these big fancy homes, saying he liked this one or that. He decided it would be 'cool' to live next to a big athlete and tried to find out where members of the Twins and the Timberwolves live." Ed scowled. "All this on a truck driver's salary! And he decided he wanted his wedding ring to have a diamond in it. A carat's worth of diamond."

Uh-oh…

"Next thing my daughter knew, she was getting bills for things she hadn't purchased—a designer tux, plane tickets to Rome, a Bentley.... When she confronted him, he told her he wanted to give her the best—and, oh, yes, could she write checks for the bills before the tenth of the month, please?"

Ed scraped his fingers through his hair, and I could feel his frustration. "I don't care if people want to beg or borrow money from me. I can handle myself. But my daughter..." He looked up and I saw raw pain in his eyes. "She dumped him, of course, and we've been dealing with the fallout ever since. She cries and won't eat, he calls a hundred times a day—what a mess! I can't believe I'm saying this, but sometimes I wonder if we wouldn't be better off without all that money. A million would be okay, but this..."

Ken and I talked about Ed's words as we drove back to my place.

"That party was proof money doesn't buy happiness," Ken commented as he turned sharply, taking a C.O.D. on the street that led to my house.

Ken is the one who taught me what a C.O.D. is. It's executed by turning a corner so sharply that if the passenger isn't buckled in tightly, he or she slides right up to the driver. He calls it a Come Over Darling and says it was much more effective before everyone got so seat belt conscious.

"There wasn't a lot of laughing going on."

"Parties in Simms are different," I pointed out. "Everyone knows everyone else very well."

"If these people don't know each other all that well, then why are they hanging out together?"

"We have a lot in common these days."

He looked at me pityingly. "You have to do what I do, darling—make sure people forget you're rich and just love you for your charming personality."

I didn't expect to feel down when Ken left, but I did. I'd seen a new side of him, the tender, funny, compassionate side. And when he departed for Simms, I had tears in my eyes.

25

I'm a sick, sick woman. I must be. I keep pouring salt into my own wounds.

I stayed off the Internet for three days after Ken left, telling myself that it didn't matter what Adam did for a living, that I knew far too much about him already. I also told myself that there was nothing but relief in my heart that his slimy charade was exposed before things went any further. Why, I asked myself sensibly, would I yearn for a charlatan who had come so close to breaking my heart?

I'm also a liar.

"Had come close" to breaking my heart?

Adam Cavanaugh *did* break it. I can imagine it fragile and shattered and lying in bits, resting all over my insides, shards poking at my gall bladder and into my appendix, chunks wedged in my stomach, all making me ill.

Okay, okay, so I'm not a doctor. But I still have a

constant stomachache that flares up every time something reminds me of Adam. Unfortunately, *everything* reminds me of Adam.

Even Winslow strikes a painful chord in me. He insists on sitting by the front door, waiting for Adam to arrive. And of course, Adam never does. Sometimes Winslow whines, lies down and buries his head in his paws as though he's crying. That, naturally, makes me feel like crying, too.

Snap out of it, you silly goose!

I also have selective hearing. I've quit listening to my own good advice.

I looked up Adam on the Web and scrolled down the page, amazed at the number of hits that came up on him.

"Cavanaugh Nominated For Second Pulitzer, This One On Children And War In Iraq. Cavanaugh Series Concerning Fatherhood And Federal Inmates Sparks National Interest. Balanced And Accurate Reporting Are Adam Cavanaugh's Forte." And there was a list of awards won by Adam spanning university faculty awards to national recognition for journalism, research and reporting, excellence and even ethics.

I did a double take at that one.

He'd written a significant piece on fetal alcohol syndrome and a dramatic exposé about corruption in countries where governments were allowing food shipments to rot at docks without distributing them. His compelling series of interviews of federal penitentiary inmates who were separated from and unable to parent their children had sparked new investigation into the topic.

Mesmerized, I kept digging until I came up with some of the articles Adam had written. Several were about children.

A knock on the door snapped me back to the present, and I felt heaviness wrapped around me like a cloak. Adam could breathe life into his subjects with his words, so that it was virtually impossible not to care about what happened to them. Unfortunately, for many of those he followed up on later there were no happy endings.

Winslow was on his feet and waiting for me to open the door in the vain, misguided hope that Adam was on the other side. I peered out the peephole and a black-eyed Susan stared back. *More flowers?* I opened the door.

"Hi, Cassia." The delivery guy thrust a giant bouquet into my hands and grinned. "Run out of space yet?"

It's pretty remarkable that the floral delivery man and I are on first-name terms, but he's visited here more in the past couple days than my own sister.

"Not yet. There's room for a couple more floral arrangements in the bathtub. And if you start bringing bamboo, I can probably keep it in my closet." I lowered my voice. "If he calls to order any more, just take them to the nursing homes, will you?"

"No can do. They come to you. But it's a great idea. Do you have room in your own car to transport them?"

I rolled my eyes. My car was another whole issue. "I'll work it out. Thanks."

Mr. Bouquet stared at me, shaking his head. "I don't

know what you did to deserve this, but with the exception of churches, banquet halls and hotels, I've delivered more flowers to you than to any other home address this week, and it's only Wednesday."

"Just lucky, I guess." I smiled brightly and shut the door.

This has to stop. My apartment is full. Ken has been sending flowers, candy and even singing telegrams. If I'd had to pick a favorite, it would have been the three-hundred-pound guy in the Fred Flintstone outfit singing a rather good imitation of Elvis's "Love Me Tender."

Ken has found his niche—taking care of me, protecting me, fighting for me, lavishing me with gifts and doing his best to be my superhero. Adam's duplicity has paved the way for Ken to leap a tall building or two and come to my rescue. He's good at it. On the other hand, twelve or fifteen bouquets of flowers would have been plenty.

I put the black-eyed Susans and company into the bathtub, grabbed a granola bar from the counter and went back to the computer to print out Adam's articles. When I was finished, I spread them out on the coffee table in front of my couch to study them.

Now I know more about Adam than I had in all the time we'd lived in neighboring apartments. Much of what I've learned doesn't jive, however, with his crass treatment of my privacy. In articles about him, words like *moral, principled* and *fair* cropped up over and over, as did *impartial, unbiased, unprejudiced* and *objective.* "Cavanaugh goes for the gut and grabs the heart," one article said. Another proclaimed, "If it's about children and it's by journalist Adam Cavanaugh, it's a must-read."

I sat back and stared at Winslow, who was studying the papers as intently as I, hoping I'd drop food crumbs onto the articles. Children and *animals,* I realized. There was something in Adam that seemed to connect with the vulnerable, the defenseless and the unlovely. Pepto was proof of that.

Articles that didn't refer to children in some way or another were few and far between. Sure, he'd covered war, famine, corruption and vice, but the single underlying theme was always children and how they were affected by the nonsensical world of the adults around them.

But if he's so noble and trustworthy, why did he betray me?

It's the question I can't answer. It is also the question that has ripped my heart in two.

I must have fallen asleep on the couch, because when I awoke I was sprawled across the pillows. Winslow had taken up guard duty and was stretched on the floor in front of the couch like a large, lumpy rug. I haven't been sleeping much, so I suppose I should have been glad for the rest, but my entire body felt as though it had been sent through a juicer. I groaned and tested the foot that had fallen asleep beneath me. It felt as though it was being stabbed with hundreds of needles and pins, and it hurt to wiggle my toes.

I didn't have long to cosset myself, however, because someone started banging on my door.

"What is this, Grand Central Station?" I addressed no one in particular as I hobbled to the door. It was my landlord.

"Hi, there," I greeted him. He was holding a white envelope in his hand. "Do you have something for me, or is it rent time already?"

"Mr. Cavanaugh downstairs asked me to give this to you after he left." He thrust the letter into my hands and stomped off.

"Wait! When did he leave?"

"Just a minute ago. He said I was to wait to give it to you, but I haven't got time for such nonsense. The plumbing is backed up in apartment twelve."

I spun and ran back into my apartment, across the floor and skidded to a stop in front of my living-room window. I could see Adam loading his laptop carrying case into his Hummer. He slammed the door, rolled his shoulders as if to release tension and glanced upward in the direction of my apartment.

Instinctively I stepped back. He didn't see me. Then he rounded the vehicle, swung into the driver's seat and drove away.

I looked after him, glad he was leaving and devastated that he was gone. Slowly I opened his letter.

Cassia,
I know you've been hiding out in your apartment. I can hear you cleaning your place at all hours of the night. Just wanted you to know that

I'm leaving on assignment and that you can come
out now.

I'm so sorry about everything.
Adam

That was it? No explanation? No nothing? And how
did he know I was cleaning, anyway?

"Jane? It's Cassia. I have a question for you."

"Shoot."

I could hear the clatter of Jane's calculator in the
background. Jane is always multitasking. She knits
when she visits with her husband, pays bills while
watching TV and either adds numbers or plays solitaire
on the computer when she's talking to me.

"I need to know how much interest I've earned on
the lottery money." It's been over two and a half
months now and probably time to ask.

There was a stunned silence at the other end of the
line. "You? Interest? Like you might spend some of
it?"

"Don't sound so happy about it. Consider it a loan
from my account. My car died in my garage, and it's
starting to smell."

"Maybe you can get it fixed and use it until I find
a new one?" She sounded as though she hoped that
wasn't possible.

"Not this time. Ken told me so. Something very
large and important seems to have fallen out of the
bottom of the car."

"Like your muffler?"

"He said something about the transmission."

"Oh, my."

"So I have to buy a new car...an *old* new car, that is, something to get me around. I'll pay myself back as I can. How much car do you think I can afford?"

"How do you feel about an entire dealership?"

I ignored her. "Nothing older than a 2000, I think. I'd like four doors because of Winslow."

"How about an SUV?"

"Great room, but lots of money."

"Oh, go hog wild, Cassia." And she named the amount of interest income I'd earned since the day of the lottery.

"Oh, my."

It felt weird the next afternoon walking into the apartment building and going past Adam's apartment without either hurrying past to avoid him or stopping to talk. I hadn't realized how big a part of my day that had become until it was gone. I felt a wave of confusion and loneliness wash over me as I stood there, helplessly staring at the door.

Then I heard a thump from inside the apartment. A thump, a clatter, a hiss and a meow. Was Pepto still inside? Surely Adam would never leave Pepto to fend for himself if he were going to be gone long—would he? I didn't think so. Then again, I don't know anymore.

Deciding to listen for Pepto in the morning and make sure that he hadn't been cruelly abandoned like me, I went upstairs to bed.

CHAPTER

26

"You mean it? You want me to actually help you pick out a car?" Randy sounded like a kid on his birthday.

"It's not that exciting," I assured him. It's actually a desperation measure on my part. I need something to get my mind off Adam's absence. It's been only two days since Adam left, and already I'm feeling the enormous gap in my life.

"Not for you, maybe. It is for me."

It isn't just about the car. Randy had been less blatant than Ken about courting—Mattie's word—me, but had he been the successful businessman that Ken is, I would probably have double the flowers around my place.

"Can I pick you up? When we're done at the car dealerships, we can grab a bite to eat."

That had the ring of "date" to it, but I let it pass. I have to get over my skittishness sometime, and Randy hasn't misled me...yet.

"I'll wait out front."

It feels good to have somewhere to go. I don't get much pleasure from being a hermit, but it's easier these days. If I run into anyone who recognizes me, I have to repeat the same conversation I've had a hundred times. "No, I haven't decided what to do with the money yet...no, I don't plan to keep it...no, I haven't lost my mind.... Have a nice day...."

I grabbed shades on my way out, hoping to disappear behind them.

At the bottom of the stairs I paused at Adam's front door. All was silent inside the apartment. Had I imagined Pepto crying in there? There wasn't a single noise coming from the other side of the door now.

Randy was prompt and obviously delighted by this turn of events. He jumped out of the car, ran around to my side and gallantly flung open the door.

"This is great, Cassia. Thanks for asking me to help you."

"You've been nagging me to get a new car forever. How could I choose one without you?" I settled into the seat and noticed a map on the dashboard. It was circled and marked with what I guessed were dealership locations.

I turned to grab my seat belt, and as I looked over my right shoulder I noticed a movement in the window of Adam's vacant apartment. I did a double take and then felt my jaw drop. Pepto was sitting in the window staring out at me. His expression was unpleasant and disgruntled, as usual.

Why had Adam left the cat alone? Unfortunately, that was no longer any of my business.

The longer I live in the city, the more of a mystery it becomes. Since many of the car dealerships Randy had chosen were in the suburbs, we passed Oak Street, Cherry Boulevard, Elm Lane and Pine Avenue. How ironic—people cut down trees to make room for houses then, in honor of the trees, they name streets after them.

"I'm bored."

Randy stared at me as if I'd lost my mind. "How can that be? We've only been shopping for an hour."

"There was a nice car at the first place we stopped. A red one."

"What make and model?"

"Red. Four wheels."

Randy shook his head in amazement. "You really don't care, do you?"

"Not beyond the basic questions—does it work, is it safe and is it cheap? Otherwise I really don't."

Randy grabbed my hand and pulled me toward another row of cars. As we walked, I caught a glimpse of something in my peripheral vision—a Hummer, like Adam's. I stumbled and was grateful Randy was there to catch me as I fell.

After the embarrassing hubbub I created in the car lot, I decided I'd procrastinated too long and was in danger of making a serious fool of myself over my reluctance to buy a new car. Once I made up my mind to just do it, buying the car didn't take long at all.

"It's between this one and this one. Do you like red or green better?" I stood back to study the pair of midsized cars I'd test driven and parked together in front of the dealership for a final look.

"It's not about the color, it's about what's under the hood," Randy said patiently.

"Then you pick it out. You're the one who's been under there."

He rolled his eyes and began to tick off the pros and cons of each car on his fingers.

"Fewer miles, cleaner, tires worn…"

After waiting patiently for him to finish, I said, "So having said all that, which one would you buy?"

Wearily he pointed to the car on the left.

"Great. I'll take it." I was pleased with his choice. I like the red one better anyway.

"I made dinner reservations," Randy said after we delivered the car to my front door. I would have been content with a sandwich, but Randy had planned something pretty elaborate.

At the restaurant we had more waiters fussing around us than cats around a dish of cream. And enough silverware spread out to do brain surgery. "I feel like a princess, Randy. You didn't have to take me to such a lavish place." I placed my hand on his and gave it a squeeze. "Thank you."

"Thank you, Cassia, for agreeing to come." He smiled shyly and ducked his head. "For giving me a chance."

"Now quit that—you're going to make me all

gushy." And I pushed away from the table and hurried to the ladies' room before Randy could say what I suspected was on his mind.

"I keep thinking I'm going to wake up and this evening will have been a dream," he said when I returned. The expression in his eyes grew soft and warm. "I love being with you. I don't want this to end. I know you're on your guard now, but that can't last forever, and I'll be there waiting when you're finally ready."

He must have seen something in my eyes that I really didn't mean to convey, because he took my hand in his and said, "Don't worry. I'm not going to pressure you right now. I just had to say it so you know how I feel."

Okay, no pressure, uh-uh—other than a sort of till-death-do-us-part promise.

I felt resentment boil up within me. This money is ruining everything. I don't dare trust the men who care for me.

Worse yet, I care for the man I don't trust.

After a turn around a small carnival we discovered set up in the parking lot of one of the malls, Randy won me an enormous stuffed pink flamingo and a teddy bear the size of Rhode Island.

"You've made my childhood dream come true," I said as I peered over Mingo's—as in fla-mingo's—head. "I would have given my eyeteeth to have these guys in my room back then."

"I'm glad you didn't have the opportunity. You look very nice with your eyeteeth intact." He stuffed the teddy bear into the trunk and put Mingo in the backseat.

"I've had a lot of fun this evening, Randy. Thank you."

"No, thank *you*. You've made one of my dreams come true, too."

Fortunately, we arrived at my building and I didn't have to respond. The bird and the bear were all either of us could manage.

"Are you sure you don't want me to walk you in?"

"Don't worry, I'll be fine. There's a security pad that we punch at night. Just wait until I get inside."

He looked disappointed. I knew Randy wanted to be invited to my apartment, but I didn't make a policy of that. Besides, I had some investigating to do. It had bugged me all evening. Why was Pepto still in Adam's apartment? I noticed a dim light burning—the small lamp Adam kept on one of his bookcases. Curiouser and curiouser.

I dragged the giant toys upstairs and propped my two new best friends next to my door. Then I walked downstairs to stare at Adam's door. Pepto hadn't exactly looked as if he was suffering as he sat on the window ledge, but even if he were being fed, it must be terribly lonely….

Wait a minute. It's Pepto I'm worrying about. He doesn't even like people.

Still, he likes me. Maybe he needs me.

I should have been having my head examined instead of creeping up to Adam's door like a cat burglar and putting an ear to the door. There was no mewing, no rustling of kitty litter being scratched in his box. I leaned closer until my ear touched the door.

That was, of course, why I tumbled into Adam's apartment when the door opened unexpectedly. I lay sprawled at the feet of a gorgeous, faintly-familiar looking man with dark blond hair and mesmerizing blue eyes.

This was not Adam, but physically he was definitely of Adam's caliber. He wore camel-colored slacks, a dark blue shirt with the collar open and a cream-and-blue tie loosened around his neck. His feet, I noticed because of my proximity, were bare.

Why the earth didn't just open and swallow me up, I don't know. How embarrassing.

"I, uh, sorry. I was just listening for Pepto. I saw him in the window when I left earlier, and the landlord said Adam was out of town…." Well, that certainly sounded lame.

Then a beautiful dark-haired woman with warm eyes and a ready smile glided out of what I assumed was Adam's bedroom. She was securing the belt of her robe around her waist as she walked. Her hair was tousled and her beautiful face makeup free.

"Chase? What's going on?" She stared at me for a moment, gathered her composure and said, "Hello. May we help you?"

"Let's help her to her feet, first thing," said the man called Chase. He picked me up off the floor as if I were a feather and set me back on my wobbly legs. "Are you okay?"

"Fine. Everything but my pride, that is. I feel like

an idiot." My cheeks were burning. When I'm embar-
rassed, I look like scalded carrots. Not a pretty sight.

Although I would have preferred to skulk out of the
apartment never to return, manners were one of my
mother's favorite hang-ups. I stuck out my hand. "I'm
Cassia Carr. I live upstairs. The landlord told me Adam
was gone. I heard Pepto earlier today and then saw him
in the window when I went out this afternoon. I just
wanted to know he was okay." I felt my cheeks redden
even more. "I didn't mean to, you know, fall in on you
like that."

"I'm Adam's cousin Chase Andrews."

So that's why he looks familiar. Family resemblance.

"And this is my wife, Whitney. My wife's office
isn't far from here, so rather than take Pepto out of his
home, we decided to stay here with him." He smiled
at his wife and looked at her as though there was no
other woman on earth. I felt a whisper of envy.

"It's our minivacation," Whitney added cheerfully.
"I get to eat out every night this week."

I liked her immediately. There was a glow and
a…something…about her that felt special.

At that moment Pepto sauntered out of the bedroom,
saw me and leaped into my arms. We both nearly
toppled, but I staggered against the wall and he stuck
all his claws into my shirt and skin and hung on. As
soon as I regained my footing, I gathered him close,
and he began purring like a semitruck. To everyone's
surprise, he licked the hollow of my neck.

"I see now why you were concerned about him. You
two are best friends," Chase said pleasantly. "He loves

Whitney, too. For a cat, Pepto has great taste in women."

"Can you sit down?" Whitney asked. "I just made tea." Without waiting for my answer, she went to the kitchen, put an extra cup on the tea tray and brought it to the sitting area.

"I really shouldn't…." *But I want to.*

My loneliness, my desire to hold the purring Pepto for a bit longer and the impulsive desire to learn more about Adam's family propelled me into a chair.

The dimness of the book-lined room, lit with candles and small lamps I'd barely noticed when Adam was here, was snug and inviting. What's more, I felt soothed when embraced by his personal effects. It often seemed that we'd known each other forever, so comfortable were we when cooking together, discussing the pets or what to do about the lottery.

Ah, the lottery. Proverbs 23: 5.

For riches can disappear as though they had the wings of a bird!

Where was that bird when I needed him?

"Where do you work, Cassia?" Whitney asked. Her eyes twinkled as though she would be delighted with any answer I gave her.

"I'm not currently employed," I ventured. "Something has come up, and I'm not able to work right now."

"Is it your health?" Chase asked. "I'm a doctor. I could steer you to one of my colleagues. I know the best doctors in the city."

"Thanks, but I'm not sick, although this stuff is

making me feel pretty squeamish." I looked at their puzzled faces. "My money, I mean."

"Your money is preventing you from working?" Whitney still looked puzzled.

"I and some of my office mates won the lottery. You might have heard about it." *Everyone else has.*

"You're one of *them?*" Whitney and Chase both started to laugh. "No kidding?"

"'Fraid not—wish I was."

"You don't sound very happy about it," Chase observed.

I explained the circumstances, and that gambling of any kind went against my belief system.

"A Christian, I suppose." Whitney clicked her tongue in mock surprise. Then she grinned and brightened a notch or two. "Welcome to the club."

"You are? Then you understand!" Relief poured through me.

"Chase and I talked about it, didn't we? What we'd do with that kind of money if it were dropped into our laps."

"I've been trying to get rid of it, but it's not working very well. I spoke to the pastor of the church I attend and two national ministries before I began to get the idea that this money is a problem for more than just me. No one wants to send the message that they're approving any form of gambling—including the lottery—because it can trap people in addictions or encourage them to spend money they don't have. It's a role model thing, I know." I paused before adding with a heartfelt wail, "But I want to be a role model, too!"

I leaned back in the chair feeling disgruntled. "I wish He'd hurry up and spend His money."

"Does Adam know about this?" Chase asked.

The hackles on the back of my neck rose. "Yessss…"

"He's the great philanthropist—a human rights, save-the-children-and-the-whales kind of guy. He'd be a great one to talk to about it."

I know.

"But I need to talk to someone who understands my faith as well as my situation. It's complicated for most people to grasp that I don't consider the money mine."

"Another Christian, you mean? Adam is…was… well, I guess we don't really know where he stands anymore. Adam and I grew up in a huge extended Christian family. We were pretty much on the same page with our faith growing up, but…" Chase frowned. "Adam has seen and experienced some pretty awful things in his work as a journalist. It's changed him, made him doubt that there *is* a God. After his recent trips we've noticed a shift in what he says and thinks. These things he sees and experiences chip away at his soul."

Was that what had happened? Had Adam lost his soul? Had he decided to use my circumstances for his own benefit because he no longer believes both good and evil exist in the world…just evil? It makes as much sense as a crossword puzzle without clues.

"I haven't known Adam very long," Whitney added. She smiled shyly at her husband. "Chase and I have only been married a few months. But I do know that he's one of the most decent, straightforward, trustworthy and honorable men I've ever met. Chase's family is very proud of what Adam does with his life. That's what's so puzzling about the changes we see in him."

Puzzling? They didn't know the half of puzzling. How could I reconcile what Adam did to me with how his family and friends see him?

With Pepto now snoring on my shoulder, I settled back and listened to Chase regale Whitney with his and Adam's childhood exploits.

Give 'em an inch, they try to take a mile.

"Cassia, it's Randy. I was wondering if you'd like to go out after work and grab a bite to eat." He's called me every evening since I bought the car five days ago.

"Thanks, but I think I'll stay home tonight."

"What's wrong, Cassia?"

"Oh, nothing."

There was a long pause on the other end of the line. When Randy spoke, I heard caution in his voice. "Did you say that in woman-speak or man-speak?"

"What do you mean?" Now I was the nonplussed one.

"When a man says, 'Oh nothing,' you can take it literally. One the other hand, when a woman says, 'Oh, nothing,' it usually means, 'Oh, something.'"

I'm more transparent than I thought. "You have an interesting understanding of women."

Randy sighed. "Sisters. Three of them, all older.

They thought I was their toy, that Mom had me just for them. They did me a favor, they tell me, by 'breaking me in' for other women. I've been trained to wait until last to get into the bathroom, share my razor and wait patiently in the car while they run into the store for 'just a minute.' I was also told that it was important that I always share my dessert with the woman with whom I was having dinner, because there are no calories in food eaten off someone else's plate."

"You're a dream man, Randy. Somebody should snap you up. I'm surprised that you have any time at all to spend with me."

"There's no one else I *want* to spend time with, Cassia."

I'm fond of Randy. He's gentle, caring, attentive and sweet. If only I didn't keep thinking about Adam…. Even when he's gone, Adam still trips me up.

"My life is too complicated right now. I don't want to burden anyone else with my dilemma."

"Not everyone sees you as having problems, Cassia. Some might say you have the *answer* to problems."

"I'm sorry, Randy, I didn't mean to complain. Sometimes God's children don't get all the details until the plan is set."

"May I call you this weekend?"

"Sure. Thank you." I hesitated. "Sorry. I hope I haven't hurt your feelings."

"You're a one of a kind, Cassia. I can't help myself. I want to keep coming back for more."

We said our goodbyes and I sat back in the chair to brood over the conversation. I need time to sort things out in my head. The truth is, not only am I stymied about the lottery money, I'm not finished processing all I've learned about Adam from his cousin and Whitney. None of it makes sense. It's as if we're talking about two different people—the noble, honest, good-as-his-word Adam and the deceiving, anything-for-a-buck, journalist-without-integrity Adam. There's no common denominator, no way to marry the two in order to discover who Adam Cavanaugh really is.

Everything feels murky, as though I'm stumbling along in a crushing fog, not able to judge or even see my next step.

Tell me, Lord! Show me something. Anything!

And the first verses of 1 Corinthians 13 came to mind. I reached for my Bible and began to read.

If I had the gift of being able to speak in other languages without learning them and could speak in every language there is in all of heaven and earth, but didn't love others, I would only be making noise. If I had the gift of prophecy and knew all about what is going to happen in the future, knew everything about everything but didn't love others, what good would it do? Even if I had the gift of faith so that I could speak to a mountain and make it move, I would still be worth nothing without love. If I gave everything I have to the poor people and if I were burned alive for preaching the Gospel but didn't love others, it would be of no value whatever.

If I gave everything I have to the poor people…but didn't love others, it would be of no value whatsoever. My mind wrapped itself around that verse and wouldn't let go. Knowledge, prophecy and generosity aren't enough without love. Nothing I can give will be enough if there isn't love behind it. I felt shivers scamper through my body.

God really makes me work for my answers, but His clues are right on target. If I gave everything I had— which these days is quite a bit—to the poor without doing so in an attitude and spirit of love, it isn't enough. It's my heart that has to be right.

My mind became a whirling cyclone of thoughts, fragments of advice and bits of Scripture that had been collecting since that fateful winning day. God can really knock me off my feet sometimes.

Sure, I'm planning to give everything I have to the poor. But am I giving it in a spirit of love? Hardly. I've been behaving like a put-upon, overtaxed whiner. I've felt imposed upon and shouldered with an unpleasant burden that interferes with the "work" I'm doing for God. Shame bled through me.

What an ego I have! The money *is* the work I'm to do for God. Granted, it is fine to be knowledgeable about where it should go and wonderful that I want to be generous about it. It's the love part that has been AWOL—that love I need to show as I give the gifts, the love I offer as a humble representative of God.

It's a dash of cold water on my feelings to realize that I haven't been trying to give the money away in the spirit God wanted. I've been trying to throw it at people as if to get a stain off my own hands. I thought of Mary Magdalene pouring costly perfume on the feet of Jesus and wiping it away with her hair. Granted, the perfume was expensive, but it was not only about the perfume, it was about the way it was offered—with love and gratitude, not grumbling and complaining.

I blew it. Clueless Cassia, that's me.

And for the first time in weeks I begin to see at the end of the tunnel a light that isn't a train.

CHAPTER

28

Adam stared out over the water listening for the loons and wondering how he'd come to this. It wasn't that his family's lake cabin wasn't pleasant or that the place wasn't beautiful. There were clean sheets on the bed, fresh towels in the bathroom and a well-stocked larder.

The only thing wrong was the company he was with—himself.

No matter how many hours he fished, how many birds he counted or the number of crossword puzzles he did, he couldn't get his mind off Cassia.

He'd come to the cabin to sort out his thoughts and make some plans, but the silence up here in the north woods was noisy, his mind filled as it was with Cassia's sputtering words and injured tone.

And the worst part of it was, Adam mused, that when he wasn't thinking about Cassia, God was bugging him. They were playing tag team with him, he decided, each taking turns demanding better of him.

Cassia was a voice for forthrightness, while God was the whisper that kept reminding him of their past relationship, their falling out and Adam's rejection of Him.

"Just leave me alone!" Adam said aloud. "I'm not the great guy either of you want me to be!"

I want you as you are.

Adam squinted toward the sky. He'd heard the message as clearly as if it had been spoken, but he knew it was coming from deep inside himself.

"Who'd want me in the shape I'm in?" Adam muttered. "Burned out, angry, frustrated, taking advantage of people who call me friend? You don't want me hanging around You."

Yes, I do. I came for people like you.

Adam recalled a time when these internal dialogues with God were natural and comfortable for him— before Burundi. Well, it certainly wasn't comfortable now.

"What about all those people I saw suffering and dying? Why are You pestering me when You have lives to save?"

Adam paused as if waiting for an answer, a defense, an excuse from the Almighty. He tensed, listening, feeling, watching, but he felt nothing.

"So now where'd You go?" he demanded irately. "If You were really God and not just my imagination, You'd let me know You actually existed!"

Still nothing.

"So You don't exist outside my imagination? Is that it?"

More silence.

"Without proof, without helping those children in Burundi, how can I know You're here? That You exist at all?"

Adam gave up the fruitless dialogue he was having with thin air when he looked up to see a doe and twin fawns only yards from him, staring his way with glistening black eyes and sweet expressions. So perfect on their pencil-thin legs, coats glinting in the waning light, they hardly looked real. What miraculous creatures they were.

Since he was a little boy, he'd loved the deer herds that roamed these woods. He'd spent his allowance money on salt licks to put near the cabin to lure them nearer. Deer were one of God's most graceful creations, his mother always said.

Funny, the family had told him that deer were more scarce around the cabin than usual this year. It was as if this little trio had appeared just for him....

Maybe God *had* sent them as a small reminder that He was in charge....

"Don't be silly," Adam said aloud. But what was he talking about? Was it silly to believe in a nonexistent God? Or was he silly playing this sad game of not admitting that God was everywhere, simply because he refused to look?

29

I'm floating in the Bermuda Triangle of men and sinking fast.

Randy…Ken…Adam…the three points of my triangle. Randy courts me like a queen. Ken's persistence in bulldozing his way to my affections is very flattering. And Adam, the most unfortunate choice of all, a non-Christian, has absconded with the goods, my heart, and is unaccounted for, AWOL, missing in action. I don't give my heart to just anyone. That's because once I give it away, I don't know how to get it back.

"There's a new show at the IMAX," Randy said, "and a new Thai restaurant opening near there. What do you think?"

"I think that people should eat more meat and potatoes. Doesn't anyone ever open a pot-roast-and-mashed-potatoes restaurant anymore?" I added, "I'd love to go out tonight. I'd like to have an excuse to get dressed up."

"Theater tickets and a restaurant downtown it is." I could hear his delight despite the crackly connection of his cell phone. "I'll see what is available and call you back." He hesitated before adding shyly, "Thanks, Cassia. This will be great."

Yeah, great.

Here I am feeling sorry for myself because a big creep betrayed me and ignoring a darling man who would turn cartwheels down Nicollet Mall for me if I asked him. Maybe Randy is what God wants for me. It obviously isn't Adam. Who am I not to give it a chance?

Okay, Cassia, the pity party is over.

At the end of our evening together, I glided from Randy's car to the apartment building in a happy haze, feeling really good for the first time in days. I enjoy being pampered and indulged, and Randy is doing his best to make sure it happens.

I allowed my hair to have its own way tonight. Randy said I looked like Nicole Kidman. I could agree with that—if she stuck her finger in a light socket. I tossed back my head to get the riot of curls out of my way and waved to Randy as he drove off.

Feeling pink and happy all over, I stuck the rose Randy had given me between my teeth and drifted toward my front steps.

I went for stylish, sophisticated and elegant as I made my way, Audrey-Hepburn-in-*Breakfast-at-Tiffany's*-like, to the doorway and resisted kicking off my snug pumps and carrying them in my hand. Playing dress-up is fun. I've been imitating a bag lady long enough. The opportunity to wear the ubiquitous little black dress that Jane had given me for my birthday made me realize that I can't hide in my apartment any longer. If I'm going to be a philanthropist, it's time to act like one.

I've lost a few pounds—nerves, I suppose—and look good. I know that because I admired a pretty woman reflected in the mirror at the theater until I realized it was me. Maybe I should wear my hair this way more often.

Humming, I checked my box for mail and sashayed toward the steps. I'd almost passed Adam's door when I realized it was ajar.

Cool. Whitney and Chase are back.

I hummed a little louder and knocked on the door. "Yoo-hoo, anybody home? I've read those books you gave me, Whitney. Should I bring them down to you?"

The door swung open and Adam filled the doorway.

At least, I thought it was Adam.

He looked dreadful. Exhausted, bloodshot eyes, stubbly five-o'clock shadow, stained and wrinkled clothing and a frown so deep the creases carved through his brow like fissures. He looked, as my grandmother might declare, like death warmed over.

We stared at each other openmouthed. I'd never seen him look so awful, and he'd probably never seen me look so good.

I am normally makeup free, barefoot and clad in jeans and a T-shirt, my hair more tamed than combed. Tonight I'd taken extra care—eyeliner, mascara, lipstick, panty hose, the whole nine yards. Talk about two strangers meeting like ships in the night.

Then, before either of us said anything, Pepto marched up to me and did a figure eight around my ankles.

"Cassia, I…" Adam struggled for words, but they didn't come. He looked as though he could drop to the floor and fall asleep where he landed.

"You've been gone," I said inanely.

"You met my cousin Chase."

At least he was equally inane. "Yes. He and his wife are very nice. Pepto likes them."

Adam looked down at the cat as if surprised to see him there. "He's going to stay with them for a while."

"You're leaving again?" I heard the quaver in my voice and hoped it hadn't been evident to him. The last thing I want him to think is that I care. I don't want to care. I want to look at him and feel nothing—not anger, disappointment or betrayal, and certainly not attraction.

So start cooperating, emotions.

What option do I have other than to forget him? I certainly can't overlook II Corinthians 6:14.

Don't be teamed with those who do not love the Lord, for what do the people of God have in common with the people of sin? How can light live with darkness?

"I doubt you'll mind, considering…everything." He looked at me so sadly that for a moment I forgot how underhanded and scheming he was. He bent to pick up Pepto and absently scratched the cat's neck. In the silence that hung between us Pepto's purring sounded like the Indy 500.

"I know it's not going to mean anything to you after what I did by betraying your trust, but I'm sorry. I knew I should have told you why...what motivated me to..." Something flickered in his eyes. "But that doesn't really matter. It was my decision to deceive you, and I have to take responsibility for my actions." He stopped himself, deciding he'd said too much. "You have no idea how sorry I am."

No? You have no idea how sorry I am, either.

He started to leave, paused and turned back to look me straight in the eye. "You look beautiful tonight, Cassia. But then again, you're always beautiful, inside and out." And he turned and shut the door behind him, leaving me standing in the hall with my jaw hanging.

I stormed around my apartment fuming about our highly unsatisfactory encounter, slamming doors and being as generally pouty and childish as I knew how, hoping that if I couldn't sleep, Adam wouldn't either. I don't know what I'd expected when we met again, but nothing this anticlimactic.

I suppose I should be happy. Adam will not be around to exacerbate my discomfort. He won't be here to remind me of how I'd trusted him and what he'd done to reciprocate. He'd apologized. And he looked terrible—thin, gaunt, miserable. Even if I were a vengeful person—and I'm not—I'd have to think he'd suffered enough.

What *had* I wanted? Anguished apologies? Resolution? No. I wanted clarity. Who is Adam? The good Adam is a humanitarian, an honest, reliable, kind guy. So who is this bad guy who has lied to me, manipulated me and been so untrustworthy? I just don't get it. I really want a *reason* for what has happened. I don't want it to be only about the money. I want to hear that Adam can justify his action. I want to trust him again. But he hadn't even attempted to defend himself. His silence makes it very clear that he had no excuse.

I stood in front of my open refrigerator staring at the contents. Carrots, lettuce, shredded cheese, orange juice and a piece of leftover lasagna. Sometimes, in my enthusiasm, I carry this healthy eating thing a little too far. Finally, desperate, I dug into my cupboards until I found a bag of chocolate chips, made myself a pot of tea and drowned my sorrows in front of a two-hour *Lost in Space* retrospective on late-night television.

Not one of my better moments, I'm afraid.

30

I groaned, wishing the Monday-morning sun streaming through my window had an off switch. How rude of it to come up now, when I was finally falling asleep....

I bolted upright to stare at the clock. Ten-fifteen!

"Oh, no, Winslow. Why didn't you wake me?"

The dog gave me a puzzled glance, as if to ask why today was the day he should have played alarm clock. After all, I'd been the one grumbling all week when he needed to go out for a walk at 6:00 a.m. I grabbed the thin cotton robe from the foot of my bed and threw it on as I hurried to the window.

I opened the blind and my heart sank.

Adam's Hummer was parked out front, engine running. The front door on the sidewalk side was open. He put a carrying crate onto the front seat, the same crate I'd seen coming into this place barely three months before. Even from a distance I could see that

Pepto was unhappy. The crate wobbled as though there were a pair of tiny sumo wrestlers hammering it out in there. For a small cat, Pepto maintains a big presence.

As I watched, Adam closed the passenger door, circled the front of the vehicle, jumped inside and drove off. Gone. This time, I deduced, for a very long time.

I automatically lifted my hand in a pathetic wave. He wasn't the man for me, but it was still terribly hard to let go.

"Schizoid," I muttered as I sat down. "Make up your mind." Adam was gone to wherever it is that Adam goes. Even the threat of Pepto had vanished.

"Well, we're free as birds now, buddy," I said to the humongous head lying on my knees.

Free as birds. If that were true, then why did I feel as if I'd just had my wings severed from my body and my heart? There was only one place to go to heal.

"Long time no see, Cassia! Welcome." My friend Greta Hanson greeted me with a hug while the six or seven people who were also in the Simms all-purpose store nodded agreement. "We thought you were never coming home. Didn't you miss us? Where are Jane and her hubby?"

"We" and "us." As usual in Simms one person feels perfectly free to express the minds of all. Though the townsfolk might debate over which church had the best potluck suppers or whether Oscar and Minnie Johnson should have painted their house bright or pale yellow, they usually formed a united front on the big issues.

"Jane is coming later, but her husband has to work."
The heads all bobbed in understanding.

"Can you go for coffee?" Greta asked. "The café still has peanut bars."

My mouth automatically began to water. The bars are simply chunks of homemade white cake frosted with creamy white frosting and rolled in chopped peanuts. Fannie's café should be recommended in every food guide in America for her peanut bars.

"Sure." I glanced at my watch. Ten-thirty on Saturday morning. I'd left the house at eight, Grandma Mattie already talking on the phone to one of her old cronies about the state of her flower garden. The fifteen-year-old boy we'd hired to water and mow had decided that it needed to be done only on an emergency basis—when he noticed something was wilted and dying.

"Running" uptown for something in Simms is true only if one is running in something viscous, like chilled maple syrup. Once I committed myself to running uptown, I knew I had better be prepared to spend at least two or three hours doing it. More than once when dashing uptown for a bag of onions or a carton of salt, I'd been waylaid and ended up dragging home hours later after having been to an auction sale, the birthing of a calf or practice for a Sunday-school musical or a coffee party.

"I'm glad you came home," Greta said, great relief in her voice. "People were beginning to talk."

We entered the café and I breathed deeply, savoring the smell of fresh old-fashioned doughnuts, oatmeal sandwich cookies with pink frosting centers and steaming coffee. I could also detect from the back a hint of the aroma of the roast beef simmering in broth, which would be served at lunchtime. How many times had my grandfather and I come here, sat in the booth at the back and ordered half a hot beef sandwich with mashed potatoes and gravy and a large orange pop? Pleasant memories washed over me, and I felt my shoulders relax.

Tulip Torgerson, waitress at Fannie's since its doors had opened in the early sixties, stalked over with two coffee cups and a steaming glass pot of coffee. Tulip, who took her job very seriously, still wore the uniform they'd required of her forty years ago—a pink waitress uniform, a white ruffled apron with pink piping and solid pink pocket, and a little white nurselike hat made of starchy fabric and lace and perched on the reddest of red artificially colored hair. Her uniform is crisp and pressed as ever. Her weathered and wrinkled face, however, could use a little ironing.

A smoker, Tulip has developed those little lines around her lips, which causes her bright pink lipstick to run hither and yon on her face. The lipstick that makes its way onto her teeth, however, manages to stay in place.

"We missed you," she said bluntly as she filled two thick china cups. "What'd you run away for?"

"I didn't exactly run away," I ventured.

"Huh. Sure looked like it to me." That put me in my place. "You'll have a half a roast beef, mashed potatoes, extra gravy, orange pop and a peanut bar, right?"

"But Tulip, it's only ten-thirty in the morning."

"It's ten forty-five now. Drink your coffee and I'll bring it out at eleven. That's when lunch hour starts around here."

I looked at Greta, who was grinning. "Oh, why not? And bring the same for my friend."

Tulip nodded approvingly and tromped off, filling empty coffee cups as she went.

"It's good to be back." I leaned back into the cracked plastic bench and sighed. "It's so much simpler here."

"Things don't change much," Greta agreed. "Best and worst is the fact that when you don't know what you're doing or thinking, someone else always does." She lowered her voice. "Tulip is a hoot, isn't she? With all that red dye she's been putting on her head over the years, I'm surprised it hasn't leaked down and rotted her brain."

"Be nice," I chided, grinning.

"Okay. I love Tulip, you know that. I'll pick on you instead. What's going on between you and Ken, anyway?"

"Going on?" I said cautiously.

"You never came home after you moved to the Cities. Ken was about as down-in-the-mouth as I've ever seen him. Then he went off to Minneapolis to see you, and since he came back, he's been whistling, singing and calling the florist every other day to send you something." Simms's idea of a florist was a little stall in the back of the Laundromat with an FDS phone line.

"He's been very sweet."

"That's it? Sweet? Cassia, you've got that guy wrapped up in a bow about you. What are your intentions?"

"*My* intentions? When did you become Ken's father? Are you protecting his innocence?"

Greta grinned. "Sorry. I just like the guy. And I love you. Will he ever be able to lure you back to Simms to live?"

Three weeks ago I would have said never. But now, who knew? I didn't, that's for sure.

"I don't know. I like it where I am. Dave and Jane are there, and the supermarkets are unbelievable. I'm teaching myself to cook Chinese food. The only thing alarming about that is fish sauce. I keep thinking about what happens in aquariums."

"Okay, I get it. You don't want to talk about it. Just remember, though, Ken isn't going to let you off the hook forever."

I was glad to see a group of hunters burst through the door of the café. Well, not hunters, exactly. There isn't much to hunt in the middle of summer, but men here like three things—being ready to hunt when the season does come around, hunting itself and wearing hunting clothes. Even my grandfather ignored it when church attendees came wearing camouflage pants and a khaki T-shirts and hung their blaze-orange hunting vests in the foyer. He considered it great progress to get them there at all.

It was an amazing mishmash of camouflage clothing and testosterone descending on the little restaurant and one of the two prized round tables in the place. Each large table held eight to twelve coffee drinkers, who solved the world's problems, elected and unelected politicians and rewrote history there every single day. One table "belonged" to the old-timers, the men who descend on the café between six and nine in the morning to drink coffee, discuss the weather and speculate about who would be doing what in the hours to come. They return again at three for a rehash, some "Yupping" and "No siree-ing."

The other table belongs to the "young bucks," everyone under sixty-five who still have to punch time clocks or report to jobs. The large tables fill with them at noon. Whoever thinks women are gossips should sit with those guys once in a while.

At four o'clock the ladies come for coffee. It's their brief respite, a calm before the storm of the dinner hour. Grandma, who has always been allergic to gossip, calls it the "Estrogen Hour."

I allowed Greta to drill me with questions for nearly an hour. She asked about everything from the lottery to my love life. I've learned to answer carefully, because talking with Greta is a little like yelling personal information into a loudspeaker. It will be all over town at the speed of sound.

On my way home it took all my willpower not to stop at the Dairy Queen for an ice cream cone. I've been preprogrammed to buy a cone every time I pass, storing up for the winter like a bear preparing for hibernation.

Grandma, who'd obviously missed Simms more than she'd let on, had every window in the house open.

The curtains were fluttering in the breeze. She'd run a load of towels and bedding and hung them on the line to dry.

"Feels good to be home, huh, Mattie?" I hugged her and smiled. She'd found her perfume and dabbed it behind her ears, too. Just like old times.

She put her hands on my shoulders and pressed me away from her so she could study me. "Is it?"

"Of course."

"Now say it like you believe it."

"Am I that transparent?"

"He's gone, honey."

"Who?" I asked, as if one of us didn't know.

"You have to get over what happened and move on."

"I am…aren't I?"

"What are you going to do with the money?"

I sat down at the kitchen table and considered the question. Many of the proposals and requests I'd received, upon further investigation, I'd found to be questionable in one way or another. "I know for sure that I can't give the money to a group that spends seventy or more percent on administrative costs," I told Mattie. "I want the money to go directly to the ones who need it. The search is consuming much of my time these days and I'm looking in directions that, on my own, I never would have chosen."

"When God closes a door, He opens a window."

I can't even count how many times I'd heard her say that over the years.

"That's it, then. God's been closing doors, and He just hasn't opened any windows yet."

Even as I said it, I felt relief. It made complete sense. My options were dwindling while the money was accruing. I no longer believed I could not in good conscience have someone else oversee the money. Besides, I had no job. Who else was there who could take it on full-time? All the signs are here that it is mine to do. Not only that, Adam is out of the picture. Any faint thoughts I might have had about our relationship turning into something more than friendship are gone. God appears to be clearing the decks for takeoff. Mine.

CHAPTER 31

Ah, Simms, the place where a traffic jam is five cars stuck trying to pass a tractor on a two-lane road. In Simms, if it's six in the morning, then you're surely up and ready for visitors.

That's why Ken arrived at 7:00 a.m. looking fresh and handsome, ready to take me on "the ride" he'd promised me. Winslow, who *had* been awake since six, was delighted to see him. I, on the other hand, needed another cup of coffee.

"You've been getting slack, Cassia. Bad influences where you've been living, I can tell. Back here I could catch you jogging past my place by six-thirty." He snapped his gum and grinned, flashing those amazingly perfect white teeth.

I couldn't help smiling back. He is a darling man, really. I've grown to appreciate him more since I have been away.

"That's what happens when I don't have a job. I get lazy." I held up a plate, "Caramel roll?"

"Just one. I want to get going—there's lots to see."

"What, exactly, is it we're going to look at?"

"You just wait, sweetie. I want you to be surprised."

And surprised I was. We drove out of Simms and toward the next larger town down the road. Winslow and Boosters sat on the bench in the back of Ken's extended cab pickup and sniffed at each other happily. They were old friends, having gone on just about as many dates together as Ken and I. The dogs were perfectly content to wait for us to finish dinner and see a movie as long as they were together. Sometimes I longed for that kind of relationship for myself—content in the moment, happy with my companion and no worries (other than, for Winslow and Boosters, at least, who would get the bigger half of the doggy treat when we returned to the truck).

We were headed toward Sioux Falls when Ken made a right off the highway and followed a wide gravel road through some rolling hills. South Dakota has a variety of terrains as one travels east to west. Sometimes there's a surprising little aberration in the prairie like the one to which Ken drove.

"A new development?" I've lived here off and on for my entire life and hadn't known this scenic little spot existed—a pond, trees and an unmarred vista of the prairies from the ledge of a hill. It is spectacular.

"My latest project. Do you like it?" For once he didn't appear supremely confident. There were lines of concern in his usually unmarked brow. Ken normally didn't really believe in worrying. He believed in *doing*.

"I love it! How many homes are going to be here? I see you've started digging a couple basements."

"Fifteen. I want the lots to be big and I don't want to crowd out the scenery."

"Have you sold many yet? They will go quickly."

"Could have sold them all by now. I've got a waiting list."

"What are you waiting for?"

He looked at me so intently that my intuition went into overdrive. Something was coming.

"I wanted you to come home and pick out your favorite first."

A roller coaster started its downward plunge in my belly. "Ken..."

He held up a hand. "Don't say anything. I know you're as skittish as a doe in hunting season. I want you to pick *your* favorite. Nothing more. Then I'll sell the rest. Most of the people who've been inquiring about sites are about our age. There's going to be a big influx of little kids in this neighborhood. You can also tell me where you think the playground should be."

Pick out my favorite lot. People my age. Children. Playgrounds. The only thing Ken hadn't done was hum "Here Comes the Bride."

Funny, but if I were still living in Simms I would have backed off, saying "No way." Today I stayed silent. Things have changed. Randy is sweet, but I'm not sure he's the kind of guy I want for a life partner. Adam, the one who might have had that potential, has messed up royally. And Ken has been becoming more sensitive and attentive to me than I thought possible. We've known each other a long time, and he has no designs on my money. And this gesture of the land...

I stuck out my hand to him. "Come on, let's go find that playground."

Ken must have been watching *Oprah*. Or perhaps he'd looked up the topic "How to woo a woman" on the Internet.

We walked most of the lots, brainstormed house designs for each and settled on two primo spots for swings and sandboxes. Then we came to what was obviously the prime bit of land in the development.

Shade trees hooded the earth from the blazing sun. From beneath the spreading trees one could stand and gaze out as far as the eye could see. The heat of the day shimmered off the earth. The colors, so dramatic when we'd arrived, were all simmering into a soft palette as our eyes filled with sunlight. It was the highest point in the development and the largest lot. It would demand a stately home to fulfill its potential.

"Log, don't you think?" Ken asked as we settled on an outcropping of rock to gaze at the view. "Not a squatty little log cabin, of course, but something majestic. A two-story, with vaulted ceilings and an overlook into the living-room area. Maybe a fieldstone fireplace or two."

"Hardwood floors."

"Of course. And lots of windows...and a hot tub."

"Professional-quality appliances."

"Stainless steel."

"Bedrooms?"

"Five. The master, three kids' rooms and something for guests."

Realizing what we were doing, I stopped myself before blurting, "And bunk beds for the twins!" Ken and I were mentally playing house. It's a slippery path to the altar when the bride's mind is fixed on the fixtures and not on who she's fixin' to marry.

I slapped myself on the thigh and started to rise. "Well, that was fun. Now…"

"Hold your horses. I've got something for you." Ken jumped to his feet and dodged behind a cluster of shrubs. When he returned, he was carrying a picnic hamper.

"Packed especially for us by Tulip. Hungry?"

Although it was still early, I felt ravenous. No matter what else Ken did for me, he'd brought back my appetite.

Tulip had outdone herself with fried chicken, hard-boiled eggs and tomatoes with plenty of salt and potato salad—the kind I love—with no mustard or pickles. She'd included watermelon wedges, Fannie's famous oatmeal sandwich cookies, bottles of juice, tea and water and—were my eyes deceiving me—breath mints. In case there was some kissing going on? What a fox, that Tulip.

"Does the whole town know we're coming up here?" I demanded, my cheeks reddening just thinking about it. I imagined the speculation going on at the café at this very moment.

"Nah." Ken looked at me slyly. "I can be dis-creet." He drawled out the word. "I'm not a clod, you know."

I burst out laughing. "No, you certainly are not. You are one of the sweetest guys on the planet." And I truly meant it.

We didn't say much on the way back to town. Ken had brought with him two big rawhide bones for the dogs and we listened to them happily smacking and chewing behind us. It was, all in all, an unorthodox but highly domestic scene.

Ken pulled up in front of the house behind Jane's car. "I see your sister has arrived."

"I wish she could have come with us, but she had to work and didn't want to leave Dave any sooner than she had to. At least she drove down for part of the weekend." I sighed, barely realizing it.

Ken did. "It still feels like home here, doesn't it?"

"To some degree it always will."

"Then *come* home, Cassia." His eyes darkened. "We all miss you—and some of us even more than others."

I put a finger to his lips. They were warm and dry and I could feel the moist heat of his breath on my fingertip. "Don't say any more just now, okay? I've had a lovely time today. Thank you."

Ken nodded and gazed at me with a look that could have melted butter. "Me, too." Then, more "dis-creet" than I'd ever seen him, he hopped out of the pickup, pulled his seat forward and loosed Winslow. The dog loped across the lawn and flung himself under a shade tree. Boosters whimpered in back, already lonely. Then, kissing his fingertips and touching them to my forehead, Ken mouthed the words "See you later."

I slid out of the pickup and watched him drive away. What a diamond in the rough Ken is. And he is a known entity, someone who had had feelings for me B.L. *Before Lottery.*

My heart and my head are more confused than ever.

32

"It's about time you got back. We were ready to send out a search party." Jane sat at the kitchen table eating an egg salad sandwich and nibbling on a pile of potato chips.

"Well, hello to you, too." I rounded the table to hug Mattie, and sat down.

"So? What happened? Grandma tells me Ken's been around a lot since you came back for a visit. *A lot.*" She waggled her eyebrows. Her short bobbed hair swung just at her jawline and her porcelain skin glowed. With the differences in our height, coloring and personalities, never in a hundred years would anyone believe we were sisters.

"I thought you didn't like Ken."

"Maybe he's not so bad, just a little annoying," Jane said with a shrug. "He's never done to you what that hunk-a-hunk of burning skunk in your building did. The familiar is looking better all the time."

Never let it be said that my sister isn't practical. When she married her own husband, Jane compiled a "pros" and "cons" list as long as her arm. Fortunately for Dave, his "pro" list was considerably longer than his "con." Dave is as laid-back as the day is long and not intimidated an iota by my calculating, meddlesome but lovable sister.

Jane reached for a slice of my grandmother's famous death-by-chocolate cake. "I thought you told me on the phone last week that you were dieting," I said.

"I snapped out of it. Thankfully this is a new day."

I pulled the plate away from her. "You can't have any cake. You said you felt chubby."

"And what business is that of yours?"

"You meddle in my love life. Therefore, I can meddle in your diet."

It was a tough choice between her two favorite hobbies, snooping and eating. Jane looked at the cake plate as if it were a dear, departed friend. "I guess I could stand to lose a few pounds."

"So you *do* prefer meddling over eating!"

"It's too juicy—you and Ken, I mean—to quit prying now. I just hope I can squeeze the details out of you before I fade away to nothing."

"You're a long way from nothing, sis." I eyed her snug jeans and T-shirt. "A little more exercise wouldn't hurt either."

She looked at me with a wounded expression. "Whaddayamean, more exercise? I shop! I did three laps at the Mall of America just yesterday."

"Were two of them around the food court level?"
Jane reddened.

"I declare," Mattie interrupted, "you two haven't
changed since high school." She stood up. "Now I'm
going to go next door and have a cup of tea with my
old neighbor. Then at four o'clock I'm going to break
my own rule and go to Estrogen Hour at Fannie's. And
I'm stopping at the store to buy three TV dinners for
tonight."

"I don't think I've ever heard you put fun before
work, Grandma," I said, ignoring Jane. "What's happening?"

Mattie grinned and her face creased into a thousand
beloved wrinkles. "I'm getting smart in my old age.
Even the Lord didn't create the earth in one day. What
makes me think I have to?

"While I'm gone, why don't you two get busy
weeding the flower beds and mowing the lawn? That
young boy who is supposed to be helping out doesn't
know one end of a lawn mower from the other."

We were sipping iced tea and speculating how stiff
we'd be tomorrow when Mattie returned home with our
wildly extravagant TV dinners. When we were kids, the
very idea of buying food out of someone else's freezer,
pan and all, was an anathema to our grandparents, so
tonight was a very big night indeed.

While our gourmet extravaganza was cooking,
Mattie joined us on the porch. She sat down by
Winslow and eyed me with compassion and a knowing
glint in her eye. "Is it easier to think here?"

"A little. When we were raking the yard I forgot for a few minutes that I'm a millionaire and a bad judge of men."

We sat rocking in our chairs as the supper-hour silence descended on Simms.

"Well, if there's one thing I've learned," Mattie said softly, "it's that you can't ignore the facts. You're still a millionaire and you're still grieving over being betrayed. There's no use pretending otherwise."

"Am I so obvious?"

"Not to others, maybe, but to family you are." Grandma scratched Winslow's neck as we talked. His fondest dream is to have someone doing it as a full-time job.

The next day, Sunday, I decided I should give the church enough money to pay for a secretary who can type.

Jane elbowed me every few seconds to point out another typo in the bulletin.

"They've used twelve different fonts." Jane snorted. "I feel like I'm reading something in those distorted mirrors in a circus fun house."

The fonts were disconcerting, but nothing compared to the information conveyed within. "Our youth baseball team plays on Wednesday. Come watch our boys slaughter Our Savior's.' Lunch to follow."

The bulletin did make the homily sound more exciting than usual. "Our sermon today, 'How Jesus Walked on the Water,' will be followed by the lovely spiritual 'Keep Me from Sinking Down.'"

Ken sat at the end of the pew next to Grandma. She

likes Ken. She'd seen the best side of him long before I'd given him a chance. What was I missing now? Who or what else had I ignored?

Lord, when the time is right, show me exactly what You want me to do. Make sure I can't ignore it or rationalize it away. Make it perfectly obvious and don't give me any wiggle room, either.

I glanced at Ken, who was studying a pew Bible intently.

And let me know the "who" as well as the what.

"What are you thinking about so intently?" Jane asked as she came onto the porch and handed me a cup of steaming tea. The night was dusky velvet, the stars twinkling more and more brightly.

"Stars. I'd forgotten how beautiful they are. You don't see stars properly in the city."

"You don't see a lot of things properly in the city," Jane agreed.

"Ever since I won the lottery, I've been trying to get my life back to normal, yet I no longer know what normal is. My old life is over. I'm reinventing myself as I go. There must be *something* simple about this. I want answers that are simple and straightforward...."

Feed my sheep.

"What did you say?" I turned to Jane.

She looked puzzled. "About what?"

"What did you say just now? Something about sheep..."

"Cassia, I didn't say a word. Certainly nothing about sheep."

"Did I *think* it, then?"

"Is something wrong?"

"No. I think that something is finally right. An idea just came to me. It was a thought so clear that I thought you'd spoken."

"About sheep?" Jane looked genuinely concerned—for my sanity.

"Feed my sheep." I slid forward on my chair and looked intently at her. "Don't you see? 'Feed my sheep.' That's it!"

"That's what?"

"What I'm supposed to do! I'm not supposed to do anything hard or complicated with the money. It's something simple and straightforward—feed His sheep! His children, the lambs of the Shepherd, don't you see?"

Clearly she didn't. Her eyebrow arched. "That's it?"

"Isn't that enough?"

"Well…you have the means to feed a lot of people, Cassia."

"Feed them both physically and spiritually, I think. John 6:51."

I could see realization dawning on her face. "Of course. John 6:51."

I am that living bread that came down out of heaven. Anyone eating this bread shall live forever; this bread is My flesh given to redeem humanity.

I knew with absolute certainty that whatever charities or petitions or proposals came my way, I could consider only those that were truly committed, both literally and figuratively, to feeding God's children. And

I knew something else, as well: God wants more than my money—He wants *me*. For whatever reason, He's enmeshed His plan for the money with His plan for the rest of my life.

CHAPTER

33

"You're going to keep in touch now, right?"

Ken's face was close to mine as he peered through the car window. I could smell his aftershave and the crisp, clean fragrance of soap. His eyes were serious.

It was Monday morning, and Mattie and I were in one car and Jane in another to caravan back to Minneapolis. Mattie's trunk was full of canned goods and things the neighbors had insisted sending along—Estelle's brownies, Helen's twelve-grain bread and three jars of Tulip's own watermelon pickles. She'd collected quite a bounty for only a week in Simms. Mattie had packed another blanket and her sewing machine, as well. Winslow, of course, filled the backseat.

"I will." I gave him a peck on the cheek. "I promise."

"And you'll think about our ride the other day?"

"All the time."

I felt warmed and encouraged by the shift in our

relationship. Ken was showing the side of himself that I liked very much.

"I love you, babe."

I reached up and put my palm to his cheek. "I know you do. I can feel it."

A smile settled across his face. "And you just keep on feeling it when you get back to that congested mess you live in. There's a wide open prairie and a wide open heart waiting for you here."

Time passed quickly on the trip back to Minneapolis. It always does with my grandmother in the passenger seat. Her favorite pastime is singing, so we belted out all the oldies but goodies—"The Old Rugged Cross," "How Great Thou Art," "Jesus Loves Me" and, just for the fun of it, a few Christmas carols.

We were about an hour from her place when Grandma turned an eagle eye on me. "So what are you going to do about those men in your life? They're circling like vultures, dear."

"That conjures up a pretty picture. What am I, roadkill?"

"You know what I mean. Ken is besotted with you and, if my instincts serve me, you're softening toward him, as well. Randy sounds like a lovely boy—so sweet and shy."

"He's a thirty-five-year-old CPA," I chided. "Not a teenager."

She shifted in her seat and negotiated her seat belt a bit so that she could look at me. "And of course there's the one you're in love with."

"You mean the black-hearted scoundrel and lying traitor that I may have had a tiny bit of interest in at one time before he lied to me, used me and dumped me for a magazine article?"

"Yes, that's the one."

"He's not for me, Grandma. You should know that as well as anyone."

"Then say it like you mean it, dear."

I hate it when Mattie does that—cuts to the quick, turns my own words on me and makes me listen to how they sound. It had been a pitiful protest, to say the least. I felt my eyes begin to fill.

"It's not about Adam. It's about why one person would do that to another, to think that the ends justify the means. It's not right! If he'd been a Christian, none of this would have happened." I felt an infusion of righteous anger just thinking about it. He lied to, used, betrayed and manipulated me and my lottery-winning friends. I resent being taken advantage of and, even more, having him stomp all over my feelings.

What I could hang on to now, however, was the fact that the focus was narrowing. My own plans and ideas were falling away.

Feed My sheep.

That was what I was to pay attention to now. Anything else, including men—Adam in particular— would have to wait.

It was nearly nine o'clock by the time I returned Mattie to her apartment, filled up with gas and purchased a quart of milk. Winslow was looking out the

window and whining, eager to be what he now considered "home."

"Maybe we could move closer to Mattie or Jane," I
said to Winslow. He cocked his head to the side and
looked faintly interested. "And it's time to get serious
about finding a new job."

I've considered going to school in the fall, to finish
my master's degree. Now I have no excuses—except,
of course, that I don't want to spend money.

So here I am, a jobless student millionaire early-
childhood specialist, who has uprooted herself from
home and doesn't trust anyone she meets. I never
dreamed I'd have a résumé like this.

The people in Simms are right. Moving to the city
isn't always what a person dreams it will be.

34

It was a shock to see Adam's door wide open as I passed.

My heart did a traitorous thump before I noticed a pair of women's shoes just inside the front door.

I stopped and knocked.

"Cassia!" Whitney looked delighted to see me. Her skin and eyes glowed and she looked, if possible, lovelier than before. "I was afraid we wouldn't get to say goodbye to you before we left. Have you been out of town?"

"I went to South Dakota for a few days."

"And how is the town of Simms?" Chase came up behind his wife and put his hands on her shoulders. "Do you have time to come in?"

I glanced at Winslow, who was pulling on his leash, nose to the ground, investigating his absent feline neighbor. His whole rear end was wriggling with delight. I unclipped him from his leash and followed him into the apartment.

"Do you mind?" I asked. "He's very gentle."

"That's more than anyone can say for Pepto. That animal has issues." Whitney eyed me. "I think he misses you. Sometimes in the evening he comes and sits on my lap and purrs."

That, about any other cat, might be considered standard activity. From Pepto it is aberrant behavior.

"So," I said casually, "what's up with you two?"

"We've been here since six, waiting for Frankie Wachter to stop by and pick up some photographs. His editor requested them, and he'd given them to Adam, negatives and all. He needs them back right away. Whitney and I came over to let him into the apartment. I don't know where the photos are, but apparently Frankie does."

Chase looked at his watch and frowned. "I hope he gets here soon. I expected him a couple hours ago."

"Chase is on call," Whitney explained. "He usually doesn't have too many uninterrupted hours in a row."

"I'll bet." I looked around the room, my head whirling. How did I ask about Adam without sounding too snoopy? If he'd *wanted* me to know where he'd gone, he would have told me, right? Still, I couldn't stand the curiosity. "Where exactly is Adam?"

Whitney shrugged and held her hands palms up, as if she was at a loss. "He left an itinerary with us, but it's sketchy. Apparently he didn't want us to know much about his agenda." She looked at her husband. "Do you remember what he was up to?"

"Not really."

Chase smiled at my puzzled expression. "Our

family is accustomed to not knowing where Adam is. He keeps a wicked schedule when he's away."

"How long has he been a journalist?" I ventured.

"Since he was about five and started using a zucchini from the garden to do a play-by-play of the game of tag going on in our backyard." Chase grinned. "We were all sure he'd be a broadcast journalist, but then he fell in love with the written word. He was smitten by it, started writing and never stopped. Believe it or not, Adam has a degree in journalism and one in advertising. He worked a couple years writing copy and marketing. Then he got tired of 'selling toothpaste,' became a journalist and never looked back."

"He has a lot of passion for what he does," Whitney said, picking up where Chase left off. "If Adam thinks something is right, he'll go to the mat for it, fight to the finish."

I wonder how he defines "right." He had these people bamboozled into thinking he's a great guy. If they knew what a creep he'd been to me...

The sound of a cell phone filled the room. Chase grabbed for it on the second ring.

"Chase, here. Uh-huh, okay, get him prepped for surgery. I'll be right there."

He snapped the phone shut and stood. "Sorry, but I have to break this up. Things have turned for a patient of mine. Whitney, honey, sorry to leave you here, but you can just let Frankie look for what it is he wants when he gets here and then take a taxi home."

"If you'd like, I can wait for this Frankie," I offered.

"Whether I sit and read the paper here or in my own apartment doesn't matter. Would that help?"

An expression of relief flooded Chase's face. "Well, we don't live far from the hospital. It would save a trip...."

"Say no more. Winslow and I will stay until he gets here."

"Great." Chase was already hurrying his wife out of the apartment. "Frankie is a tall, skinny guy with a scraggly beard—or maybe it's been shaved off by now. He knows where to look. Just lock up after he goes. And listen." Chase smiled in a way that made the family resemblance between him and Adam very apparent. "Thanks."

"Go. Leave. Go. You've got a patient waiting." Even if it meant sitting in Adam's apartment, memories flooding down upon me like a torrent of rain, at least I could do something to help someone.

And that, I realized, was part of what was wrong with me. I had been so stymied by the money that I hadn't made myself useful.

The buzzer rang and I jumped to my feet, startled. I'd been half-asleep in the chair, the paper on my lap. I glanced at the clock. It was after eleven.

I punched the intercom button. "Who is it?"

"Hey, Whitney, it's me, Frankie. Can you let me in? Sorry I'm so late."

I buzzed him in without explaining and waited for him at the door.

"Hi, Whit. I didn't mean to stand you up, but something came up...." He frowned. "You aren't Whitney."

"Sorry. Chase had to go to the hospital, and I said I'd wait for you so Whitney could go home. I'm Cassia Carr. I live in the apartment above this one."

Frankie is a tall, thin man, the kind who is likely gifted with a metabolism that just doesn't stop, who can eat as much and often as he wants and still not be able to keep his jeans on his hips without a belt tightly strapped around his middle.

He wore faded jeans with a rip above the knee, a pale gray sweater and a jacket with so many pockets, pouches and compartments sewn into it that he could have housed a week's worth of groceries in there. They were all, of course, sprouting with things like lenses, film and light meters and whatever else photojournalists need on a moment's notice.

He currently didn't have a beard, but his hair was long and scraggly, as if he'd cut it himself with a kitchen knife. His eyes were the same gray as his lightweight sweater, watchful and unreadable. His skin, slightly pockmarked, was fairly sallow. All in all, he looked tough, unhealthy and a little wild.

This is a man with whom Adam had spent a good deal of time. Would unraveling the mystery of Frankie do anything to solve the puzzle about Adam?

"Come in." I stepped out of the doorway. Winslow's head came up and he looked interestedly at our new visitor. "Chase said you'd know where to look for what you wanted."

"Not really. But it shouldn't be hard to find." He sauntered over to Winslow, allowed the dog to smell the back of his hand to gain his approval and then began to scratch Winslow behind the ear. They were immediately BFF.

Best Friends Forever. It doesn't take much with Winslow.

"It should be in a large, padded manila folder. I sent it to him, so my return address will be in the corner. I can look in the bedroom if you don't mind checking around out here."

I was the one to find it, tucked under the couch as if Adam had chosen to keep it out of sight.

"I think this must be it." I held it up to show Frankie.

"Probably. Let me check." Frankie slid his finger along the already broken tape at the seal, plunged his hand into the packet and pulled out a stack of eight-by-ten black-and-white photos, each with a sticky note attached to identify the subject matter.

"Ah…"" he said with satisfaction. "Bingo. These are what I need." He sauntered to Adam's kitchen table and spread them out to study them.

Good manners, courtesy and curiosity did battle within me. Curiosity won. I inched toward him, trying to get a peek at the photos.

Frankie, without turning his head, sensed I was there. "Want to see them? These are some of the best photos I've ever taken—and the worst."

I looked down at the glossy paper scattered across the table and gave an audible gasp of dismay before I drew back from the images.

The photos were mostly of women and children. I didn't see an adult male anywhere, even in the background. That, of course, may have been

Frankie's choice. The subjects captured in his lens said it all.

First was a mother sitting on bare, hard ground, holding a lifeless child. She stared down at the infant…toddler…youngster—it was difficult to tell the age. Her face was blank, her features numb, except for a single huge tear rolling down her cheek. The mother's body, hands and wrists poked from beneath her clothing looking sticklike and frail. The tear seemed to overwhelm her face, the emotions of a grieving mother all captured in a single tear.

There was a second child in the picture, a live one, hovering in the background. His eyes were round and dark as black opals, his stomach bulged over scrawny hips and sticklike legs. The boy was obviously emaciated, and it was clear that this mother would be shedding another tear soon.

I wanted to turn away from such intimate grief, but I couldn't move.

The photos were set in a landscape as arid and barren as the craters of the moon. A cooking pot lay on its side, empty but for a bit of sand drifted over its lip. It had not been used for a very long time.

There was a photo of, astoundingly, children playing. Little boys with sticks and rocks, listlessly poking at them in some made-up game. Every child had the same bloated belly, the same spindly legs and the same resigned expression. The photo, had it been hanging in a gallery somewhere, might have been titled "Playing While Waiting To Die."

There were dozens of them. A little boy holding a

bowl and looking upward to an adult off camera, with resolve and hope on his face. Orphanages with their little residents lined up out front, not a smile to be seen. Aid workers unloading a truck as children milled around them.

"Where is this?" My voice sounded strangled, even to my own ears.

"Burundi," Frankie said absently, still studying the photos. "The Great Lakes Region in Africa. There was a civil war there in the nineties. Well over a million people were forced to leave their homes. Half the men were killed or taken from their families. Thousands and thousands died." He pushed the photos around with his finger. "Fortunately, the governments are at least trying to work together now, but there are still a lot of nasty flare-ups and human rights issues to deal with. That's why Adam and I were there."

"You and Adam?"

"He never said anything about Burundi?" Frankie frowned, and then his face cleared. "Oh, that's right. The apartment above this one was vacant when we left. You hadn't moved in yet."

He straightened and turned away from the table. "This was a rough one. He and I have done a lot of human rights stories together—that's his area, his forte, I guess you'd say. If Adam does a story in that niche, people take notice. He's not the kind of guy who distances himself from his stories, that's for sure."

I recalled what I'd read about him on the Internet.

A troubled expression crossed his face. "I wish he

had kept a little more distance on this one." He paused. "I wish I had, too, but it's hard not to get pulled in."

"What are you saying?" Between these photos and what Frankie was articulating, my heart was thumping like a jackhammer in my chest.

"Refugees from the Congo are still wandering into neighboring countries. Add that to the already displaced people in Burundi and you have masses of people who need assistance. There are warring factions that still ignore human rights and protections. Parts of the country are still at war, while leaders are trying to put a stop to corruption and start addressing the fundamental issues that plague the region. Put all that together and you can imagine the logistical nightmare of taking care of the children. They're the victims of everyone else's failures and completely unable to fend for themselves. Watching them suffer and knowing they have no idea why this is happening to them is agony. A child shouldn't have to accept malnutrition as a way of life." Frankie traced his finger over a little sticklike figure.

"No," I agreed.

"That's why neither Adam nor I can get it out of our minds. It's why I'm going back. Every photo I took represents a thousand children going hungry. I have to find a way to document it even more fully, to wake people up to what is happening. We can't continue to go our merry way tossing scraps of food into the disposal and turning off the images that haunt us."

I heard the quiver in Frankie's voice and felt myself wanting to cry. It was so unfair. *And so far away.*

Like a clap of thunder it came to me. Intellectually I may have known about the problems and issues of this land and its people, but not emotionally. I was as distant from true pain and suffering as a human being could be. Never having lacked food or love for a day in my life, it was not just difficult for me to understand what those children were going through, it was unimaginable.

And if something were far away…out of sight, out of mind, so to speak…then it was far easier to ignore.

The scales fell from my eyes.

I stumbled backward, staring at the table, and almost tripped over one of Adam's many exotic handmade rugs.

"Are you okay?" Frankie looked alarmed.

Feed My sheep.

This was the direction God had been pointing me all along. I'd prayed for a plan, and when the time was right He'd given it to me. The connection between knowing I was to "feed His sheep" and what Frankie's photos revealed was overwhelming. I'd asked. He'd answered. Just like that. The blinders were gone and I knew with certainty that this was the path I was meant to take.

I was as surprised as Frankie to hear myself saying, "I want to go with you to Burundi. How much time do I have to get ready?"

CHAPTER

35

"You're going where? When?"

Jane was not ecstatic about the news that I was leaving for Burundi as soon as I could pack, get my inoculations and do whatever else was needed to enter a Third World country. Frankie, fortunately, was willing to help expedite matters. It's Jane's own fault that I have an up-to-date passport. She thought I'd use it to accompany her to Ireland and Scotland someday soon.

I sure fooled her.

She sat on my couch looking as though she'd been sucking on pickles. Frustrated and not comprehending why I had gone off the deep end without warning, my sister came grudgingly to bat for me. That was, in no little part, thanks to our grandmother.

Mattie sat with Jane, looking as sweet as Jane did sour.

"Are you sure that between you and Cricket, Winslow won't be a problem?" Winslow has been worried since the moment I opened my suitcase and started packing. He is not a dog to be left behind, and I know that my departure will be traumatic for both of us. As if he knew what I'd said, he whined and sadly lowered his head to his paws.

"He'll be fine. Dave loves him. They go driving together in Dave's convertible. Winslow likes to feel the air on his face and his ears flapping."

"And Cricket?"

"You've seen that enormous dog run she built at her house thinking that someday she'd have a collie. Winslow can break it in for her." Jane's eyes narrowed. "You're scaring me, Cassia. Just how long do you plan to be gone?"

"I have no idea."

We'd gone through the whole *feed My sheep, giving out of love, the scales off my eyes, Burundi* thing over and over. It was important that I not just send representatives to do my work for me. God called me to this. I didn't want to take the easy way out. However, cautious Jane didn't approve of anyone, especially me, flying off to the Congo with a man I'd just met, in an attempt to save the world.

But Frankie isn't going alone. His wife, a smiley, earth-mother type who wears Birkenstock shoes and consignment-store jeans, is going with him. Elise is every bit as fired up to do something in Burundi as Frankie is and delighted to know that he's hooked up with someone who has several million dollars to get the job done. With a master's degree in economics, Elise is one smart cookie, and has already begun researching the most efficient and effective ways to make the money work for us. It took us approximately twelve seconds to become good friends. I felt safer embarking on this adventure with Frankie, the world traveler, and Elise, the savvy businessperson, than any other couple I could imagine.

God does provide. And now that He's started, His rapid-fire provisions are blowing me out of the water.

Later, as I was folding clothes, I stopped to stare at my grandmother. "You knew this 'anointing' stuff was coming all along, didn't you, Mattie?"

"It's His standard operating procedure," she said mildly. "At least in my life experience."

"So if it's got God's blessing for whatever it is you're doing, it seems to go more smoothly?"

"He certainly knows how to smooth a path when He wants to. My whole Bible study group will be praying for you, Cassia."

Off on a wing and a prayer. I'm not usually the impulsive type, and here I am, tripping off to Africa with people and money that were dumped into my lap, in an attempt to save children from starving to death.

It's been a busy week.

There is no one but God for me to depend upon to get through this one.

And the rolling in my stomach has turned from dread into excitement.

CHAPTER

36

Without Winslow my apartment is like a morgue. Sometimes I forget just how much company the big lug is to me. I even start to fill his bowl with water before I remember that he's at Jane and Dave's house. I have no doubt that he is in good hands—they just aren't mine.

Fears and questions started to set in as dusk approached. By this time tomorrow I'll be winging my way across the world doing what, I feel sure, is God's will for my life.

When one prays as Isaiah did in chapter six, verse eight, "Lord, I'll go! Send *me*," it opens up, as Mattie says, a whole new can of worms. There's wisdom in the old cliché "Be careful what you pray for—you might get it." I prayed that I could serve God with my unplanned winnings. Little did I know that it would involve inoculations, hiking boots and antidiarrheal medication. Ewww.

I've grown spiritually through this, that's for sure, stretched and pulled like a piece of stiff elastic. The more I stewed and flapped about, the fewer answers I got. But now my bags are packed, my apartment cleaned, the refrigerator emptied, the newspaper and mail stopped, the bills paid and my goodbyes said. Nothing left to do but wait.

Saying goodbye to Ken had not been easy.

"Have you lost your mind, Cassia? Burundi? That's the edge of the earth! Go there and you'll fall off."

"Earth's round, Ken. Have you heard?"

"Don't be cute with me, Cassia. How can I be sure you'll be okay?" There was real apprehension in his voice.

"God's my travel agent. We'll be fine. I'm traveling with a couple who have been to Africa several times. They know the ropes."

"Cassia, if anything were to happen to you over there…"

"Ken…"

"Cassia, I love you. I couldn't stand it if something happened to you. The world is a better place with you in it." He drew a deep breath. "But I'm proud of you, too, because you're doing the right thing. And sometimes the right thing is the hardest thing to do." Ken's heart is pure gold.

Randy wasn't much easier. "You can't! You've got the money—hire someone to go for you and check it out. Let them write up a proposal for your approval. Philanthropists aren't this hands-on, Cassia!"

"Some are."

Randy's groan across the line sounded as if he was being filleted as we spoke.

But ultimately he, too, gave in and gave his blessing. "I'll be waiting for you when you get back."

"Randy…"

"As a friend. Far be it from me to stand in the way of God."

I am free. That, alone, overwhelms me. And it scares me spitless.

I was grateful when the doorbell rang. Someone had arrived to distract me from my own racing thoughts.

The man on the other side of the door introduced himself as Terrance Becker, Adam's agent. He stood on my welcome mat awkwardly shifting his weight from one foot to the other, dressed in crisp dark pants, a pristine white shirt and striped tie. I had a hunch he'd left his also-perfect suit coat in the car.

"What can I do for you?"

He looked uncomfortable. "Frankly, I'm not sure. I really can't even explain why I came other than…a feeling."

Nothing surprises me these days. After all, I'm a lottery winner ready and willing to fly to Africa in the morning. A literary agent I'd never met before appearing on my doorstep is small potatoes.

"I feel there's something you should know."

I let him in, then cocked my head and waited for him to continue.

"I'm partly responsible for the lottery story Adam is writing." His face flushed red. "He came back from a trip to Africa completely burned out. He told me only a fraction of what he'd seen and done while there, and even that was difficult for me to hear. I can't imagine all he and his photographer faced."

I nodded. I couldn't imagine it either.

"He was ready to quit writing altogether. I suggested that instead of going from difficult story to difficult story that he look for some 'brain candy' to write about. I thought that if he did something that wasn't so intense, he'd remember how much he loves his work. Not having Adam Cavanaugh on the job would be a blow to the human rights groups that depend on him to get the word out about what's happening in the forgotten parts of the world." Terrance hung his head and his shoulders slumped. "I had no idea that it would tear him up even more."

"I don't understand."

"He'd committed—actually, I'd committed for him—to people who wanted to buy the story. Adam's a man of his word, but he felt really low about not telling you that he'd been 'spying' on you. He wanted you to know what was going on, but we both assumed that you'd say no if we approached you." Terrance looked pleading. "You don't know how unique you are—a Christian woman accidentally winning the lottery and dead set on giving it all away. Cassia, I don't ever remember hearing a story like that before."

"Probably not," I agreed, "but that doesn't make what Adam did right…."

"He knew that. He'd decided to tell you what was

up. Had he been earning the money just for himself, he would've backed out and returned the advances."

"What do you mean, 'had he been earning the money just for himself'?"

"He's giving what he earns on your story to relief groups working in Burundi. His earnings are going to provide funds for children there. I know I didn't help, telling him I could get a book contract...."

"A *book* about me?" I squeaked, more surprised than angry. "That could earn money?" *Oh, puleeeze!*

Terrance named a sum that, before the lottery fiasco, I would have thought exceedingly significant.

"And that's why he kept this secret?"

"At first he thought it would be easy to tell you. Then, as he got to know you, he felt like no matter what he did, he was going to betray someone. He realized that you wouldn't tolerate his toying with your life."

"You've got that right."

And he thought it better to betray me than the children. I didn't approve of his deceit, but Adam's struggle was coming into clearer focus. Good intentions and bad deeds.

"If he'd just told me..." I couldn't finish. I don't know what I would have said or done. We'd barely met. I was in shock. Terrance was right. Once I realized how many crooks and scam artists are out there, I might have turned him down flat or chased him off with the faux Aunt Naomi.

Terrance held out the manila folder he'd been clutching. "Something compelled me to make a copy of this and come over here. I'm sorry if I intruded."

"Something compelled" him, huh? It occurs to me that if this were dusted for fingerprints, God's would be all over it. I took the folder.

Terrance, obviously a suave and sophisticated man, seemed completely unnerved. "I just wanted you to know how much Adam struggled with deceiving you. I'm sorry."

"Where is he? Why doesn't he apologize for himself?"

Now the agent looked really miserable. "I don't know. Adam was down on himself and the world when he left. He said he needed to get away." Terrance shuffled his feet on my floor. "There's no one in the world who can take better care of himself than Adam. But this is the longest I've ever gone without hearing something from him." He smiled lopsidedly. "On the other hand, he often takes time after a tough assignment to regroup and rest. The Greek islands are a special favorite of his."

I felt the anxiety rolling off him in waves, and it wasn't helping my disquieted state of mind one bit. "You're worried, aren't you?"

"I can't help it. I've known him a long time and never seen him quite like this." He looked at me speculatively. "You have the ability to tie him in knots, you know."

"It's *my* fault now?"

Terrance smiled. "That's not the kind of knots I meant. Adam's hard to read, but he values your friendship…a lot. He's grieved over losing it."

Just once I wish people would let me decide what I'm thinking and who I want in my life. *Just once!*

Holding the battered file to my chest, I walked Terrance to the door and let him out.

Adam is a grown man who can take care of himself. Worrying about him is not my job. What transpired between us is over. Actually, I should be grateful to him. He, through Frankie, was the first one to point the light in the direction of Burundi. Still, the fact is, Adam has disappeared off the face of the map and I don't like it one bit.

Adam had run away and he knew it.

"What a tangled web we weave when first we practice to deceive." He'd done a great job of it. A humorless grin pulled at one corner of his mouth. He was a regular webmaster of the insect type and feeling low as an earthworm's belly to boot. He'd not only hit the bottom of the barrel, he'd explored its underside.

But enough beating himself up, he chided himself. Leaving the Cities—and Cassia—was cowardly, but it was also necessary.

Not only had he deceived his journalistic target, he'd fallen in love with her. At first she'd been only a means to an end—albeit a worthy one—but it had taken only hours before she'd begun to thaw the ice he'd thought permanently encased his heart.

He sat in an airport restaurant for over two hours watching people walk by before moving to his gate.

Now he scrutinized the businessmen and women carrying briefcases or poking at their laptop computers. They all looked like people on a mission, knowing where they were going and what they were doing. There were families waiting to embark on vacations, college-age young adults toting backpacks and plugged in to radios or CD players, oblivious to the hum of voices around them.

For the first time in his life Adam didn't have an agenda. No, make that the second time. He hadn't planned to fall in love with Cassia or get caught in the ethical conundrum that had ensued. He'd believed he was smarter than that. Unfortunately Cassia seemed to have the ability to muddle his brain with a look or a smile. A guy whose friends teased him about being a "man of steel" where clear thinking and logic were concerned wasn't accustomed to being putty in anyone's hands.

But there was no use torturing himself by playing the "what if" game. He'd blown any chance he might have had with her by not being up front with her. All that was left to do now was find a new path for his life.

Maybe he'd do some "extreme travel" articles about mountain climbing in Nepal or winter camping in Siberia. And he'd always had an interest in China. Maybe he'd walk the Great Wall.

If only he'd never met her, he wouldn't have this sucking wound in his chest…but he *had* met her. That, Adam told himself firmly, was then. This is now.

"Buck up, old boy," he muttered to himself.

Then the ticket agent called his row. He hoisted his backpack to his shoulder and headed in the direction he knew he could go.

CHAPTER

38

Although I'm flying today, I'm not going to put my full weight down quite yet.

Experienced travelers, Frankie and Elise tucked themselves in for a long nap almost before we were airborne. I, having scared myself silly reading the precautions I should take for a lengthy overseas trip, was busy scoping out exits, scouring information pamphlets and eyeballing people in the escape rows to decide if they were fit enough to wrench the doors off in case of an emergency. I was diligent about taking walks and doing exercises in my seat to prevent blood clots, and I was, of course, praying full tilt the entire while. I felt it was my Christian duty to keep reminding God we were up here, practically in outer space, and that we were depending on Him to keep the pilot awake and on task.

I've shoveled snow for hours at a time and found it easier than this.

The hours after we landed were such a blur that, if pressed, I'm not sure I could recall what I saw or where I was. It was a kaleidoscope of color, sound and smell. Hot dry air, languages foreign to my ears and exhaustion were overriding my senses. Worn out, I leaned back into the competent care of Frankie and Elise, who seemed to know exactly what they were doing and how to get to our hotel. I barely remember getting to my room or falling asleep.

"Hey, in there, are you awake?" Elise's chipper voice on Friday morning was a stark contrast to my semiconscious state.

"Come in," I muttered, opening my door. "And don't be too cheerful. I'm exhausted."

"Jet lag. It takes a bit to recover."

She sat down on the end of my bed and grinned at me. "But while you were lollygagging in bed, I've been busy making appointments with people who can help us carry this off. The relief funds and Christian charities I contacted stateside gave me names and locations. We should be able to start spending your money very soon. And I've learned," she continued, "that a group of countries, including Burundi, Sudan and Rwanda, are establishing a system for monitoring orphaned and vulnerable children. There are so many more children ill or orphaned as a result of AIDS that they see the need for a concerted response to the problems. Perhaps we can use some of that research to find the neediest ones more quickly."

Finally I'm in action. God has all the puzzle pieces in place, and the larger picture is emerging.

"I've also made contact with an orphanage and a school that may be able to help us build more of both in rural areas. There are local churches willing to help in any way they can."

"You did all this in the hours we've been here?"

"Most of this information came through sources in the states. I'm not a miracle worker, but I have acted as a fund-raiser back home. It's all in whom you know."

"God strikes," I told her. "Not only does He introduce me to the people who can take me to Burundi, He also throws in a professional businessperson and fund-raiser who can do in weeks what might take me years."

"But you're the one with the money. We need you and we need to work fast. We can't stay here long, you know."

I felt a flutter of concern in my belly. We hadn't come to the safest place on the planet, that's for sure. Bujumbura, the capital, where our plane had landed, maintains a curfew. Rebel activity in the outlying areas is common. It amazes me how calm I feel in this circumstance in which I can't rely on myself for anything. God must get me through.

"By the way, Frankie is going to the village where he took those photos," Elise informed me. "I'm going to stay here and see what I can learn about the local feeding centers. Apparently they use a highly nutritious formula to bring starving children back to health. After that they switch them to the same stuff in a solid. Providing more might be a great place to start, and quick, too. After all, we won't need the schools and orphanages unless we save the children first. Do you want to go with me or ride along with Frankie?"

It was tempting to stay with Elise. Having business meetings and making plans sounded safe. Bouncing off into rural Burundi is not in my comfort zone.

"I'll go with Frankie."

"Do you trust me to make decisions for you if anything comes up? I don't want to do anything without your stamp of approval."

"You're the experienced one, Elise. Besides, I won't even have a vision for the types of things we can provide until I visit some of the villages, right?"

She stood up and wrapped her arms around me in a big hug. "You are the bravest, most generous person I've ever met."

I hugged her back. "Actually, I've always thought of myself as cowardly and tightfisted, but maybe I do have some potential in those areas." I glanced heavenward. "Through no fault of my own."

She walked toward the door. "Don't forget sunscreen, a wide-brimmed hat and extra water. And tell my husband not to drive like a maniac."

I gave Frankie the message, but either he didn't hear me or he ignored me. We bounced along the rough trail in a stripped-down Jeep that made my old car look like a brand-new Porsche. Frankie drove at full tilt until my breakfast turned into a milkshake.

"What's the hurry?" I yelled over the engine noise. I sat on my sun hat to keep it from blowing away and hung on for dear life. Frankie, familiar with his own driving, had strapped his camera and gear down in back so that it wouldn't be thrown from the vehicle.

"I want to take as many rolls of film as I can of this village. Elise plans to put together portfolios for more fund-raising, and Adam's agent asked me to bring back more photos."

"More fund-raising?" I squeaked, my teeth rattling like a pair of fake choppers. "Don't I have enough money?"

Frankie looked at me in surprise. "Elise must not have told you about her latest idea. She thinks that if you build schools, orphanages and feeding centers, perhaps churches and other charitable organizations will agree to take on the day-to-day operational costs. It's actually not that much in U.S. dollars. If so, then you can continue to put infrastructure in place…wells, hospitals, churches…."

And I thought *my* dream was big.

"There are lots of places that can use your help, Cassia. If it's planned properly, we can stretch out your money, make it last a long time and do a lot more good."

"Oh." We hit a rut that threatened to swallow us.

What a switch. Now I was concerned that I wouldn't have *enough* money. I sat back, relaxed in my seat and decided to go with the bumps. Not a bad decision for my life, either.

I'd expected Africa to be all arid desert. This hilly, even mountainous country was a pleasant surprise. Frankie, my travel guide, said that there was a plateau in the eastern part of the country. Lake Tanganyika is in the west. Tang-ga-nyi-ka. I like the way it rolls off my tongue. I'd never expected to see it, however.

"Not much farther," Frankie advised me.

I was enjoying the scenery and was a little sorry our destination was now on the horizon.

A small community came into view, certainly not like the neighborhoods I'm accustomed to at home. Frankie drove directly to the far side of the village and pulled up at a small building with children playing outside. Two or three adult women seemed to be in charge.

"Here it is," Frankie said, as if this explained everything.

"Okay, but what *is* it?"

"This is where Adam and I spent a lot of our time. Most of those pictures I took were in the outlying areas around this village. This building is part orphanage, part hospital, part church."

A small boy ran up to Frankie's side of the truck to stare, and others followed. I had no idea I could be so interesting.

I plopped my squashed hat on my head and some of the children giggled.

I turned to ask Frankie if he knew the names of any of my little admirers and was thunderstruck at what I saw.

CHAPTER

39

In that one moment my entire love life passed before my eyes.

Adam rounded the corner of the building and strode toward Frankie. His step slowed. The expression in his eyes told me I was the last person he expected to see. I felt the world decelerate until we were all in slow motion. Time stopped and I devoured the look of him—slimmer, hair shaggier, beard, and lines of weariness etched so deeply into his tanned face that I wanted to touch them with my fingers and smooth them away. He wore an air of sadness like a heavy cloak.

Unaware that time had stopped for the rest of us, two children ran up to Adam. One of the little boys flung himself against Adam's leg and practically shimmied himself into Adam's arms. Without looking at the child, he automatically reached to pick him up.

Then the world accelerated again.

"Frankie? What is going on…Cassia? What are you doing here?"

"I'm working?" I wasn't quite sure myself at what.

He shook his head as if to clear cobwebs. "Nobody told me…" He turned to Frankie. "You…"

"Cassia is with me, Adam. She and Elise have some things going on."

"Elise is here, too?"

"Back in Bujumbura. She has an afternoon full of appointments."

"What kind of appointments could Elise possibly have in Bujumbura?"

The little boy in Adam's arms snuggled in, rested his head against Adam's shoulder, stuck a finger in Adam's hair and began to roll it between his forefinger and thumb the way most children might stroke the silky edge of a blanket. As we stood there talking, I saw the little guy's body relax and his eyes droop as he fell asleep in the safe haven of Adam's arms.

"Like I said, she and Cassia are doing some business together," Frankie offered enigmatically. "Listen, I'd love to stay and chat, but I've got work to do. You two can entertain each other." And like a puff of smoke, Frankie and his camera vanished.

The silence between us was punctuated by the voices of children and the occasional instruction of one of the adults. Finally, uneasy with the silence, I said, "So this is where you went."

A frown etched the furrow in his brow even deeper. His arms and face were brown from the sun, and there was a dramatic contrast between his light shirt and dark complexion. "There are things here I have to finish."

"What things?"

Adam looked at the child in his arms as if noticing him for the first time. "Digging wells, playing with the kids, working at the feeding center, a little of everything. I and another guy, a missionary from Oregon, have been designing a drainage and septic system for this place. Next we're going to lay a concrete foundation for a new hospital. It won't be much, but it will free up this building to make room for more children."

He grew more engaged the longer he talked about the project. "A few cots, some blankets and pillows and it will look like the Hilton."

"I see."

He looked at me strangely. "Do you?"

The question sent a pang through my heart. Did he think I could miss the poverty and the need right before my eyes? Did he think I wasn't human?

"You might be surprised how much I see and know," I snapped.

He digested that slowly.

Anger and longing were warring within me. Instinctively I knew he'd built an invisible barrier around himself just to keep me out. My very presence is a source of painful reminders for him. It's clear that whether or not I forgive him doesn't matter as long as he refuses to forgive himself.

"Terrance told me why you did it."

He looked dumbfounded. "Terry? Told you what?"

"How the idea to write a story about me got started

in the first place. That you agreed to do it because you could channel the money you earned into places like this one. That no matter what I thought or what experience I'd had with you, you were an honorable man." I studied his still, passive features. "He's afraid you might give up writing completely."

Adam didn't argue.

"He also told me I was the 'fluff' that would make you enjoy writing again."

"And see how well that worked out." He tipped his head toward a big old tree. I followed him to it. Somehow he managed to slip to the ground with his young charge in his arms and not wake him. Adam leaned against the base of the tree, and the youngster slept soundly against his chest.

I dropped down by the two of them. "You must be very good friends."

Adam looked down fondly at the child. "We're buddies, James and I." He noticed my surprise and added, "That's what he's called here. His parents both died of AIDS some months back. He was pretty sickly when I first saw him. I started feeding him at night when Frankie and I were around the village. I practically needed an eyedropper at first, but once he got the hang of having food in his belly again, he turned into an eating machine. He was so desperate for affection that sometimes I let him hang out with me while I wrote. After I left, I was afraid he'd go backward, but he's done pretty well. He hasn't forgotten me, though."

None of us have.

"I'm surprised you came back here. I thought when

you left you were going off to write, rest, or 'find yourself.' All there is to do here is work."

He smiled crookedly, which made him look rakish. "Finding myself isn't a bad idea. I lost a part of me when I was writing your story behind your back. I'd never be able to work for a tabloid, I've discovered." His eyes became shadowed. "I'm ashamed of myself, but I just didn't think you'd let me do the story if I told you what I wanted to do. You were clear on that." He smiled ruefully. "The good news is that I must have some moral principles left after all."

"I wish you'd said something."

"I might have, if I'd figured out what it would be. 'Hi, Cassia, I want to use you to make money for children in some forgotten mountainous country in Africa. Don't worry, I'll spend it wisely.'"

I winced. He was right. I would have told him to take a flying leap off a Burundian cliff.

"Terry also told me to ask you straight out for money for my pet cause. I've watched you in action. I know how that would have gone over."

He did indeed. I'd railed more than once about people coming at me with hands extended for me to fill them. I now know that it wasn't because they were bad causes. What was holding me back was knowing somewhere deep inside myself that God had other plans for the money. *Feed My sheep.* And it wasn't His healthy, could-lose-a-few-pounds sheep, either. He'd led me to a hotbed of the neediest on earth.

"How long will you be here?"

Adam thoughtfully eyed his surroundings. He'd lost

weight doing hard physical activity. "I don't know. I've been working eighteen hours a day and I haven't even scratched the surface yet. I'm the little Dutch boy with his finger in the dike, and the rest of the dike is crumbling fast."

"What would help most?"

A woman came up to Adam and held out her hands, indicating that she would take the sleeping child from him. Somewhere in the distance a bird or chicken squawked. It was an odd punctuation in the silence between us.

"Where would I start? Good wells and sewers, a decent building to house the hospital, food and other provisions for these kids. Feeding centers, schools, vaccines... Once I start the list, I don't know where to stop."

"If villages each had a hospital and feeding center, a school and people and supplies to run them, would that help?"

I saw Adam take a deep breath and expel it shakily.

"It would be a dream come true."

"This, then, is your lucky day."

He looked at me with the same sort of absent-minded tolerance he'd displayed when the little boy had come running to him. He was willing to hold him, but he did have more pressing things on his mind.

"That's why we're here. Elise has a vision for how my money can be best used to do what we've been talking about. Frankie can tell you more about it than I can, but she thinks that if we can put everything structurewise into place in a village, then other charities and faith groups would be capable of taking them over and running them. Ideally, they'll train the residents how to run their own hospitals and schools and then move on."

"What?" His voice was strangled.

"Just what I said, you big goof." I watched him sit straight and lean toward me.

"You aren't making this up, are you?"

"Of course not. Ouch! You pinched me!" I rubbed the spot on my arm where he'd reached out and twisted the skin.

"Just making sure you're real. I don't want this to be a dream I'm going to wake up from soon."

I smiled and pinched him back. "There. Real enough for you?"

"For a skinny little thing, you have strong fingers."

Welcome back, Adam.

By the time we got back to our hotel with Adam in tow, Elise had returned from her own meetings and was doing a little two-step in Frankie's and her room.

"I thought you'd never get here!" she screeched as we entered. "I have got so much to tell you…. *Adam?* What are *you* doing here?"

Adam ran his fingers through his dark hair and grinned sheepishly. "Why does everyone who sees me ask me that?"

Elise clamped her arms around him and gave him a bear hug. "Because we worry about you when you disappear. Because we love you. And other than that, I can't think of a single reason." She started clucking like a mother hen. "And shame on you for not telling anyone where you were."

She turned on Frankie, who was arranging for himself an innocent face. "Did you know about this all along?"

"Not exactly…"

"What does 'exactly' mean?"

"He never said he was going here. I just figured that this was probably where he'd come," Frankie said. "I know that *I* can't get this place out of my mind."

Adam's eyes glazed and he glanced away from me.

Something in my heart softened, melted like snow in the first warm spring rain. I understood now how deeply and passionately Adam cared about these people and this place. This big, strong, stoic man was brought to tears over dying children he felt helpless to save.

I knew in that instant that Adam would have moved heaven and earth to do something to help. Why should I be surprised that he'd write a story about me—even without my permission—if he'd thought it would make a difference here?

I slept so hard on the plane ride home that I drooled on my little airplane pillow.

The rest of my party was no better. One week in Burundi was like a year at home. Fortunately, there were a lot of empty seats on the return flight, so everyone was able to spread out.

Frankie and Elise were tangled together asleep across three seats. Frankie, bless his heart, snored like a steam engine. Elise, smart woman that she is, wore earplugs. Adam, who on impulse had decided to come back with us, looked handsome even in his sleep.

Frankie snored, while Adam did not. Frankie's mouth fell open, giving everyone a view of his tonsils, but Adam's did not. Frankie's hair went berserk and made him look as though he'd been electrocuted. In contrast, Adam's fell gently over his forehead and made me want to brush it away from his tanned face. And while Frankie made me feel like dropping a blanket over his face so I didn't have to look at him, I could, and did, stare at Adam every chance I got.

He kept me at arm's length since we met in the village. He's cautious and watchful, like an ice fisherman testing thin ice—eager to be fishing but terrified of drowning.

He's smiling more now, however. Elise's work was productive, and things are falling into place. She made a connection with an organization that has been building hospitals and schools on the eastern plateau side of the country, and they were ecstatic about having actual funds to work with, not piecemeal donations and their current pay-as-you-pray financial policy. They employ locals in the villages, which brings some money into the community. They also pay with goats, ducks, cows and any other food-producing creature, so that by the time they complete their projects and leave the village, there is an ongoing supply of milk and eggs, as well.

Elise has notebooks filled with ideas, names, addresses and information to take back to the States to sort through. Her business training has kicked in, and she is showing less of her Birkenstock style and more of her Brooks Brothers for Women mode.

And I'm at peace. There's not a single niggling doubt that there's something more I should do or say. The money is being channeled into the right places. I've given up fighting the fact I'm rich and begun maximizing it so that not a dime is wasted that could be going to someone in need. And due to Elise's persuasiveness, I've resigned myself to the fact that I can pay myself a salary for the work I do for the Feed My

Children Foundation we're starting. I won't be rolling in money, but I will be able to pay the light bill and buy dog food. A dandy compromise if ever there was one.

But there is still one big gaping hole in my life, and it will be waiting for me when I get back. Ken, Randy and Adam. Adam skirts around me as if I'm an electric fence ready to zap him. Ken will have flowers on my doorstep the minute he knows I'm home. And Randy will rev up his cell phone for frequent check-ins to monitor my emotional temperature.

Lord, You've handled everything else, so I give my feelings about Adam to You, as well. I ask for release. He doesn't believe like I do, Lord, and I refuse to relegate You to only a corner of my life. Love me, love my God. We're a package, You and I. I ask You to protect me from the pain of loving someone like Adam.

Maybe I'll sneak into my apartment under the radar for a few days just to get my bearings.

"Cassia!" Jane squealed so loudly that the woman standing next to her in baggage claim clamped her hand over her ear. "You're home!"

Translation: "I was sure I was never going to see you again. You scared me out of my skin."

"Are you exhausted from your trip?"

Translation: "Don't you ever do anything like this again. You look terrible."

"We missed you so much."

Translation: They missed me.

"I'm okay, Jane. Terrific, really. It was an amazing trip. God provided everything we needed." *And more.*

"Dave's outside with Winslow, and Grandma is waiting in the car."

Now, when everything is fine, I feel tears in my eyes.

"Just a minute. I want to say goodbye to the others." I turned back and waved to Elise, who had just collected her things from the baggage carousel.

"Thanks for everything," I whispered in her ear as I hugged her. "You were awesome."

"Thank *you* for the privilege of having a part in this amazing thing we're doing."

Frankie slipped his arm around Elise's waist. Funny, when I'd first met him, I'd thought he looked wild and rebellious. Now he looked like a soft teddy bear and a very safe place to fall. "When will we be in touch?"

"I want a couple days to regroup before I do anything. I have a hunch that by then, Elise will have a 'to do' list for me as long as my arm." I glanced around. "My family is ready to go, but I just wanted to say goodbye to you and Adam."

"He took off already," Frankie said. "He told me to tell you both goodbye."

"Without saying anything to us?" Elise looked indignant.

It's me he's avoiding, I know. I understand now why Adam did what he did. Although I have forgiven him, he's not willing to forgive himself, so not *everything* to do with the money is sorted out yet.

If Adam's rebuff at the airport had hurt me, Winslow's elation at my return almost made up for it.

When he saw me, he emitted a yelp of pleasure and began to wag his back end so vigorously that he almost knocked over a businessman in a suit and tie. As the gentleman stumbled off wondering what had hit him, Winslow tugged at his leash until I thought he might choke himself.

I couldn't even get to Dave to give him a hug. Winslow planted himself between us, and when I bent to pet him, he cleaned every bit of makeup off my face with his tongue.

"Calm down, big guy. I'm home to stay."

Half whining, yipping, he indicated that he didn't quite believe me. Adam is afraid he can't regain my trust. Me? I'm trying to win back my own dog.

"Do you want to go to our house or your own?" Jane asked when we were in the car. Mattie had given me a greeting almost as effusive as Winslow's but without the tongue part.

"My house, if you don't mind. I feel like I can't spend one more minute away."

"We thought so. Dave and I brought you some groceries, and Mattie made a hot dish and a pie. We'll eat there."

Bliss.

Comfort food, my favorite people and my dog. I hardly noticed that Adam's apartment was dark when we arrived.

Well, maybe just a little.

Okay, okay, I noticed a lot. Worse yet, I was disappointed. Somehow I still harbored the notion that we could pick up where we'd left off before the money-Burundi-lottery-story fiasco. That goes to show I'm an optimist, I guess, but this time my optimism failed me. I have the sinking feeling that Adam isn't coming back at all.

"Cassia? Where'd you go? You look as though you're a thousand miles away." Jane waved a spoon in front of my face to get my attention.

"Sorry. I was a thousand miles away, or maybe more."

"You haven't said much about your trip," Mattie commented. "We're eager to hear everything."

"Okay," I said, mustering the energy to share my experiences with my family. "But hold on to your hats—this trip was a very wild ride."

CHAPTER

41

"Hey, Chase, it's Adam. I just got in. Any chance I can bunk with you for a couple days?"

"Hiya, bud. Sure, come on over. Whitney and Pepto will be thrilled to see you."

"Whitney, maybe. But Pepto? I don't think so."

"You never know. Having these women in his life has mellowed him."

"Women?"

"Whitney and Cassia. We met your neighbor and discovered that the misanthrope in cat's clothing adores her. She's a great gal, isn't she?"

"Yeah, really great." *And the reason I need to stay at your place until I get my head straight.*

Cassia was popping up everywhere, like a beach ball in a swimming pool, Adam thought. He'd push her out of sight in one place, and she'd show up somewhere else.

"Are you okay? You sound funny."

"Just tired. And by the way, my cab is only a few blocks from your place right now."

"At least you know you're always welcome. I'll tell Whitney you're on your way. She'll want to feed you."

Adam felt every single bone, muscle and fiber in his body as he carried his bag toward Chase's front steps. There wasn't a spot that didn't hurt, including his brain cells.

"Look at you!" Chase stood in the doorway and greeted his cousin. "Is the beard your new look?"

"Only until I can get a razor." Adam dropped his bags and the two embraced.

"Come inside. Whitney is making an omelet and fresh coffee. I think you have a lot to tell us."

After four or five cups of coffee, the omelet, bacon, a stack of toast, two slices of pie with ice cream and half a dozen homemade cookies, Adam finally felt like talking.

Pepto, who had been giving him the cold shoulder as punishment for abandoning him, forgave him in trade for a slice of bacon, and deigned to claw at Adam's pant leg in welcome.

Whitney and Chase chose to regale Adam with stories of their becoming friends with Cassia.

Here she is, popping up again. I can't get away, even here.

"You're pretty quiet," Whitney observed. "You do like your neighbor as much as we do, don't you?"

"Sure, I like her." Adam shifted in his chair and sighed. "I'm just ashamed to face her." Seeing the look in his hosts' eyes, he told the rest of the story.

Whitney and Chase were silent when he finished.

Finally Chase whistled. "A little ethical conundrum, huh? A moral lapse?"

"You certainly get to the point," Adam growled. He scraped his fingers through his hair. "And I don't even know why it's a big deal. I'm not the first journalist to step on toes to get a story, and I won't be the last. It's not as though I said something bad about her. She comes off in a great light—a heroine, actually."

"You're right. No big deal," Chase agreed cheerfully.

"I mean, really, I've blown this all out of proportion."

"So true. It's really insignificant in the scheme of things. What's one woman being upset when you can help a lot of children? She can handle herself. Do you want another cup of coffee?"

"Yeah, I…" Adam glanced up sharply. "What are you doing?"

Chase's eyes danced. "Not a thing. Just assuring you that most people wouldn't give it another thought, Adam." He reached for the carafe and poured coffee into Adam's cup.

"I didn't think I'd ever hear that from you, Mr. Moral Upright God-Fearing Citizen."

"Of course, *I* wouldn't have done it, not without her permission. But I suppose that's why I'm a doctor. It's always clear what my responsibility is—the patient."

"Well, it's not that big a deal, Chase!"

"Excuse me? Who's beating himself up for a choice he made? Adam, if it's such a big deal, say you're sorry!"

"I have."

"Did she forgive you?"

"I think so."

"Have you forgiven yourself?"

Adam grimaced. "Obviously not."

"Has God forgiven you?"

"What does that have to do with anything?"

"It used to have everything to do with it." Chase leaned back in his chair, crossed his arms on his chest and grinned. "That God you decided you didn't believe in, the One you lost in Burundi, must still be a big deal. If not, you wouldn't care whether or not Cassia was upset."

"I can be ethical and not believe!"

"Of course you can. But there's more to you than ethics, Adam. There's conscience. And there's that annoying but effective Friend of ours, the Holy Spirit."

"Don't go there with me, Chase. Don't make everything a sermon."

"Okay, okay," Chase agreed, still exasperatingly cheerful. "You figure it out for yourself. But I'd bet you anything that the Holy Spirit is trying to get to you any way He can. He's not crazy about hardened hearts, you know."

"You'd *bet* me? Chase, gambling is what got me in all this trouble in the first place!"

Adam stood in the shower and let the hot water pour across his skin. He turned the showerhead flow until the water came out like painful little pellets. As he stood there, he scrubbed his skin with a bar of soap and a washcloth, as if trying to wash his frustration away.

Chase was right. This was no big deal. Cassia didn't hold grudges. She'd said as much. On the plane ride home she'd told him it was fine to publish the articles, since they were being used to further "our cause." She'd even said that if he actually thought someone would be foolish enough to buy a book about her, the lottery and Burundi, he should write it—after she'd approved it, of course. The only thing she insisted was that the part her faith played in all of this be included, and also how God had led her to the place she needed to be.

Adam turned off the shower and shook his head like a big wet dog, sending a spray of droplets around the bathroom. He hated it when Chase was right. God *was* more important to him than he cared to let on.

God was the One sitting on Adam's conscience. And Adam was learning that when God wants a person's attention, He can make himself very weighty and conspicuous.

CHAPTER

42

Not home yet?

I'm beginning to feel foolish, tiptoeing several times a day, as I do, down the stairs to see if Adam and Pepto have arrived.

That man has a way of appearing and disappearing like vapor!

That's another reason Adam and I would never have worked together as a couple. I like attributes like stability and steadfastness, and adjectives such as *unchanging, rooted, committed* and *reliable.* I like, as my mom says, "somebody whose feet are under your dinner table every night." Adam's feet could be under a dinner table anywhere in the world at any given time. He'd be the boat and I'd be the anchor. He'd want to set sail, and I'd drag him back to the warmth and security of home.

Ken and Randy. Now, those are stable men. I wouldn't have to worry about losing either of them to Rwanda, Calcutta or Timbuktu.

My phone rang, arousing me from my disgruntled musings. It was Whitney.

"Hi, Cassia, have you seen Adam around?"

"No. Should I have?"

"Not necessarily. He's been staying with us, but I thought he'd stop at his place today. I wanted to tell him to bring over Pepto's toys when he comes. If that cat is going to stay here, he has to have something to do. He's decapitated half a dozen catnip mice already."

No kidding. Pepto should run a cemetery for the creepy little things.

Then what she'd said sank in. "Pepto is staying with you?"

"It's not completely settled but, knowing Adam, he'll be off again in a few days."

"Oh." My voice sounded tinny and small in my ears.

"That guy has itchy feet. They can't stay in place long."

Certainly not under just one person's dinner table.

"Anyway, give him the message if you see him. He's got Pepto with him right now. He's having his teeth cleaned at the vet's." Whitney's throaty chuckle drifted over the line. "Tomorrow I'm going to watch the obituaries for former veterinarians and their assistants."

After I hung up, I paced until Winslow determined that *I* must need to go out for a walk. He took his leash, which was lying on a chair, and carried it to the door, where he stood patiently, waiting for me to notice.

His was as good an idea as any, I decided. Exercise

is an excellent way to vent frustration, and boy, am I frustrated. Angry as I've been with Adam, disappointed as I am that he's neither a Christian nor a homebody kind of guy (translation: marrying kind) I still care. Just once, could he reciprocate by communicating with me? Is that too much to ask?

I picked up the pace and raced Winslow through the walking paths around Lake Harriet.

Winslow finally wore out and called it quits on the walk. I'd hoped to sweat Adam right out of my system, but it had been only a partial success. Still, I felt better as we walked home.

The floral deliveryman was trying to ring my apartment when I entered. His face showed relief when he saw me. "Oh, good. I'm glad you're home. Now I don't have to come back with these."

He carried two bouquets. One was twenty-four yellow roses that smelled divine. The other was a summery bouquet made up of bright splashes of color—red, yellow, pink, purple and lavender. The first would be from Ken, the second from Randy.

"Did you have a good trip?" Mr. Bouquet asked. "You were gone for a while."

"How did you know that?"

"There was a dry spell in the floral industry. I wasn't delivering here every day."

"It's an embarrassment of riches." I took the bouquets, one in each arm, and looped Winslow's leash over my index finger. "But they both just found out I'm back in town and are relieved I came back alive. I really can't blame them."

My floral friend shook his head. "You must live a very interesting life."

I sniffed at the roses. "Not intentionally."

I almost didn't see Adam with my vision blocked with flora, but I did stop when I heard his voice.

"Need help with those?"

I peered at him through the shrubbery. "Sure."

He lifted the roses out of my arms and stepped aside so that I could continue up the stairs.

"So you're still here."

He looked at me in surprise.

"Whitney called to have me tell you that if you were going to leave Pepto with them any longer, you should bring more mice." I eyed him carefully. "*Are* you leaving again soon?"

He followed me into the apartment, and we set the flowers side by side on the table. For something to do in the awkward silence, I opened the gift cards. After a cursory glance, I laid them on the table. I was right. Ken was the roses.

"Why?"

"Just curious, that's all."

"I'm thinking about it."

"Where will you go?"

"Burundi, I suppose. I can write from there if I have to."

"Why can't you do it here?"

He looked uncomfortable. To distract himself, he absently picked up the gift cards on the table.

"Oh, lots of reasons…" His voice trailed away and his eyebrow rose.

I glanced at the full message on the card.

Now that I've got you back alive, marry me!
Ken

Before I could grab it away, he looked at Randy's card, too.

Welcome home! We need to get together and talk about our future.
With love—Randy

"Doesn't look like you'll have time for neighborly visits anyway." Then he added obtusely, "Why do you care when I go?"

Not many things pet my fur the wrong way, but I did not appreciate this. I felt myself morphing into the proverbial fiery redhead.

"Why do I care? Oh, I don't know. Maybe because I thought I was your friend. Maybe I assumed we both enjoyed the time we spent together when I first moved here. Could it possibly be because I spoke my heart to you and hoped you'd handle it carefully? Or is it the fact that we watched movies, made popcorn and played with the pets several nights a week? That we shared our suppers potluck style?"

I took a breath and plowed on. "That I thought you actually *cared* about me? What kind of idiot was I to assume that? You are disgraceful, Cavanaugh. Who are you anyway? The famous journalist humanitarian? An anything-for-a-buck reporter? Sincere friend? Traitor? It doesn't really matter to me, but I'd like to know. Make up your mind, Adam. You've got to be something!"

CHAPTER

43

A firecracker with a short fuse.

He'd lit it unintentionally, but now he had no idea how to douse the blaze. Adam stared at the irate beauty, taken aback. Fire in her eyes, she quivered with indignation, revealing a new side of Cassia, one he hadn't known existed. It was the side capable of righteous anger, of standing up to injustice and to thoughtless men.

"You're right. That was a rotten thing to say. I've been having my own pity party lately. Maybe I need to try a little Ben & Jerry's. I was out of line...."

Humor did not work.

"You sure are out of line. You're so far out of line you're...you're..." She sputtered to a halt. Building up new steam, she added, "And what makes you think you can draw your own lines anyway?"

How do I answer that? Adam wondered. But the odd question piqued his interest. As Cassia stomped to the sink muttering and drew water to top off the flowers, Adam's mind began to spin.

Who does draw the lines in my life? Who makes the rules? Me? Well, I haven't done the greatest job of it lately.

To be honest, life had been easier when he'd allowed God to call the shots. But God had disappeared in Burundi. All Adam had found there was pain and trouble....

He watched Cassia as if from a distance, noticing the high color in her cheeks, the curve of her flushed neck, the graceful way she held herself even when she was angrily clanking pans and emptying the dishwasher.

As he looked at her, he wondered—had his experiences in Burundi all been trouble, or had he missed something?

If his experiences had been nothing but trouble, what had brought Cassia there with her millions of dollars? How had she managed to get into his life at all? She'd even connected with Frankie and Elise with their combination of compassion, professionalism and familiarity with the issues. They were two of the people most likely able to get things done in that country. What had compelled Cassia to a country she'd barely heard of until recently?

Everybody loved her—Chase, Whitney and even Pepto. She seemed to scatter a trail of blessing wherever she went.

Maybe God *had* been in Burundi after all, Adam mused. Maybe he just hadn't been looking for Him in the right places.

Lord, I'm so sorry. I've been a fool. It's better when You're in control. Forgive me. And Adam lifted his hands in a gesture that, if someone had been watching, might have been equated with an equestrian handing the reins from one rider to another. The reins of his life.

Then he realized that Cassia was still grumbling about him as she stomped around the apartment. "Used to be a Christian, but gave it up to become a jerk. Just my luck... 'You'll meet lots of interesting people in the city, Cassia.' What does Jane know? Interesting people aren't always good for you. Adam's proof of that. What have I ever gotten from knowing him but aggravation...."

She looked up to find him staring at her. "Well, you are! Aggravating, I mean." She stood, arms akimbo, daring him to disagree with her.

"You are absolutely right. I am. I even aggravate myself. But it's going to change. You told me once that God hit you over the head with your grandmother. Well, I think He's just hit me over the head with myself."

Cassia's eyes grew wide and her mouth gaped.

"Well, it's a big deal, but you don't have to look that stunned."

"Winslow. He's gone." Her hands flew to her cheeks. "I dropped the leash when I came in, but I didn't shut the door."

"He'll be fine," Adam said. "He can't get outside. He's just wandering the halls. Then his eyes widened. "And I didn't shut my front door. Pepto..."

"Winslow!"

And they raced downstairs, afraid of what they might find.

"No blood" was Adam's first comment as we approached his doorway. "That's a good sign. And we didn't hear any howling."

I closed my eyes and willed myself to breathe deeply. In my mind's eye I saw Winslow crying and whimpering, with Pepto's claws embedded in my dog's big licorice gumdrop nose. I know that if Pepto wanted to do serious damage, he'd go for that vulnerable nose, bury his claws there and hang on. Winslow could run in circles, shake his head, drag the cat on the floor and still never extricate himself.

"I shouldn't have left the door open, Cassia. I'm sorry…." Adam stopped so quickly that I ran into his broad, warm back. He turned and took me by the shoulders. "I'm sorry for everything—especially for being a jerk. I'm going to ask God to help deal with it, okay? If He'll forgive me and you forgive me, then I can forgive myself—for the articles, the subterfuge, the jerk-ness."

Delight coursed through me. "I'm overjoyed to hear you two are on speaking terms again."

"*I* quit talking to *Him. He* never quit talking to *me.* And—" Adam drew a deep breath "—I think He used you to get my attention."

"Adam," I reminded him, "Pepto's got Winslow. We can talk when the rescue mission is complete."

"Right." He grinned at me, and for a moment I almost forgot what we were up to.

"Not in the bedroom," Adam reported.

"Nothing in the bathroom."

"They wouldn't have gotten out somehow, would they?"

"None of the people who live in the building would have let them out."

"Then where are they?"

Suddenly Adam began to chuckle. "Hiding in plain sight."

I spun around to see what he was looking at. There was Winslow, taking up Adam's entire couch and—I nearly dropped my teeth. Well, at least I would have if they'd been false.

Between Winslow's massive paws lay Pepto, purring, as Winslow patiently cleaned the cat's fur with that tongue the size of Adam's shoe. As we watched, Pepto and Winslow traded jobs. As Winslow drooled happily, Pepto started to groom him. How nauseating. They were like a lovesick couple who couldn't keep their hands off each other.

"Talk about Isaiah 65:25!"

Adam eyed me expectantly, waiting for me to translate.

"'The wolf and the lamb shall feed together, the lion shall eat straw as the ox does, and poisonous snakes shall strike no more....'"

And we burst out laughing.

Later, after dinner, which we prepared together in Adam's kitchen while he told me of his own rocky journey back to God, we sat on the couch watching our two lovebirds. Pepto had forgotten how crazy he was about me, and Winslow didn't seem to know Adam existed anymore. They had eyes only for each other.

"BFF," I murmured. "Best Friends Forever."

"Who are you talking about? Them or us?"

"I'd like to think both, but it's your call."

Adam watched our pets doze on the floor. This time Winslow lay on his side with Pepto draped over his front legs. One of them snored.

"Look how long we kept them apart because we thought they wouldn't—shouldn't—like each other."

"I guess they showed us."

Adam moved a stray curl from my temple. "We wasted a lot of their time thinking they wouldn't be happy together."

"Hmm."

"I think we may have wasted a lot of our own time, too."

I could feel his warm breath on my ear.

"You think?"

"Definitely."

Then he shifted so that he could take my face in his hands and look into my eyes. "What do you think about making up for lost time?"

"What do you mean?"

"Like having a very short engagement."

A flutter of happiness moved through me. "How short?"

"Very short. What are you doing next month?"

"I'll be busy. I'm going to a wedding. Mine."

"Cassia, will you do the zipper on my dress? I'm having trouble getting it past my waist. It feels a little snug." Jane shuffled across the bedroom we'd shared in Simms when we were girls.

"You haven't gained weight since we measured for your dress, have you?"

"It's not a big deal. If this dress doesn't fit, I brought another along just in case. You've only got one bridesmaid. Who will know?"

"I knew I should have gone with plan A." I tugged on the zipper of the body-hugging sheath Jane had chosen for the wedding.

"Have a dog for a bridesmaid? I don't think so!"

"He doesn't gain weight overnight—he'd be cheap to outfit." I gave her a chastising look. "And he doesn't talk back."

Jane's dress is an elegant aquamarine that reminds me of the seas in the Caribbean. I like it because the color is a perfect backdrop for the flowers we are carrying for the wedding.

As usual, I couldn't make up my mind, so I went to the florist and chose one of just about everything they had—except carnations, of course—and the riot of color creates a flowery celebration.

I chose the menu for the sit-down dinner in much the same way. The one-of-everything general store managed to find large white tents so that we could have our reception in the backyard of Grandma's house, which is spectacular in late August and early September, and I made a list of everything Adam and I liked to eat and we chose from that.

Frannie's is catering their wonderful roast beef, mashed potatoes and gravy, and those great oatmeal sandwich cookies no gala should be without—made in miniature, of course, and each decorated with a tiny pink rose. Adam insisted on corn on the cob since it's in season, and homemade ice cream to go with the cake. Since his entire family is coming, as well as everyone in Simms, we ordered enough food to feed all the attendees at the Super Bowl.

I'm also amazed at the number of Adam's coworkers, publishers and VIPs that are coming. We've even had to figure out a place to park limos during the festivities. The elementary school principal offered the parking lot and playground area at the school. If the limo drivers get bored, they can hang out on the jungle gym.

I frowned as I tugged at Jane's dress. She caught my look in the mirror.

"It's going to fit, isn't it?"

"Eventually. If you promise not to bend or breathe."

"Oh, good." Jane gave a sigh of relief, which pooched out her belly and made the zipper slide backward. "Then what were you thinking about?"

"The cake."

"Oh, that." She looked at me, bright eyed. "I think you're very brave, you know."

"'Brave' isn't exactly what a bride should have to be concerning her wedding cake."

"Brave is what you have to be to allow Tulip full rein decorating it."

"I was feeling a little too benevolent toward the community of Simms when I agreed to that." I thought everyone would enjoy having one of Tulip's cakes, but I had a momentary memory lapse and forgot about some of Tulip's past designs.

The woman is an artist, there's no doubt about that. Or maybe I should say *artiste*—fickle and fussy where her creative muse is involved. Sometimes Tulip suffers delusions of grandeur. There was that Volkswagen-sized football cake she created when Simms had a successful year on the home turf. Well, maybe it wasn't a Volkswagen, but it was as least as big as the little red wagon in which she had to haul it. Her cakes were decorated with everything from sparklers and party favors to entire historical depictions of the first pioneers settling in Simms.

"I've been trying to imagine what she might do, and drawn a blank."

"Who knows how Tulip's mind works? She'll think of something."

"That is what I'm afraid of." I got the zipper to the

top and turned Jane around by the shoulders. "What do you know, you look great!"

"You doubted that for an instant?" Relief was written all over her face. "Now it's your turn."

I glanced at the clock, and the jittery butterflies in my stomach all took flight.

"Am I doing the right thing, Jane? Adam and I are very different."

"Are you happy?" Jane opened the closet door and removed my dress.

"Blissfully."

"Do you love him?" She spread the elegant satin creation across the bed.

"With all my heart."

"Does he love you?" Jane unzipped the zipper.

"With every fiber of his being."

"And he's a Christian. What's the problem?"

"Our lives are so different. A globetrotting journalist and a woman who wants to make a home and work with children."

"But your passions are the same." She picked up the dress. "Now hold up your arms."

I squirmed into the dress, thinking hard. "We do care about the same things—God, family, Burundi, doing good in the world, pets…."

The dress fell around me in a graceful puddle.

"Like I said, what's the problem?"

I breathed in when she zipped the dress, but I didn't have to. It glided into place.

"There's no problem except the one I'm trying to make."

"So quit it." She took my cheeks in the palms of her hands. "Honey, everyone is happy for you. Everyone knows it's right. All your friends from the lottery are here—Stella, Cricket, even that lady who carries her purse clutched to her chest—and the strangest little couple. They said they were 'Mrs. Carver and George.' Do you know who they might be?"

"Neighbors." I wanted to smile. "Watchful neighbors."

"Even Ken and Randy gave you their blessing."

Jane is right. I couldn't have asked for more beautiful responses to the news about Adam and me. Randy says he's still kicking himself for not speaking his feelings earlier. "I could have had a chance, Cassia. I blew it."

The good news is that Randy has learned something from our star-crossed relationship. Parker Bennett recently hired a new accountant, a pretty blond, blue-eyed one. Randy liked her immediately and didn't waste any time telling her. They promised they'd be here for the wedding.

Ken took it the hardest. He was angry at first, then hurt, and finally, after hours of our talking together, he was happy for me. Not happy in a giddy, how-fabulous kind of way, but glad that I'd found someone like Adam.

"You know, Cassia, I never wanted to think it, but I guess I've been afraid of this happening for a long time. I've always been a little rough around the edges and forget, sometimes, that it doesn't always come off as endearing." There were tears in his eyes when he added, "I've always loved you and, no matter how I feel, I want you to be happy."

I don't think I'd ever loved Ken more. He did the right thing, even when it was the hard thing.

"Is Ken going to be at the wedding?" Jane asked.

"No. He said it would be too difficult." I heard a quiver in my own voice. "But he sent us a gift."

"No kidding?"

"Look." I pointed to an enormous gift basket on the floor by the dresser.

"That thing is the size of a twin bed!" Jane shuffled to the basket, but was careful not to bend over. "What is it?"

"A supersize Ken's Custom Homes' Welcome Home basket. Pounds of coffee, chocolates, toilet paper, coupons for milk, everything he leaves in his clients' new homes."

"Okay…" Jane backed away looking puzzled.

"And in the bottom there's a gift certificate for all the materials needed to build a house—at cost. He said he'd have them delivered anywhere between Rapid City and Minneapolis, but if we want to build outside the two-state area, we have to pay shipping fees. Ever practical, that Ken."

Jane's jaw dropped. "Well, that's the best gift you'll be getting!"

"No, the best gift is that we parted friends."

There was a knock on the door. "Honey, can I come in?"

"Sure, Mom. We're almost ready."

My mom looks a great deal like Jane—dark hair, pleasant features and she carries and fights the same roly-poly gene my sister inherited. She took my hand.

"You are a vision, Cassia. Have you even looked at yourself?"

I turned toward the mirror and gasped. At Adam's request, I'd more or less left my hair in its natural state, a red curly cloud. My skin, which doesn't really tan but goes directly from lobster colored to peeling, and my pristine white dress made me look fragile and ethereal. I'm neither, but it's a look I like.

"We are so glad for you, darling." Mom's expression clouded. "I wish Dad and I could have been more a part of this romance of yours."

"Trust me, Mom, you wouldn't have enjoyed it. I didn't exactly enjoy most of it myself."

My poor mother, who has no idea of all the confusion and miscommunication that has gone on, smiled weakly. Ignorance is bliss sometimes, and that's what I wanted for her today—bliss. There will be time later for Adam and me to unroll the entire story of our meeting and falling in love.

"Is Daddy ready?"

"He's been at the church for two hours. It's a big day when he gets to walk his daughter down the aisle and then marry her to her new husband."

"And Mattie?"

"Holding court at the door of the church with your friend Whitney. She's in her element."

"Well, then," I said, "I guess it's time."

My heart pounded so hard as I stood at the back of the church that I feared it might thrash its way out of my chest and escape. Even the prospects of that, however, couldn't make me take my eyes off the most handsome man in the world, the one who was waiting for me at the end of the long, white-carpeted aisle.

Adam's white teeth flashed in his deeply tanned face when he smiled. He and Chase are a devastating duo. The ladies in Simms will have much to talk about at Estrogen Hour on Monday. Adam's hair, just the length I like it, made my fingers itch to touch it. I'd never seen him in a tuxedo before, but it does even more for him than those trim jeans and soft shirts he wears.

Dad fidgeted like a nervous bridegroom while Adam looked calm and collected, as if he did this sort of thing every day. When the music started I put my foot forward, the first step of the journey into my new life.

"Don't you dare give Winslow another piece of cake!" I instructed Adam. "He'll be sick."

Adam had planned ahead and arranged for a little mesh zippered tent from which Winslow and Pepto could watch the festivities. Winslow looked happy enough in his extra-extra-extra-large bow tie. Pepto only tolerated the white velvet bow tied around his neck, but he hadn't shredded it either, so I took the fact that he hadn't destroyed his wedding garb as an indication he was having a wonderful time at the party.

"Why not? There's plenty to go around."

We turned to look at Tulip's most outstanding masterpiece yet. The cake was a series of tiers, bridges and waterfalls laced in elaborate frosting lattice and lace. There were plastic swans swimming in the mirrored glass pool at the bottom of the cake. Even she knew she'd outdone herself, and was proudly giving out business cards saying "Tulip's Cakery."

The children of Simms were playing soccer in a field visible from the yard, while neighbors and friends were wearing out both eyeballs and tongues discussing the interesting group of people Adam's side of the wedding invitation list had brought. Adam's family, which is huge, just as he'd warned me, mingled easily with everyone. Dad and Adam's father, who I've only just discovered is a professor of religious history, were involved in a spirited discussion. Mom and his mother were regaling each other with "When Cassia was little she…" and "Before Adam was potty trained he…" stories.

Everyone was so busy, in fact, that no one seemed to notice when Adam took me by the hand and led me to a secluded corner of the yard.

"Well, Mrs. Cavanaugh, what do you think about this party and your new status in life?"

"I've never been happier, or more grateful. God is good, Adam."

"Psalm 119:65," he said.

Lord, I am overflowing with Your blessing, just as You promised.

Amen!

* * * * *

QUESTIONS FOR DISCUSSION

1. What would you do if you accidentally won the lottery the way Cassia does? Did you learn anything from Cassia's handling of her windfall?

2. Do you think Cassia could have found happiness if she'd married Randy or Ken? Why or why not?

3. Among Cassia's family and friends, who did you think was helpful to her as she tried to discern what she should do with the money, and who wasn't helpful and why?

4. What did you think about Cassia's relationship with God? Is it similar to or different from your own relationship with God?

5. Did you think Cassia's response to Adam's lack of honesty was appropriate? If you were deeply disappointed by a man, how would you react?

6. Adam had a rationale for his behavior that he ultimately found unsupportable—do you judge him as harshly as he judges himself? How could he have remained true to his goal of helping the Burundian orphans without deceiving Cassia?

7. Did you think of Winslow and Pepto as characters in the same sense as Cássia, Jane, Adam, Randy,

etc.? Do you have any favorite books where animals play prominent roles, and how does the "humanizing" of animal characters add to your enjoyment?

8. Have you ever gone through a crisis of faith like Adam's? How was it resolved?

9. Were any of the secondary characters in the novel especially appealing to you? Who and why?

10. Have you ever faced a situation like Cassia's where a decision led to a radical change in your life or lifestyle? Did you feel you had divine guidance in the situation and what form did that take? How do you feel about the decision and the changes now?